STANDING LESSONS

STANDING LESSONS

A NOVEL

Norval Rindfleisch

Writer's Showcase
San Jose New York Lincoln Shanghai

Standing Lessons
A NOVEL

Writer's Showcase
an imprint of iUniverse, Inc.

For information address:
iUniverse, Inc.
5220 S. 16th St., Suite 200
Lincoln, NE 68512
www.iuniverse.com

Any resemblance to actual people and events is purely coincidental.
This is a work of fiction.

ISBN: 0-595-21798-2

Printed in the United States of America

To
the one
who said softly

I'll string along with you

C O N T E N T S

▼

It is a trite but true observation
that examples work more forcibly than precepts:
and if this be just in what is odious and blamable,
it is more strongly so in what is amiable and
praiseworthy. Here emulation most effectually
operates upon us, and inspires our imitation in
an irresistible manner. A good man therefore
is a standing lesson to all his acquaintance, and of
far greater use in that narrow circle than a good book."

—JOSEPH ANDREWS
Henry Fielding

"In matters of fashion, go
with the tide—in matters
of principle stand like a rock."

—Thomas Jefferson

PROLOGUE

▼

Epitaph
The Crypt Kensington School Chapel

Thomas Stevens Beckwith
1862-1931

Ordained a minister in the Episcopal Church
June 12, 1887

Founder and for thirty-one years first
Headmaster of Kensington School (1895-1926)
Endowed with intellectual gifts of a high
order, he was a humble and godly man, apt to
teach, persuasive in discourse, judicious in
counsel, firm in purpose, pure in word and
spirit. He won the love and gratitude of two
generations of Kensington boys.

Ethel (Codgell) Beckwith
1865-1947

Wife and helpmate, endowed with those
virtues that adorn her sex—gentleness,
kindness, and understanding—she served
students and alumni of Kensington School for over
fifty years.

PART I

▼

ON THE EVE

CHAPTER I

▼

The first three days of April were sunny with the bright clarity of early September. Warm breezes dried the fields of eastern Connecticut and melted the last crusty remnants of crystallized snow in the shaded recesses of stone walls and between the dark, sinewy, surface-roots of great trees. On Thursday afternoon Jack Bartley officially began his fifteenth season as Kensington School's third form baseball coach by conducting the first outdoor practice. He began again with the certain knowledge that, unless some sort of miracle occurred, he would complete by the end of May his fifteenth losing season.

They had had cals and throwing drills in the gym for almost a week, but he couldn't tell much from that. He had heard that two or three players were decent athletes, but when they were assembled for the first time on the third form diamond, he knew there would be problems; too many of his players had copper-perfect tans from three idle and probably frivolous weeks of spring vacation in exotic and romantic places like Barbados and Jamaica, where it had never been his good fortune to visit, and eight of his fifteen players wanted to try out for second base. The tans would fade in the pallid early New England spring, restoring within a week the de facto, if illusory, appearance of socio-economic equity between students and faculty, but the worst team he had ever coached had begun with twelve players trying out for second base. It was a sure sign of trouble. The opposite principle, the sure sign of a potentially strong team, was the number of players trying out for catch. His best team ever began the season with four catchers.

He ran them through his usual infield and outfield catching and throwing drills. Most had never played baseball before. They conveniently misjudged fly balls and grounders, scrambling judiciously out of the way of a direct confrontation. He soon realized he had only two or three coordinated athletes and no catcher. It was clear that he would have to go back to basics: throwing drills, catching drills, running drills, sliding drills. He had no illusions, though this year the hope he always felt each spring was quickly dissipated. Ironically, it was as a coach he saw himself as a true moral educator, not of the courage and judgment and endurance that varsity coaches liked to think they instilled in their players, but of prudence and humility and long suffering, the Christian, stoical virtues he was by reason of his own athletic incompetence perfectly suited to teach.

Now that the spring coaching had begun and the push past World War I to the final exam was underway in his American history classes, he knew he would have little time for relaxation until June. After his last class Saturday morning, he decided to steal away to the Kensington Center Golf Course for his first and probably last round before graduation. He wasn't a good golfer, really a duffer who shot in the high forties on a good day, but he fantasized that perfect round all winter and he had played enough to believe he might someday put thirty-five perfect shots together in sequence.

He didn't really love golf so much as the golf course itself, bordered by stone walls, with fairways slicing through copses of hardwoods and white pine, terraced greens cut into the sides of hills, and the flooding stream that wandered through the middle of the course. Players crossed the stream several times on bridges constructed of oak timbers and pine slabs. The course was hilly, full of irregular contours. He rarely hit a flat lie. Every shot was different, even the putts. It was this wonderful irregularity that attracted him to New England. He had spent two years in the Navy in New London and on liberties explored the coves and beaches from Old Lyme to Stonington and upland into the hills and woods of eastern Connecticut.

After the service, he returned to the Midwest and finished his interrupted undergraduate program at Northwestern and then completed his Masters in American history at Wisconsin. Toward the end of his graduate program, he came across by chance a notice in the placement office for a job teaching American history at the Kensington School in Connecticut. He needed a break from the graduate school grind, so he sent off a letter of application. During spring vacation he drove East, interviewed for the job, and with no other job in sight he accepted an appointment when it was offered a month later.

He had not intended it to be a permanent position. It was just to be a break for a few years. Each winter in his first years he announced that he was quitting to do something more important with his life like graduate school to finish his doctorate or the Peace Corps. Then it was a larger prep school, and finally law school. They were mostly fantasies that he entertained but never did much about. Early each spring Headmaster Woodbridge called him in to his office for his annual lecture and pep talk which invariably succeeded in "screwing Bartley's head back on straight again."

In time, he and Karen were married and his daughters arrived soon after. Also in time, he became the master of his own destiny. It wasn't a very grand destiny, but he was master of it. He was appointed chairman of the history department in his fifth year, revamped the curriulum shifting the focus away from the purely political to the social, economic, and cultural, and hired teachers compatible with his own style and approach. His dissertation on Jefferson would never get beyond note cards of sources, but each year his understanding of American history widened and deepened as he told again the story of the Great New Beginning here in New England where it all began 350 years before and repeated itself as it moved westward in ever widening circles of inclusiveness and toleration. Except for his mediocrity at golf and his losing baseball teams, his life was comfortable and satisfying.

He found his clubs and cart in a darkened corner of the basement. He dragged them into the light near the bottom of the stairs and, extracting the clubs one at a time, began wiping off the bits of dried grass and dirt with the towel attached to his bag. He checked the pocket for balls, found two unopened packages that he could not even remember owning, and stored them away again.

The door at the top of the stairs opened. He looked up to see two blond pony tails surrounding an indistinguishable face.

"Is that you, Daddy?" The voice was artificially bold.

"Of course, it's me. Is that you, Annie?" The door opened all the way and she came bounding down the stairs.

"Of course, it's me. Who else would it be?"

"Oh, I don't know. I was surprised to see you so I asked a dumb question. I thought you had gone with Mom to the chapel to do flowers."

"I did but I came back." She stood before him in the full light at the foot of the stairs. She wore jeans and white sneakers and a dark red, hooded sweat shirt with "Kensington" spelled out in white letters across her chest. In the light her face shone pink and chubby, and he thought he sensed a look of hopefulness or expectation in her eyes. Or was it loneliness or boredom?

"Didn't Mom need your help?"

"I suppose so, but Rach was along and wanted to help too, and if I'm there then I just do everything because she can't reach and then she gets mad, but I get bored waiting for her because it takes her about a month to drag the chair up to the altar and climb up and get a vase and hand it to Mom and then climb down and move the chair, et cetera, et cetera. Do you get the picture?"

"Yes, I get the picture."

"What are you doing?" she asked.

"It's so nice out I thought I'd play a round of golf. First of the year."

"Do you need a caddy or a scorekeeper or anything?"

"Are you sure Mom doesn't need you? You've been helping her with the flowers a long time now."

"I suppose she needs me, but I talked to her and told her that I was kind of growing out of helping with the flowers and that it seemed that Rach was kind of identifying with her a lot lately and that maybe I should just take off and let her set the altar today and not compete because when it goes so slow I get bored."

"Identify? Where'd you learn that word?"

"In social studies. We learned about identifying and role models."

"Who told you about them?"

"Mr. Seznowski."

"Mr. Seznowski? That doesn't sound like his subject."

"He was talking mainly to the boys about baseball and playing sports and being on a team and learning teamwork and spirit from a coach."

"What do the girls do when he's talking to the boys about sports?"

"Oh, we get bored and think of other things and try not to laugh at him because he talks so loud and gets carried away. The boys sit there staring up at him with their mouths open. He doesn't teach social studies, Daddy. He teaches sports. All the time, even in math. I hope you teach history in your classes and not sports. I'm sick of sports. There's no teams for girls except being a cheerleader. Yuk." He picked up his bag and cart and began to lift it up the stairs.

"If you want to come along, you have to promise not to get bored and want to leave. We'll be at least two hours on the course, maybe longer because I'm going to play a couple of practice balls."

She jumped ahead of him up the stairs.

"I'll get the doors." She opened the door ahead of him as he carried the clubs up the stairs. Then she rushed to the entry door and opened it and ran ahead of him behind the dorm to their station wagon.

"I won't get bored, Daddy. If I do, I'll just kind of go off by myself and enjoy nature, look for frogs or wild flowers or something."

Before stowing his clubs in the back of the car, he showed her how to spring the wheels of the cart into place and unfurl the handle until it caught. She took the handle, tilted the cart forward and pulled the clubs around the car.

"That's easy," she said. "Can I keep score too? Will you teach me?"

"Nothing to it," he said. "Just count the strokes and write the number down in the space after the number of the hole. I'll show you when we get a card at the course."

They collapsed the wheels and handle and loaded the clubs into the back of the wagon. She climbed in after them and sat next to the clubs. Bartley walked around the car once before getting in. He shook his head at the rusting rocker arms and fenders. It was virtually an embarrassment, something of a joke—a decaying Country Squire with fake wooden paneling—a symbol of those American values of bigness and waste he held in open contempt. He had bought it, a used nine-passenger wagon, to haul students to games, off campus movies, concerts. One semester, a group of his more radical students had dubbed it in good-natured mockery the "bourgeoismobile." Perhaps, this was the spring to make a change. He started the car then shut it off and turned around to Annie.

"Hey, Pal, you better use the bathroom before we go. It'll be at least three hours before we get back." He didn't want her to use the public toilet in the club house.

"O.K." She climbed over the seat and opened the door. "Besides, I have to leave a note for Mom. She'll want to know where I am. We're supposed to do the baking later for the dorm feed. I'm your assistant tonight. Mom's going to the movies with Mrs. Martin, so I get to put everything out." She shut the car door. "I'll be right back." Then she paused a moment and asked, "Are you O.K.? Have you gone to the bathroom?"

He laughed. "Yes. Besides, boys don't have to worry about that. We just go behind a tree in the woods."

"Girls can do that too, you know."

"Behind a tree? Girls?"

"Oh, Daddy, not just by a tree. In the woods. Where no one can see. It's not very complicated."

Somehow, now that he was assured that she wouldn't have a problem, he didn't like the idea.

*   *   *   *

Two hours later, they drove back to the campus and parked behind the dorm. Annie ran into the house to begin her baking and Bartley took his clubs to the basement and began cleaning his irons. When he had finished he went upstairs and flopped into an overstuffed arm chair in the corner of his study opposite his desk. They had draped the chair, bought at a year end dorm auction, with a bright red throw to hide the white stuffing that bulged through the worn upholstery of the arms and seat cushion. But it was comfortable. When he prepared for class there, he placed a writing board across the arms and placed the book he was reading or the papers he was grading on it. Just as often though he fell asleep. Once, in his first years at Kensington when the history department was small, they decided to read examination blue books together after dinner. He brought in a rocker and two other easy chairs from the living room for the other members of the department. Each opened a can of beer. They held a short business meeting and then began to read. Karen found them all asleep at nine o'clock. When he needed to get work done, he went to the library, found an uncomfortable wooden chair, and sat bolt upright at a table. Right now, he relaxed and recalled the few good golf shots of his mediocre opening round.

A short hallway connected his study to a bathroom on the right and the kitchen beyond. The doors were open and he could hear Karen's and Annie's voices echoing down the hall from the kitchen where they had already begun baking for the dorm feed. He listened passively, intermittently at first, then with sharpened interest, then with dismay, then with anger and finally with humiliation and despair.

"So what did you do with Daddy this morning?" he heard Karen's voice over the gentle whirl of an electric beater.

"Oh, I pulled the golf cart and kept score, looked for lost balls, chased some frogs, put up with a couple dumb fourth formers."

"Was it fun?"

"A little. Mostly boring though."

"Did you learn anything? Would you find the cookie sheets in the drawer under the oven? And we'd better double the cookie recipe. Daddy says there aren't many boys off on weekends."

Bartley heard the sliding metal and the clank of the drawer.

"Not much really. Keeping score is easy. All you have to do is add. There are lots of rules though. They're on the back of the card and they're different on every golf course." He heard some more clanging and then the conversation was obliterated by the high whine of the beater. In about a minute the beater quit suddenly, leaving a dramatic silence for several moments.

"I learned something else. Not like learning at school or anything."

"What was that?"

He sensed a deliberate hesitation in the pause that followed.

"Daddy cheats at golf."

"Daddy cheats!!" Karen almost shouted and then began to laugh.

"How?" she asked.

"He takes extra shots, and he moves the ball to make it easier to hit. He played two balls and sometimes he told me to put down the lowest score. And once he didn't count all his strokes. He used algebra instead. Hey, Mom, that's right. Daddy taught me algebra today. That's the neatest thing I learned lately. Algebra—using a letter like x or y to stand for a number especially if the number is enormous. X is an unknown number and even if you know the number, it sounds better to put down x instead of some awful score like 14, which is what he *really* had on the fifth hole, but we put an x down instead."

"That's not exactly cheating unless he put a smaller number down instead of 14 when he added the score."

"He didn't do that. He was honest with the total score. He put down 46 + x. It's different with what's called Mulligans and winter rules. And it's really strange with that kind of cheating because there are rules."

"Rules for cheating? That certainly is strange. What kind of rules does Daddy have when he cheats?"

"Well, in Mulligans you can take a second shot without a penalty on the first hole only. But if you decide the first shot was terrible and you want to take a second shot, called a Mulligan, you have to play the second ball even if it's worse than the first."

"Why is it called a Mulligan?"

"I asked him, and he said it was originally some kind of ethnic slur against the Irish. Isn't Daddy Irish?"

"He's half Irish."

"Is he Jewish?"

"No. He's Irish and English. Why did you think he was Jewish?"

"Oh, he explained something about another cheating rule called a Shapiro. He said that was originally an ethnic slur too."

"What's a Shapiro?" Karen asked.

"According to Daddy, *it's the best of an infinite number.* That means you can hit about a thousand balls off the first tee and you play the best one. You can only do that when there's nobody else on the golf course, I think. It's a way of warming up. Daddy said it was probably given a Jewish name because Jewish people are so smart."

"I don't think he should have told you about a Shapiro even if he tried to make it complimentary."

"I think he was just trying to entertain me. He thought I was already bored, but I wasn't. I didn't get bored till about the fourth hole when we caught up to the two fourth formers and Daddy played with them the rest of the way."

"Would you check the cookies in the oven. We'll put the cake in later. When we put the cake in, would you go over to the Martins and get Rachel. I don't want her crossing the highway alone."

"O.K. Here's another cookie sheet ready."

"You said Daddy moved his ball too."

"Yeah. There's a rule on that too. It's called winter rules or preferred lies. But I told him it was April, and he said April in New England is like February in Florida where they have special conditions. Anyway. You get to move your ball a few inches so you won't have a bad lie. You can't tee it up or anything, but Daddy moved it around until it sat up nice in the grass. They don't do that in the tournaments on T.V. I watched and they *never* move the ball with their hand or the club. But I guess it's O.K. because on the card it said winter rules were permitted under certain conditions."

"That doesn't sound so bad."

"No. I guess that wasn't bad cheating. But there were a lot of times he didn't have to move the ball at all. The grass was nice and smooth and the ball was easy to hit, but he moved it anyway."

"What were the boys like?"

"Typical fourth formers. One boy's mother is that *awful* Aunt Sarah on that *terrible* soap opera."

"What's a typical fourth former? I didn't know fourth formers were capable of typical behavior."

"Oh, smart alecky, show offy, silly. Mostly for each other. Especially dirty words. When we were in the rough looking for Daddy's ball on the hole he had that humongous 14, they used D, H, S, and F words, mostly showing off to each other that they were mature or something."

"Didn't you say anything, tell them to stop or anything?"

"No. Why should I? We hear those words all the time coming out the windows of the dorms. Rach knows all of them and she's only six."

"I certainly hope you don't use them."

"Me? Why should I? I don't have to prove to others that I'm grown up. Girls know they're growing up. They don't have to prove it."

"Check to see if that sheet is cooled down a little. We'll fill it up once more."

"I was wondering about one word though. Is *pathetic* a dirty word?"

"No. It means sad. How did they use it?"

"They called Daddy's baseball team pathetic and that he was a pathetic coach. But sad doesn't seem to fit Daddy. He's always happy coaching, cheering his players and everything."

"In the sense they are using the word, pathetic means hopelessly incompetent."

"Just my luck. That dumb Bobby Bennett talks all the time about being the bat boy for the Kensington varsity because his father's the coach. There probably isn't such a thing as a bat girl, and if there was, what fun would it be being a bat girl on a pathetic team?"

"Maybe Daddy's team won't be as pathetic this year. Why don't you ask him if you can help?"

"I've been thinking of that, but I don't want to start and have that stupid Bobby making fun of me because the team is pathetic."

"Your father's not a pathetic history teacher."

"History teaching doesn't count much in the sixth grade, Mom. It's only coaching that counts in the sixth grade."

"You'll find that changes as you grow older."

"I know, but *now* is when Bobby is the varsity bat boy, not ten years from now."

Bartley heard the oven timer ring, the clanging of the doors, the sound of sliding thin metal and the closing of the oven door again.

"Daddy is funny though and the boys really liked him. They were awful players. I probably could play better than them. Daddy started giving them lessons, how to hold the club and hit down on the ball. He let me hit some practice shots on a short hole and I did better than they did. Then he tried to talk them into taking history, but they were afraid of Mr. McLean grading them too low. It was really funny how he teased them and pretended that if they didn't take history, he'd get them if they ever came before the Discipline Committee."

"Your father has a way with students. How he gets away with what he does, I'll never know. He's a mystery, but it's best not to ask questions about mysteries like your father. Just let them happen."

Annie laughed out loud.

"He was *so funny* in the car coming back talking to the boys about his score. 'If this, if that' he'd say. Instead of shooting 46 + x which equals 60, he decided his *real* score if everything had gone right would have been a 48 or so. I mean it was really funny the way he replayed some of the holes and cut two or three strokes off his score, and he decided he really should have had a 6 not a 14 on the third hole."

The timer bell sounded.

"That's enough cookies. It's not possible to make more than they can eat. We'll just quit now and put the cake in. You wash up and go get Rachel. I'll leave everything here in the kitchen. You let Rach help you frost the cake later and help Daddy take everything to the dining room table about ten. I should be back from the movie by 10:15 or so to finish up."

"O.K., Mom. Swell talking to you."

"Swell talking to you, Annie. We'll have to do this again. You know, you really ought to ask Daddy about being a bat girl for his team."

"I'll think about it. See you later."

Bartley heard the kitchen door close and the screen door slam. He sat stunned for several moments and then he bent forward, stood up slowly and walked to the kitchen. Karen stood with her back to him, looking out the window down the pathway leading toward the Main School Building. She wore a denim skirt and high-collared beige blouse. Her legs were bare and she wore webbed sandals. When he called her name, she turned around smiling her crooked smile (that he once called "naturally wry") and automatically brushed her bangs with one hand and fluffed the back of her hair with the other.

"Hi. Where have you been?"

"I've been sitting in my study for about ten minutes."

"Annie and I have finished the cookies. Annie really is something. She baked most of the cookies herself. Talked my leg off in the process."

"Yes, I know. I heard most of the conversation."

"What? You eavesdropped. You should be ashamed of yourself, Jack. That was our talk. None of your business."

"None of my business. Dear God, I'm shattered."

"You should have shut the door if you didn't like what you were hearing. And what are you shattered about? It was an ordinary conversation."

"Do you have many like that? About me?"

"We have many conversations like that. You are not usually the subject."

"Did you hear what she said."

"Of course, I heard what she said."

"I'm devastated."

"Oh, Jack. Quit over-reacting. It was just Annie, her way of saying things bluntly."

"But she thinks I cheat at golf."

"Well, don't you?"

"No. I play according to local agreements, not tournament rules. We take Mulligans because we don't have a chance to warm up. We take preferred lies because the Kensington Golf Course isn't exactly the Great Platonic Country Club in the Sky, you know. It's a disaster. Most New England golf courses are disaster areas until June or July. The tournament golfers play on manicured courses. No one is permitted to play on them for weeks before a tournament. Their fairways are better than our greens. When the Kensington course is in *perfect* condition, I'll play according to tournament rules. Good lord, Karen, everyone cheats at golf. It goes with the territory. It doesn't mean I'm going to cheat on you or embezzle money or cheat widows and orphans in scams." He paused. "I mean, every time I drive the car I break the speed limit. That doesn't make me a murderer or traitor. Players just

all agree beforehand whether they are going to take Mulligans and preferred lies."

"What about putting down x instead of fourteen?"

"We do that all the time, too, especially in match play when you
lose a hole, you lose a hole. It doesn't make any difference by how
much. If the other player beats you with a 5, then you can have a 6 or a
12 or a 100. You just lose one hole."

"You better explain all that to Annie."

"What good would it do now? She not only thinks I'm a cheat, she
thinks I'm *pathetic*, and your definition didn't help—'hopelessly
incompetent.' You could have said outmatched or poorly equipped to
compete. She's already too ashamed even to ask me if she can be my
bat girl. And besides, we're not pathetic. It's the schedule that makes us
look bad. We play tough teams."

"She'll understand that if you explain it to her. She's very understanding and sympathetic."

She turned away from him and poured the cake batter into the pans.
She opened the oven doors and placed the pans on the wire racks and
closed the door. He sat down on a kitchen chair and watched her prepare the frosting.

"I shouldn't have taken her along."

"Jack," she laughed, "you can't be the perfect father forever. Children grow up. They sense a larger world. They become critical, discover flaws, imperfections in their parents."

"I guess I've got my work cut out for me."

"We have our work cut out for us."

"Maybe it's time we started looking for another prep school for her.
Send her off and defer her awareness of our fallibility."

"When Kensington goes coed, she may want to come here."

"Unofficially, Woody implied in the department heads meeting the
other day that we are going coed a year from now. The Trustees will
officially announce it during their spring meeting." He paused. "I
hadn't thought of that. Not Annie coming here, but that she will have

to live with other students' opinions of us. That could be dreadful for her. Especially if her father is already both a pathetic coach and a cheat at golf, and a 'mystery that defies explanation.' You told her that too."

He had calmed down, even managed a smile at her final characterization of him. He returned to his study, his anger and humiliation had turned into a reflective sadness. He sat at his desk and listened to Karen move about in the kitchen. Finally, he spoke down the hallway.

"Did you know something, Karen. That just being yourself, just existing in the presence of others is a terrible responsibility, but to have children is awesome."

He did not hear her come down the hallway. She was behind him before he knew it.

"I'm sorry I teased. You really are hurt, aren't you?"

He tried to smile.

"No. Not hurt. I know I'm a lousy golfer and a pathetic coach. I'm frightened for Annie now that she knows it too."

"Don't worry. As she grows older, she'll find new and better role models to emulate and in time she'll forgive us." She returned to the kitchen.

"What do we do until then?" he shouted.

"Why, muddle our way through as best we can."

He knew that was true, but somehow that didn't seem adequate any more. That's what he did with other people's children.

*   *   *   *

Later that afternoon as he sat in his study, he heard a knock that was so light and tentative that at first Bartley thought it was the door rattling. Air currents from doors opening and closing at the opposite end of the dormitory would set his study door vibrating. He again made a mental note to fill out a work order for housekeeping to tighten the door or pad it with insulation.

He was reading through sixty-three responses to Question #3—Turner's Thesis—on the departmental examination. It had been one of his questions, one that he had insisted politely, as department chairman, be included even though his colleagues had objected, politely, that though the closing of the frontier was not irrelevant, it did seem to them that Bartley was "flogging a dead hobby-horse," but they acquiesced; he volunteered to read the responses to Question #3.

The door rattled again. Clearly now it was a knock, timid and hesitant, but insistent. It was probably a third former who had lost his key, couldn't find the prefect, and desperate, had ventured to invade his privacy. At the first dorm meeting in the fall, he had warned them about losing keys. Coming to get his master key, unless a matter of life and death, was an intolerable invasion of privacy. It was one of his few absolutes. He knew they believed him to be one of the more liberal masters, lenient and friendly, so they were reluctant to alienate him, especially since there were so few minor rules that either he or his wife had not compromised out of kindness.

He finished the response he was reading and called Karen, who he thought was in the kitchen, but she didn't answer. He decided she had taken the girls for a walk. Whenever he graded papers at home, Karen protected him from intrusions from the dormitory. The knock sounded again, this time forceful and demanding. He prepared himself for a brief episode of indignation.

Standing before him was his prefect, Peter Colby, his clenched fist raised, about to knock again. He dropped his arm abjectly. Bartley looked for Peter's eyes, but they avoided him, first glancing at over Bartley's head to a framed World War I poster of Woodrow Wilson, surrounded by flags and bunting and boys in uniform on the wall above the desk, and then to the floor. Bartley had never known Peter to avoid a direct engagement of eyes. He was notorious for his forthrightness—a straight-arrow, direct, no-nonsense young man. Peter entered Kensington in the third form from Iowa, the son of an alumnus who had gone west to seek his fortune as the president of a bank purchased by his family.

In spring of his third form year Peter led a gentle revolt against the brittle sophistication and cynicism of Kensington's "negos," mostly sixth formers who had exhausted the social and intellectual possibilities of a pastoral boarding school and were thinking already of the new and promising life of sin that awaited them in Cambridge and New Haven and New York. Peter received permission from the chaplain to speak at Tuesday evening chapel, often led by a faculty member or student. He read to the school a newspaper article about "squares," sent to him by his mother who had clipped it from Peter's hometown newspaper in Iowa. The article was about "square deals" and "square meals" and being on the "square." Peter concluded by declaring he was proud to be a "square."

It was a daring feat for a third former to challenge the reigning opinion makers of the school, but he survived the mocking epithet of "poso" leveled at him and went on to be a leader of an "era of good feeling" that had become the spirit of the school ever since, a spirit gratefully welcomed by a faculty grown weary of student distrust and hostility.

"May I speak to you, sir...privately, if possible."

"Sure, Peter. Come in." Bartley motioned Peter to a captain's chair alongside his desk. Peter wore his crew sweats with leather patches on the seat, a towel around his neck tucked inside his sweatshirt, and those wonderful, fitted, soft leather sneakers that Bartley always admired and would have purchased from the Athletic Association had he been able to decide a practical use for them.

"Just back from the Crew Lake?"

Yes, sir. The bus left me off behind the dorm."

"I assume you're first boat again this year."

"Yes, sir. So far anyhow."

Peter's modesty was genuine. He probably really felt someone might displace him as the stroke of the first boat, which had won the first boat fours at Worcester the previous spring by two lengths, but everyone else knew that he could generate more power with more perfect rhythm and timing than any oarsman at Kensington in recent memory. He was a tall, powerfully built young man and a dedicated athlete. He played tackle on the football team and wrestled light-heavyweight in the winter. He was good at football and wrestling because he was strong, but he lacked finesse. In crew, he was gifted, certainly capable of Division I college level rowing though his intention was to attend a small college in the Midwest, either Grinnell or Carleton. That he had chosen to be Bartley's advisee and dormitory prefect was an indication of serious academic aspirations as well as athletic. Bartley, though enthusiastic, was a decidedly mediocre coach of lower level teams, an assistant in third form soccer, and head coach of third form baseball— a team whose perennial performance was something of a joke among students and faculty alike.

"Is the ice out?"

"One end near the finish line is still frozen, but we've been able to get in a good workout. There's plenty of open water at the upper end."

"It's been early this year."

"Yes, sir. Last year the ice didn't melt until almost the first week of April."

"Well, we're still indoors in baseball. The field is all mud. Not that I mind, of course. We don't get much done in the gym. It defers my realization of just how bad we're going to be. It also sustains the players' illusion for another week or so that I know what I'm doing."

Bartley laughed at the joke on himself, but Peter could manage only a flicker of a forced smile. He leaned forward in the chair with his hands on his knees and began to stare at the floor. Bartley sat down at his desk and leaned back in his chair. He looked past Peter to the plaque in the shape of a shield that he had been given at an athletic awards dinner in his tenth year at Kensington. It read "For ten years of meritorious service to Kensington players and teams and for enthusiasm above and beyond the call of duty." That too was something of a joke. He waited several moments and then, sensing a real problem, he spoke.

"What's wrong, Peter?"

Peter brought his hands to his face and shook his head. For a moment Bartley thought the boy might cry, but when Peter looked up at him and engaged Bartley's eyes for the first time, Bartley saw a face flushed with embarrassment, the color rising in Peter's cheeks to his hair line.

"I meant to come and see you earlier in the week, sir. Actually I almost came in Sunday night when I got back from my weekend, but I just couldn't."

Once again he looked down at the floor. Bartley began to feel a rising tension—there was something wrong, so serious that the boy couldn't speak of it. He felt some terrible confession was hovering on the horizon, an admission of drug or alcohol involvement, plagiarism; his imagination quickly ran down the list of all the major offenses punishable by dismissal in the K book.

"Do you want this conversation to be considered confidential? Are you asking to invoke the discretionary clause of the disciplinary procedures?" As soon as he had spoken, he felt ashamed for suspecting Peter. There had never been the slightest hint of suspicion about Peter about anything in four years. Peter looked up startled.

"Oh, no, sir. My problem isn't disciplinary, it's personal. I wouldn't break a major school rule now, two months before graduation and at the beginning of the crew season."

Bartley watched the color in Peter's face subside. Bartley could detect a setting of face muscles. The boy licked his lips."Sir…" he blurted and halted, stumbling for words. Then he seemed to give up again. Bartley didn't know whether he should help with questions or wait patiently for it all to come tumbling out. Patience was usually the best strategy when a confession was impending. Finally, Peter blurted,

"You're a Catholic, aren't you, sir?"

Bartley sat motionless for some time, not so much bewildered by what seemed an irrelevant question as intrigued by the connection of the question to the personal problem that was about to be revealed.

"Yes, I'm Catholic, more or less. I don't practice regularly any more." He felt irritated at himself because he knew the tone of his admission was defensive, that he might have conveyed that he was ashamed of being Catholic. He wanted to add that he was a Midwesterner, like Peter, and a graduate of Wisconsin and Northwestern, which were the very reasons Bartley had been hired in the first place when Headmaster Woodbridge decided to diversify the student body and faculty in the late fifties and early sixties. The school had become so diverse, so tolerant of differences over the years that he had not thought about how strange he felt in those first years a decade and a half ago when Kensington was still considered a country club, a restricted preserve for the sons of Wall Street brokers and financiers living in the Fertile Crescent of affluence from Cold Spring Harbor to Darien.

"Could you answer some questions about Catholicism for me, sir?"

"I guess so. As much as I know, which is as far as being raised Catholic and Catholic high school took me. Why me though? You can go down to Kensington Center and talk to Father Burns at St. Michael's or you can talk to Mr. Le Clair in the French department. He's a professional Catholic. I'm only a lukewarm amateur."

"I couldn't ask anyone else, sir. You're my adviser. It's personal. Besides, what I want to know is about Catholic morality." And he flushed pink to his ears again. Bartley guessed the drift of Peter's problem.

"Should I close the door?"

"Yes, sir. I think that would be better. I wouldn't want Mrs. Bartley to hear."

Bartley got up and closed the door into the kitchen. As he returned to his chair, he asked, "Are we going to talk about last weekend?"

"Yes, sir," Peter said with resolve, now that Bartley had carried him across the emotional barrier, the shadow line of his humiliation.

"Oh, God, sir. It was terrible. What happened was just awful."

"I've already gathered that much. You're not helping me understand your problem by lamenting your fate. Do you want me to help you? Do you want my advice or am I just a listener?" He had to take Peter seriously on this the only occasion in four years he had come to Bartley with a problem.

"Oh, I need your advice, sir. I didn't come here just because I felt sorry for myself."

"Then, begin at the beginning, please, and lead me out of this wilderness where you have managed to lose me."

"Yes, sir. I'm sorry. I jumped to the end because I can't get Sunday out of my mind. I'll go back to the beginning. I took a weekend last Friday night."

"That much I know. I had the duty for three days in your absence."

"I went to Jennifer Powell's home near Worcester. We've been dating for almost two years now. Her dad picked me up after crew practice. She took a weekend from Randall Hall. We wanted to be together just once before crew season began. We won't see each other again until the spring dance in May. I've got to row every Saturday until the Regatta."

"So far you haven't told me anything I don't already know." Bartley knew from Peter's weekend permission slip where he had gone.

He knew Jennifer Powell well enough. She was one of several young women assigned to their apartment at the Glee Club Dance two years ago when Peter first met her.

"Listen, Peter. We're going to be here all night if you plan to explain every trivial detail. I happen to know, it's a matter of common knowledge here, that you've been going with Jennifer for over two years, that she's been your guest for two dance weekends, and that she's Catholic, if that's important, because I drove her to mass once."

"I've got to get to it in my own way, sir. I just can't jump into it."
There was a touch of petulance in his voice.

"O.K. I'm sorry." He spoke gently now. "Let it come out the way it
has to." He suddenly realized that it was his own curiosity that made
him impatient. He knew generally what was coming and he wanted to
get to the essential details.

"I'm going back home in June. Chances are we won't ever see each
other again. She's going to Smith, and I'll probably end up at Grinnell.
It's what my parents want and I guess I want it too. I've attended at
least one of my dad's schools, so long as I return to the Midwest, I can
go to any school I want so long as they approve of it."

"I thought you really liked Grinnell and Carleton."

"I do. It's just that my choice is ending up to be their choice too,
and it's too late now to apply back here. Because now I wish I were
going to come back east again next year."

"And so your last real weekend together turned out rotten?"

"Yes, sir. It was supposed to be perfect and it turned out worse than
rotten. We were going to see each other only once more before graduation—at the spring dance here when she will be coming for the weekend; but dances are so crowded and busy, there's no privacy…"

"And restricted."

"Yes, sir. Restricted. I should say we were going to see each other
once more. Now I'm not going to see her at all."

Over the years Bartley had desensitized himself from a too ready
responsiveness to student unhappiness. He had been something of a
Pied Piper in his first years at Kensington—seeking out student misery,
engaging and often exacerbating it, and then rescuing the victim with
his compassionate understanding and wise counsel. He needed that
when he was a new teacher, needed to be of personal value to each student, needed student approval, needed to be their friend—not just an
authority or judge or taskmaster. Soon he found himself with no time
to himself. Students with problems from all over campus sought him
out causing some envy and bitterness among colleagues who felt he was

interfering. He worried all day over a student's anguish that he became aware of after a morning class only to discover by evening that the student couldn't even remember being upset earlier in the day. As he gained experience, he began to detach himself from student problems unless they became obvious through chronic recurrence or dramatic obtrusion. He tried to keep alert to signs of serious emotional disorders, potential self destructive behavior. He knew Peter's pain was routine, there was not danger here, but Bartley owed Peter more than sympathy. He sensed for the first time Peter's misery. The boy's pain was so real it was palpable.

"Go ahead. I really don't know how I'm going to be able to help you, but…" He shrugged.

He heard the front door open and after a few seconds, slam; then the chatter of his children Amy and Rachel and Karen in the kitchen. He got up and opened the door, and as he greeted the girls he signaled to Karen with his eyes that he was in a personal conference. She nodded and after he closed the door and sat down, he heard her shepherd the children down the hallway to the other side of the apartment. When he sat down, he knew he should be quiet until Peter told his story.

"Anyhow it all started off great. Mr. Powell picked me up on Friday night after crew practice. He had already picked up Jennifer and we drove to their home. Mrs. Powell made a great dinner. Then we all watched TV together. The next day Jennifer had the car and we went all over together. We played tennis and climbed a small mountain. She gave me a tour of the day school she had attended before she went to Randall Hall. Then we went home, and I helped Mr. Powell with a cookout. They had some friends in for drinks and supper. Some of their friends were really neat; one guy had rowed for Cornell and we talked about rowing. Anyhow, all of the adults went out to some tennis or country club to a party and dance. We stayed home to babysit for Jennifer's sister. After Jennifer's little sister went to bed, we went to the recreation room to watch TV, but it was lousy so we turned it off and put some records on and danced."

He stopped to regroup his emotional forces. During this general narrative, he had looked at Bartley directly. Now he dropped his eyes again to the floor.

"We danced for a while, and we began to neck and then we were on the couch sitting, and then we kind of stretched out." Peter broke off and stared at the floor.

"Am I to assume," Bartley said, "that something happened?"

"Yes, sir," Peter groaned.

"And good Catholic girl that she was, she became angry at what you did?"

Peter looked up with a strange expression of surprise, almost wonder on his face.

"Oh, no, sir. I didn't do anything just on my own. She wanted me to. She moved my hand. I wouldn't dare by myself."

"What's your problem then?"

"She came in. Mrs. Powell. They came back early from the party. She had a headache or something. Mr. Powell was putting the car away. We had music on so we didn't hear them drive up or the doors open or shut."

"I take it that Mrs. Powell wasn't too happy with what she saw?"

"She became so angry, so absolutely enraged she was almost out of her head. I thought she was going to have a stroke or a fit. She sent me to my room and took Jennifer to her room and they talked half the night."

"Mr. Powell never became part of any of this?"

"No, sir. Even the next day when Mrs. Powell treated me as though I was some kind of turd, he acted as though nothing happened. I went to mass with them and sat there like a dummy or like some murderer or thief, and poor Jennifer was on the edge of tears all day."

"What did Mrs. Powell say to you?"

"Nothing. She didn't say a damn word, sir. I wish she had. She just looked with this cold stare or else turned her back. Sir. She is the iciest bitch I have ever met in my life. You'd swear I'd killed her daughter."

"I'm afraid you may have done much worse."

"She didn't talk to me, but she told Jennifer that she couldn't see me again. She's made it absolutely clear that Jennifer won't be able to come to Kensington for the spring dance…Sir, what did I do that was so horrible?"

Bartley decided he couldn't probe any further. He didn't need any details. He didn't want to be a priest in a confessional. He was instantly transported over twenty years backward in time to his own adolescence, to his religion class at Christian Brothers Academy in a remote, Midwestern city and Brother Augustine, his home room advisor, almost eighty years of age. He remembered the lectures on purity, the prohibition of virtually everything, the man-to-man talks when Brother Augie exhibited his familiarity with worldly expressions like "French kissing" or "wet dreams" or "starched shorts." He almost broke into a smile as he recalled the classroom scene, each student repressing laughter as best he could, but the silent undercurrent of mockery conveyed by eyes and the coarse and erotic movements of hands beneath and beyond the awareness of Brother Augie, who stared at the floor and the ceiling between bursts of rhetoric.

"Peter, I can clarify matters very simply. Everything is forbidden. Today, the morality hasn't changed, but there is less emphasis upon sexual purity; but when I was young, and more importantly, when Mrs. Powell was young, any illicit picture, movie, book, or activity, including dancing too close, that might lead to sexual contact or intercourse was officially forbidden—the domino theory of inevitable sexual progression. At school dances, if you danced holding your girl too closely, a brother would sneak up behind you and tap on your shoulder and advise you to leave room for the Holy Ghost between you and your girl."

"Are you putting me on, sir?"

"No, I am not, Peter. What you were doing is explicitly prohibited, or rather, whatever you were doing is probably prohibited. In my young manhood, I was told over and over that chastity was the most sacred, most hallowed virtue. Indeed, I associated the loss of my childhood innocence almost exclusively with my developing sexuality, though I should have lost my innocence with a growing awareness of injustice, or evil, or death, or suffering, but such was not the case with me or probably with Mrs. Powell either." He had unconsciously lapsed into his pedantic, teacher's voice.

Peter hunched his shoulders, absorbing what he heard, and nodding his head sadly as he realized the full implication of what Bartley was saying. Finally, he spoke steadily, without apparent rancour.

"I think that's the stupidest, most unnatural attitude I've ever heard. Jennifer is the first girl I've ever touched like that and I didn't do it for two years."

"You may be right, Peter, but what you believe is not what Mrs. Powell believes about Jennifer and your relationship with her."

Peter leaned forward again and with his elbows on his knees, placed his head in his hands, and sat staring at the floor, reflecting, silently weeping—Bartley couldn't tell. If Bartley didn't know that Peter was devoid of the least capacity of hokum, he would have been repulsed by what appeared to be melodramatic posturing.

As he sat waiting for Peter to speak again, he felt a gradual detachment from the moment and from the person he had become. He wondered what he was doing here in this study, in this remote New England boarding school, listening to a trivial tale of sentimental woe which fifteen years ago he would have dismissed with contempt. But he was here, not only listening but advising and commiserating with a young man whose monumental suffering amounted to little more than the denial of a date to a spring dance—a denial he probably deserved.

"Would you help me, sir? Would you help me write a letter to Mrs. Powell to apologize, to beg her, or whatever I have to do, to let Jennifer come to the spring dance? I'll do anything."

"Maybe she'll relent all by herself. Maybe you should wait her out a while. She may realize she over-responded. Surely Jennifer told her mother the truth, and if she comes to believe it was the first time and that it won't happen again now that you understand her attitude, she'll come around of her own accord. Do you communicate with Jennifer? Write? Phone?"

"I call her almost every night and charge it to my home number."

"Well, give it some time. Jennifer will let you know in a week or so if there is any relenting."

"O.K. I'll wait. But in the meantime would you help me prepare a letter to Mrs. Powell in case she doesn't change her mind?"

"I really shouldn't, Peter. I've really done about all I should as an adviser." Actually he had no business doing anything as an adviser. Peter's problem originated beyond the school's jurisdiction. Bartley could listen, he could commiserate, help Peter deal with his disappointment, but Mrs. Powell was not a Kensington parent. Yet he owed so much to Peter. The boy's good will and positive attitude had kept the spirit and morale of the dorm high for two years now. Peter had saved Bartley hours of counseling and disciplinary litigation by sensing potential trouble and defusing it before it came to Bartley's official attention. Peter did all of Bartley's unofficial early warning and he steered boys with emerging personal or academic problems to Bartley before they became serious. Prevention was ninety percent of Bartley's job and Peter had done fifty percent of the prevention.

He saw the disappointment in Peter's eyes.

"I tell you what I'll do. I'll read your draft and make suggestions, but you're going to have to write the letter yourself."

"Do you have any suggestions now?"

"Yes. Be honest, but remember Mrs. Powell believes in the sacredness of her daughter and you threaten her idea of her daughter. She is still a child to her mother."

Peter stood up preparing to leave. For the first time a smile broke across Peter's face.

"You'll have me sympathizing with her point of view pretty soon." He opened the door and disappeared into the hallway.

Bartley heard the door close behind Peter. He closed his eyes for several moments and opened them again and focused on the spines of books arranged on the shelves to the right of his desk aesthetically by color rather than alphabetically by author. He turned to stare across the room at the door Peter had just shut behind him. He hoped Peter's problem would go away. He had already found Mrs. Powell guilty of arrogant abuse of her moral authority and felt a rising anger against her. He did not want to re-open the spiritual wounds it had taken years to heal. He smiled as he said a brief, silent prayer that Peter's problem would go away. He shook his head in wonder. The indelible marks were indeed indelible, and the anger and guilt would always lie, just below the surface of his consciousness.

✳   ✳   ✳   ✳

Later that evening, Annie and Rachel popped four grocery bags of popcorn and frosted the cake. When Rachel fell asleep watching the TV, he took her to bed, made a tour of the dorm, and returned to play cards with Annie until the movie in the gym was over. Karen returned a little after 10:00 and hurried to the kitchen to check that he and Annie had done everything she had told them to do.

"How was the movie?"

"I don't know. I couldn't tell whether it was any good or not. I was so angry through most of it, I couldn't concentrate. I should have left early but Janet wanted to stay."

"The usual student disruption and barnyard observations?"

"Yes. But I can deal with that. It's Skinner. He was the O.D. He stopped the film three times, threatening the students with disciplinary action. All he had to do was ignore the comments and they would have shut up. He was wearing his marine fatigues with captain's bars and every time he stopped the film, he walked to the front of the gym and stood glaring, his feet set apart and his hands clasped behind his back. He's been out of the Marines for five years now. When is he going to grow up and realize all he does is provoke the students. He's such an ass."

Bartley smiled at her outrage. Skinner, math teacher and varsity basketball coach, was an ineffectual macho joke among the students. They probably went to the movie because they knew he was on duty and wanted to antagonize him, safely, with anonymous catcalls in a darkened gym. It was something of a sport.

"It takes all kinds," he laughed.

"It does not take all kinds. There is no justification for Skinner. He's a menace. He's awful, Jack." She turned around and stamped her foot. "He treats Marilyn like a chattel possession and he humiliates his basketball players too, screaming at them during the game. I used to love the basketball games, but I can't go any more. He must be awful in the classroom. I just don't understand why Woody rehires him. I don't understand how you tolerate him. He stands for everything you have always hated."

He winced. She spoke the truth. Fourteen years ago, he would have shared her rage. Did he know more now or care less? He tried to assuage her anger by justifying himself. He pretended to a lightness of tone though he spoke as much to convince himself as her.

"First of all, you would not be so angry if you realized just how little influence he has among students. They probably went to the movie just to challenge him tonight. If he really had any influence on student values, I'd feel your anger. But he doesn't, and Woody tolerates him because he is, like it or not, an adequate math teacher in a time when math teachers are hard to come by. Besides, he's willing to coach varsity level sports at a time when many of the present faculty are either unwilling to do so or, like me, are incompetent to do so."

She had turned her back on him and carried the cake to the dining room. He didn't follow her. He knew she was right, of course. Skinner's presence at Kensington was a mistake, but he also knew that the school was slow to correct mistakes. Woody could get rid of Skinner in time, through gentle pressure, hints of displeasure, limited raises, until even Skinner would get the message and resign to save face after he already had a job at some other school. That's the way it happened, quietly, politically, in some ways compassionately. It wasn't that Karen didn't understand that. She just didn't accept it as he did. She didn't care that Skinner didn't have any influence in the school. All she knew was that he hurt people—his wife, students, colleagues.

Annie answered the knock on his study door. For about five minutes the boys filed in and sat quietly on the living room floor watching TV until Bartley invited them into the dining room with an announcement.

"Tonight we shall not talk about Mr. Skinner, the recent Discipline Committee recommendations, or the New York Yankees."

Kensington was halfway between New York and Boston. Bartley was a Red Sox fan, but several of the boys in the dorm were from New York. Bartley was also on the Discipline Committee.

He did not talk much during the dorm feed. He listened as the students spoke to Karen as though he weren't there, of surreptitious disciplinary violations, personal anxieties, fellow students they hated. He learned more about what was truly happening at Kensington at a dorm feed than he did in classes or school meetings.

He watched Karen move about the room, passing more cake, stopping to talk to two or three boys at a time, sometimes to listen and nod and laugh. She was best with individuals and small groups. He had never been comfortable with private counseling. He was at home in discussions or debates of public or historical matters, confrontations of values. It was she who had made him sensitive to the anguish of homesickness and loneliness, of the fear of being hazed and excluded or ridiculed, of the fear of failure in academics or sports, of letting down the hopes of parents who lived vicariously through their children—children who had become by virtue of attending Kensington investments in parental status or the symbolic validation of dubious genes.

He still couldn't believe his luck in finding her. He met her at a summer party at Fox Lake, a reunion of sorts of friends from Northwestern. He had been teaching at Kensington for two years. She was staying at her parents' cottage nearby. She had graduated from Madison and was working in Milwaukee. She went east twice that fall to visit him, once for a dance weekend and again at Thanksgiving. She quit her job. They were married the week after Christmas in Wisconsin. She moved into his apartment for the beginning of the second semester and assumed her new role as though she had been born to it. From the first day she performed her duties with sensitivity and grace and restraint. Then, after Annie and Rachel were born, she went back to graduate school for a year to gain certification, began teaching math as a substitute at nearby middle and secondary public schools and occasionally at Kensington when members of the math or science departments were sick or off to a conference.

Lost in reflective admiration, he did not at first hear the voices raised and directed to him.

"Mr. Bartley, how's third form baseball look this year?" It was Steve Wharton, one of the varsity baseball players in Pierson, but it could have been any of the four sixth formers sitting on the floor around the coffee table. When he looked at them, he saw smiling, artificially innocent faces.

He couldn't resist. It happened every spring. The faces changed, but the tradition persisted, and he played his role straight, permitting himself to be baited, knowing the teasing was good natured. Each spring there was a subtle change in the sixth formers after spring break. They groped toward the language and terms of a greater equity with the faculty and they began to put up barriers of distance between themselves and underformers.

"Lots of promise," he lied. "Lots of promise. I see an undefeated varsity four years from now, if the J.V. and varsity coaches handle the material right after I pass them along."

"That's not what Mr. Henry said. He came down to varsity practice after watching your practice the other day and he told Mr. Bennett that the incompetence of the third form team was exceeded only by the ineptitude of their coach."

"What's Mr. Henry doing down at varsity baseball? You'd think that after twenty years of coaching, he'd find something else to do on spring afternoons than snooping around, looking over Mr. Bennett's shoulder. He's behaving like old man Boyden at Deerfield. Ninety years old and hanging around everywhere for years after he retired, second guessing teachers, coaches, his successor. Tell that to Mr. Henry, when you see him next, that he reminds me of old man Boyden, wandering around the fields, sitting in the back of classrooms, refusing to let go."

Bill Henry, chairman of the English Department and recently retired varsity baseball coach, had told Bartley about Boyden. "The old fart rides around in a golf cart everywhere stopping to buttonhole strangers, students, faculty, whomever. Advanced state of anecdotage, Bartley. When I get like that I want you to shoot me, put a bullet right through my head, and put me under the sod."

There was a silence around the table for several moments and then the question came. Every year it was different.

"Mr. Bartley, Carrington and I had an argument the other night and we're interested in your opinion. What was the greatest period in baseball? The Yankees domination under Stengel with Mantle or the Yankees under McCarthy led by Ruth and Gehrig?"

"Neither," he began firmly and with the authority in his voice of the experienced lecturer. He sensed the attention of the younger boys had turned toward him. "Neither, Wharton. In fact, from the historical and national perspective, both periods can be considered the Dark Ages of baseball." He watched the eyes of some of younger Yankee fans widen incredulously.

"Those were times of concentrated economic power, times similar to the years before Jackson when eastern banks controlled the money supply and stifled the westward expansion. The baseball expansion period in the fifties and early sixties parallels Western expansion in America; consequently, the breaking of the economic stranglehold of the banks by Jackson and the emergence of anti-trust laws under Teddy Roosevelt. During the two great Yankee epochs baseball was not the National Pastime, it was a New York pastime. From the perspective of those of us from out West, the Stengel and McCarthy epochs were bad for baseball, bad for America."

He paused briefly, an automatic hesitation he had built into his lecture style so that students could catch up on their note taking. "Baseball arrived truly as a National Sport after desegregation but especially after expansion when teams from Milwaukee and Minnesota, Atlanta, Oakland, San Francisco, Los Angeles—even if they were transplanted New York teams—faced each other in the World Series. Baseball was liberated, democratized, pluralized and the domination of the National League this past decade—the truly democratic league—the first to use large numbers of Blacks and Latinos is proof of the triumph of the Jeffersonian spirit in the National pastime. I say the decline of the Yankees has been good for baseball and good for America."

"Do you really believe that argument, Mr. Bartley? What would baseball be if it weren't for Ruth and Gehrig and Dimaggio and Mantle?"

"That's not the right question, Wharton. What would baseball have been if Dimaggio had played for San Francisco, Mantle for Houston, Ruth for Baltimore and Gehrig for the Cubs?"

He was pleased that he had remembered his argument. He had even embellished it a bit this time with the analogy to trust busting. Each spring he vowed to write an article, half serious, half in jest entitled "Jefferson vs. Hamilton on the New Frontier or Baseball as Microcosmic Reflection of the Problems of Balancing Freedom and Order in the Fifties and Sixties." He could see the article already in print, his name JOHN BARTLEY in bold letters under the title, perhaps in *The Atlantic*, or even *The American Scholar*. Then he added. "Yankee Hating is more than a personal passion, Wharton. It's a world view, a national view, a philosophy, a theology, a religion." He disappeared into the kitchen accompanied by a chorus of boos and catcalls.

Peter stayed behind to help clean up. He hauled the soda cans and paper plates out to the dorm wastebasket and helped Annie wash the silver and serving plates. He appeared to be in a good mood, animated and articulate, clearly the center of attention of the younger boys to whom he must have seemed like a god—prefect, commodore of crew, football star, and scholar. It was clear he was something of a god to Annie. Now that he thought about it, Annie had followed Peter around the apartment during the entire dorm feed. Just before Peter left, he withdrew from his rear pocket a folded sheet of paper.

"I've got to get out in the dorm for check-in now. Would you read this when you have time, sir? I've worked on it for at least three hours. I'm not sure of the tone. I think it might be O.K., but I really can't tell."

"I'll show it to Mrs. Bartley and see what she thinks of it."

"Oh, God, no, sir. Don't do that. I don't want her to know anything. I mean, this letter wouldn't mean anything to her unless you told her everything. I couldn't bear that. It's bad enough telling you."

"O.K." Bartley laughed. "I won't show it to her, but I'm not sure I can do much without her advice. I usually tell her everything and she tells me what to say or do, and I get all the credit."

"We all know that, sir, but do this one alone. I'll take my chances."

Later, after Annie went to bed and as he and Karen sat in the living room reading, she apologized.

"I'm sorry I said anything about Skinner tonight."

"What did you say that was so unfair or untrue that you need to apologize?"

"About him nothing, but I was unkind to you."

"Do you mean about my tolerating him?"

"Yes."

"You're probably right. I suppose I should be more sensitive to what he says and does. It's not that I don't care. It's just that he's such a fool, I don't regard him as a threat. He defeats himself. Besides, he's wonderful comic relief sometimes, such a buffoon. But you're right. Fifteen years ago, I might have gone to Woody and said—take your choice—fire Skinner or fire me."

"Now, you're shackled with a wife and two children and can't take that kind of stand."

He knew she was teasing but he also knew she wanted a re-affirmation.

"You know that's not true. Why couldn't I go in and demand Skinner be fired now. My position has never been stronger. I can get another job. I just don't think Skinner does much damage. I feel secure in the atmosphere of values Woody has created here."

She waited for several moments before she continued.

"I was talking to Maggie Henry at the Day School Fair the other day and one thing leading to another, she asked, right out of the blue, 'Do you know what has been the most profound change at Kensington School in the past twenty-five years?' I guessed all the usual sorts of things—changes in admissions, curriculum. She shook her head at each of my suggestions. Then she said that she and Bill had discussed the question over cocktails the other evening and they agreed one change stood out above all others...."

She stopped and pretended to go back to her reading. He waited several moments and then looked up.

"Well, what was it?"

"What was what?"

"The profound change that Bill and Maggie were talking about?"

"Oh, I didn't think you wanted to hear. I didn't think you were listening with your head in that dumb magazine. You always do that. Stick your head in some book or magazine when I'm talking."

"I was listening. I wasn't reading. I was just looking at pictures." He showed her the magazine. "My God, Karen, it's a *National Geographic.* I was listening to you."

He knew she was right. He couldn't break the habit. At cocktail parties the first thing he did was examine his host's library or coffee table and select something to read. He simply didn't feel secure without reading material in his hand. When Karen scrubbed the kitchen floor and spread newspapers out until it dried, he found himself leaning over reading four months old articles or want ads. Now she pretended to read, but he could detect around her mouth the edges of a smile. He returned the magazine to the coffee table and returned to his chair.

"I'm empty handed now. I'm looking right at you, paying attention."

"I forget what I was saying."

"You were going to tell me what Bill and Maggie Henry agreed was the single most important change at Kensington School in twenty-five years. I would bet it's Bill's idea and Maggie just agreed with him."

"Yes. Well…" she paused. "Maybe I shouldn't tell you—you might get angry. You promise you won't get angry?"

"Why should I become angry? I might disagree with their conclusion, but I'll hardly get angry over a difference of opinion."

"You don't know their opinion."

"No, I don't and I probably never will know if you keep putting me on and off about it. I'm about to give up and go to bed."

"All right. Go to bed. I'll tell you in the morning."

He stood up now and assumed his most menacing air above her.

"Dammit, Karen, tell me now or I'll beat you."

She laughed. "I've provoked the mild-mannered Jack Bartley into threats of violence." He drew his arm back.

"Sit down and relax." She pushed him away. "I'll tell you. I just wanted to make sure you cared about what I have to say. Sometimes, Jack, I rattle on and I don't think you listen to me or care about what I'm saying."

"You know that's not true. I'm just pre-occupied—I think about my classes, the dorm, my baseball team. Right now even Peter, of all people, has a problem."

"Peter! I can't believe that."

"Well, he does. A real one."

"Can you tell me?"

"I'm not going to tell you anything until you tell me what Maggie Henry told you."

"Oh. It wasn't very original. I agree with her. She said the most significant change that she and Bill have witnessed in the past twenty-five years has been the mellowing of Jack Bartley—from rampaging radical to institutional stalwart, a pillar of the school. As I said, I agreed, but told her that it wasn't the mellowing itself that was as important as how you have rationalized those changes."

He sat for some time without answering.

"I suppose you can think of it that way. I suppose they're right. I think of it the other way."

"What other way is there?"

"Just think how much the school has changed to accommodate me."

"That's why I love you, Jack. You can see two or three or even four sides of every issue and you're never indecisive. You always know which one or two of the ten sides you believe in."

"That's why I have you tell me what to believe. That's what everyone says. That's what the opponents of co-education were saying about my committee recommendation last year."

In a decidedly male dominated institution she knew that they were considered as a couple that shared a job, that she was not just an ornament like a tea service or Christmas tree or decorative presence at school functions, or like poor Marilyn Skinner, a chattel possession. Bartley stood up.

"Well, I guess I'll go to bed. Need to get my sleep, be ready to seize every opportunity that might happen tomorrow to define my role as pillar of the community."

"Can you tell me Peter's problem?"

"Not really. Something happened when he spent last weekend at his girl's home. The girl's mother won't let her daughter come to the spring dance now. He's upset. Wants me to help him with a letter to the mother. I just hope it'll all go away in a week or so. I don't need Peter's problems. I have enough to do the way it is. Incidentally, did you notice Annie following Peter around all evening. Every time I saw Peter, there she was right behind him, looking up with worshipful eyes and a beatific smile on her face."

"Oh, Jack, are you just noticing. She's had a crush on Peter since we began using him as a babysitter last year. Whose idea do you think it was to use him in the first place? Who didn't want him to be prefect because he wouldn't be able to babysit any more?"

"Annie's?"

"Annie's."

"You know, Karen, this started out to be such a great day. Two good classes on the causes of World War I. Beautiful weather. My first round of golf, and then, KABOOM. Everything goes to hell. Annie discovers I'm a pathetic cheat. You tell me that community opinion has decided I've gradually sold out my principles to the forces of political and moral reaction. I belatedly realize that my oldest daughter has an emotional fixation on my prefect and for almost two years now I've been unwittingly aiding and abetting the relationship. My prefect, an otherwise perfect young man, has a personal problem and has been pestering me to help him solve an unsolvable dilemma, and I can't say no because I owe him so much I'd feel guilty denying his one appeal for my personal help in four years."

"Jack, you have a gift for exaggeration, distortion, and self-pity."

"How would you characterize my day then?"

"Well, I'd say Annie has broadened the basis of a realistic sense of her father and taken an important step toward maturity. The school community has come to recognize your maturity and qualities of responsible leadership, and you have come to recognize and accept an important step in Annie's normal and inevitable development as a person."

"What about Peter's problem?"

"What happened between him and his girlfriend's mother off campus at their home a week ago is really none of your business."

CHAPTER 2

▼

They were in the house no more than ten minutes when he heard a knock at his study door. He didn't answer at first, hoping the person would decide he wasn't home and go away, but the knock sounded again. Karen had put some water on to heat for tea. The light was beginning to fade outside. He turned on the TV and searched the channels for a golf tournament, found nothing, and then hearing the knock again knew it would not go away. Whoever it was knew he was home, perhaps had seen them return in the car.

He opened the door to Peter Colby, leaning against the wall in a muddy sweat suit, his face flushed, carrying a pair of sneakers.

"Hi, Mr. Bartley. Got a minute?"

"Sure, Peter. What have you been doing? Don't you get enough exercise rowing six days a week?"

"Oh, we didn't get much exercise. We were playing Kensington's version of rugby on the old JV soccer field."

"What does Coach Dennison think about that kind of activity on Sunday for his first boat stroke and crew commodore?"

"Not too much. He came by and saw us and made all the varsity crew members quit. He gave me hell, but I think he'll either forgive or forget by tomorrow."

They walked through the study into the living room.

"I'd better not come into the living room, sir. I'm pretty muddy."

"I wasn't going to invite you to sit down. Want a cup of tea or coffee?"

Bartley turned the channel selector again but then turned the set off.

"No thanks. I just came by on my way upstairs to see if you'd read my letter. I was going to do some more work on it this evening before I start serious study."

"Your letter?"

"Yes, my letter to Mrs. Powell. I gave it to you last night after the dorm feed."

"I'm sorry, Peter. I forgot about it completely." He shrugged guiltily. "We went to the beach this afternoon for a hike. It's been the nicest day so far this spring. What with chapel and school dinner, I haven't gotten around to reading it yet." He was irritated at himself for feeling guilty about not doing something he really shouldn't be doing at all.

"That's O.K., sir." Peter was clearly disappointed. "I can handle it myself."

"No. I said I'd read it and I will. Can you give me an hour? We just got back."

"Sure. That would be great, but you don't have to, Mr. Bartley. I shouldn't have asked you to start with."

"You come down after supper. Are you going to the dining hall?"

"No, sir. I'll finesse the cold cuts and macaroni. After I shower, I'm going to get a couple of microwave chili burgers in the tuck shop."

"See you in an hour or so, Peter. I'm sorry I forgot."

"I'm sorry I asked you. I hate to be in such a hurry, but it's kind of urgent. It's already been a week since…."

He read the letter after supper. It was dreadful. The tone was tinged with anger and frustration. The apology was reluctant, with implicit reservations. Peter vowed to promise anything if Jennifer could come to the dance, but he admitted no guilt. It was honest, sincere, and direct. It was honorable and certain to alienate Mrs. Powell even more than she already was.

Bartley had yet to sense the person of Mrs. Powell. She remained generic in his mind so that his suggestion to Peter later that evening had to do with tailoring the language of the letter to persuade a person of conservative moral disposition, authoritarian, but reasonable, and capable of thinking matters through. The new letter they put together in his study was addressed to a hypothetical identity—a fair minded, concerned parent whose perspective deserved to be respected (handled nicely, Bartley thought, in a subordinate clause), but who was essentially trusting. Peter as a guest apologized for betraying the trust and by failing to respect Mrs. Powell's values and expectations.

When they were finished, Peter admitted the letter might be more effective than his first draft, but he had reservations. He read it over several times as he sat in Bartley's study.

"It's good, Mr. Bartley. I just want to make sure I'm not apologizing for having touched Jennifer. I'll promise her I won't touch Jennifer again and I won't, but I'll be damned if I'll accept her morality."

Bartley felt a certain pride and confidence in the subtly articulated refinement of language they had worked out together. He assured Peter once more that the letter did not compromise principle.

"You are apologizing for not being sensitive to her expectations of proper behavior by a guest in her home. You are not apologizing for what you did *per se.*"

"I guess you're right. I'm just not so sure. I don't want to sound unappreciative. I'm going to send the letter. It's the best we can do, but I'm not entirely happy about it. It splits hairs just to win an argument. I remember in American history last year you talked about people who used language the way we have here. You called them sophists. I think we're sophists."

"You're the sophist. I disclaim any responsibility. I'm only your adviser. If you send the letter, you accept the consequences. Don't blame me if she rejects it."

"She's already rejected me. There's nothing left to lose. To hell with everything." He stood up with resolve. "I've just got to try. I just want to be with Jennifer once more before I go back to Iowa."

When Peter left, Bartley read through the final version of the letter they had typed together and which Peter was going to copy in his own hand. It was without question a shameless piece of sophistry.

*   *   *   *

Sunday evening after check-in, Bartley delivered his Doomsday speech in his living room. He told the subdued students about sixth formers who had been dismissed from Kensington just minutes before the faculty assembled for the graduation procession. He warned them that there would be no relaxation of school rules just because they were arriving at the end of the school year. The rules applied now just as importantly as they did in early fall. Afterwards, Bartley began his preparation for the unit on the New Deal by re-reading his lecture notes from previous years and re-examining some of his sources, but preparing for the Great Depression was a matter of emotional rather than factual retrenchment. The department would be divided over everything from the personality of FDR to Social Security to the NRA. He suspected that the real purpose of the department party in late May was to reconcile the factionalism that splintered the department every year over the New Deal.

When he first began teaching at Kensington, he was the only member of the the school who was remotely liberal except for two or three sixth formers the faculty believed were psychotic. He was perceived by students and colleagues as a flaming radical. Within ten years the more radical students considered him a reactionary for defending the New Deal, which they considered a sell-out of principle, a hopelessly compromised political solution to the failure of capitalism, which in turn was the cause of racism, sexism, and nationalism. Somehow the New

Deal had become the principal cause of Viet Nam, and FDR was personally responsible because he had saved capitalism.

Recently, the spectrum had begun to swing the other way. FDR was once again considered the chief villain in American history, but now because he had begun deficit spending as a solution to a stagnant economy. The country was now reaping the sad consequences of his spend-thrift ways—spiraling inflation, irresponsible waste in government agencies, unhealthy bureaucratic centralization of power. He didn't know what the disposition of this year's students would be, but he sensed recently an incipient fascism and elitism in the rising popularity of the old Hamiltonian trickle down economics and what he called the "new" freedom to screw your neighbor or to ignore suffering entirely. He found the democratic spirit carried him through all the polemics and charged issues. He prepared for the unit on the New Deal by reading Jefferson.

*   *   *   *

Monday morning he found Bill Henry alone in his basement classroom toward the end of third period. He walked in, pulled up one of the chairs and sat with his chin propped in his hand with his elbow resting on the writing arm. Henry was reading and didn't look up. They sat like statues for some time. Behind Henry was a bookcase and in one corner stood three metal filing cabinets. Henry was one of the few faculty who had his own classroom. Henry's room doubled as the office of the Summer School, a small co-educational enrichment program that had served as a pilot project for Kensington's Co-education Planning Committee. In June, Henry would put a shingle over his door, import some office equipment and supplies, and administer his summer program out of the cool of the basement. Now it was full of chairs with writing arms. A portable blackboard stood against one wall.

At one time or other, Henry had been the College Counselor, Chairman of the Discipline, Curriculum, and Dorm Heads Committees, advisor to the school paper *The Kensingtonian* and to the literary magazine *The Prism*. He graduated from Harvard during the late thirties and enlisted in the RAF, was shot down in 1941 and spent the rest of the war as a POW, an experience he mentioned occasionally to lament the loss of the four best years of his life. He had coached varsity baseball twenty years but had finally given up to his assistant.

Henry finally spoke. "Boyden, eh? You told Wharton to ask me about Boyden?"

"It was just a suggestion, Bill. I just remembered what you told me about him, hanging around like that until he was a hundred. You told me to shoot you if you ever did it."

"I remember, but I didn't think you'd take me literally. It was metaphorical, but I guess you're right. I stand corrected."

"I was just reminding you of the metaphorical meaning." Bartley said.

"Get off Bennett's back?"

"Right." Bartley laughed. He could tell the voice bore no anger, but he knew Henry would retaliate in a jibing sort of way and so he added "And off of mine."

"But I told the truth about you. I watched you for almost twenty minutes and I couldn't tell whether the coach or the players were more incompetent."

"Christ, Bill. It was the first practice outdoors. And I had to move along. The AD has already scheduled us for a game within a week."

There was a long pause now as Henry placed his book face down on the desk and folded his arms.

"Did you ever stop to think, Jack, why you remained the third form coach for almost fourteen years now. During all that time you never moved up to J.V. or even assistant varsity coach."

"I never asked to be moved up. I've been happy with the third form team."

"That's true, but I never asked you to move up either. I always moved a new coach in ahead of you when the J.V. spot opened. Did you ever stop to think why I never asked you?"

"I assumed you never asked because you knew I was satisfied."

"Not true, Jack. There were several reasons, educational and otherwise, but two stand out in my mind as I reflect upon the years from the distance of my retirement. The first reason was aesthetic, almost purist. You know, Bartley, you are not much of an athlete. In fact, you're embarrassingly awkward. Something in me balked at letting you take a J.V. team, replete with the Kensington uniform over to Pomfret or St. Georges and conduct drills before the game. It stuck in my craw. I didn't want to be humiliated. It didn't make any difference that probably nobody noticed. I just didn't want anyone at Pomfret or Westminster or St. Georges to think we had a coaching staff of graceless clods. Somehow coaching the third form team didn't count. Besides, nobody ever watches those games anyhow."

"I don't mind being rejected by anyone with such purity of ideals and purpose. You were right."

"But that was a personal, aesthetic reason. There was another, more explicitly educational reason that I hate to admit now because it is complimentary."

"You mean I did something right?"

"Over the years, Jack, you accumulated such a storehouse of special knowledge about coaching kids who couldn't play baseball, that, in my humble judgment, you are unique. There is probably no one else in the whole goddamn world with your expertise. Do you realize, Jack, that when you lost 15 or 20 to nothing, you achieved great victories. I could never understand it. I left some of your games bewildered—how you kept the score under 20 runs a game, besides the fact the sun set, was a feat of absolutely brilliant managing—making all the right moves, changing your personnel, working pragmatically to get one out at a time regardless of how many runs might score. That's your genius, Bartley. You play for outs, any way you can get them, and that's why I never asked you to come up to the J.V. or Varsity. You were indispensable where you were."

"You know, I didn't come here to talk about my great skills as a coach. I came about something else."

"Well, speak up. I've still got reading to do. If you hadn't come in here and sat there like a sphinx staring at me, we could have been done and I could get back to preparing for class. I've only a few minutes the way it is."

"I wanted to talk to you about something Maggie said to Karen the other day—something about me, something to do with, as you put it so euphemistically, my mellowing. You said the most profound change at Kensington in the past twenty-five years was my mellowing, but I take it to mean my creeping conservatism. I just wanted you to know that I reject your assertion."

"I suppose I overstated your case. There may have been some more radical change than your mellowing, but the spirit of what I said was true. It seemed absolutely true and right after my second martini."

"Well, I don't think I've changed at all. I'm still consistent with the liberal principles I came here with. In fact, with the young "coordinated" gladiators we seem to be hiring here every year, I find myself taking more liberal positions as I grow older."

Henry laughed out loud.

"You are something, Jack. Coming here, trying to pretend you're some variation on John Stuart Mill, growing more liberal with age. You're a sham, Jack. I remember you when you first arrived. Jack Bartley, students' buddy, advocate of student rights and freedom, elective athletics, sign-out privilege in the dorms for all forms, student power. A kid had to commit murder while under the influence of alcohol and drugs while raping the Headmaster's daughter in a stolen car before you'd even consider voting to fire him."

The bell rang. Henry stood up, picked up his attache case from the floor, opened it and inserted a pile of papers and some books. He snapped the case shut, and walked around the desk. He shook his finger at Bartley.

"Shame on you, Jack. Coming in here, trying to defend the indefensible. No. You've mellowed. In fact, it's worse than mellowing. From what I hear you and your bosom buddy Brewster have been running your dorms like concentration camps. Oh, no, you've changed all right. To hell with your liberal principles, Mr. Middle-of-the-Road, moving to the right with the times. I've heard, it's the scuttlebutt since spring vacation that you're forming a neo-fascist coalition with Skinner to bring corporal punishment back to Kensington."

Bartley got up and left the room, smiling at the outrageousness of Henry's charges. But he couldn't argue even with good humor. What could he do? Bill Henry was his mentor, his ideological guru. What was a respectful disciple to do?

*   *   *   *

At the noon school meeting Charles Brewster, the senior master and head of the dormitory committee, reminded all dorm heads and prefects of their meeting in his apartment immediately after lunch. It was one of the few meetings Bartley could not and would not miss. As soon as Brewster rose from his table at the closing bell, Bartley excused himself from his table and fell in beside Brewster as they descended the steps leading to the quadrangle. For over a decade now, Bartley and Brewster had been partners in supervising Howe and Pierson dormitories cooperatively, alternating weekend duty and providing solace and counsel to each other during times of disciplinary crises. Their friendship had grown slowly, a strange and improbable liaison that stood as a testament to each man's spirit of toleration.

"Have a quiet weekend, Jack?"

"So far as I could tell."

"Any of my boys unruly or riotous?"

"Not so far as I could tell by occasional tours of your dorm. We've been lucky with our prefects this year."

"It's not luck, Jack, and you know it. We picked kids with character and a commitment to our rules and with the courage to enforce them."

"I give credit to their size. Both of them are big enough and strong enough to be forces of intimidation. That always makes rules more compelling to the inmates."

Brewster took a left fork in the pathway that led behind the Main School Building and to the back entry to his dorm apartment.

"Care for a cup of coffee before the troops arrive? The coffee is instant. I also have an apple turnover left from Sunday's breakfast that I'll split with you."

"I'll take some of both."

"Not that it matters, since I never go to chapel on my off-duty weekend, but I hope the preacher Sunday was a theologian and not a sociologist or a musicologist like Hal. I just think the boys ought to graduate from Kensington with some notion of what has passed for religion for the past two or three hundred years in Protestant America—something they may never discover if all they experience is the usual Sunday sermons of Shepherd's pop sociology and leftist politics. I sit with eyes closed, half asleep, listening to Hal preaching, I think I hear William Sloan Coffin again and I start up and wonder what the hell he's doing in the Kensington Chapel again and not in jail where he belongs."

Bartley laughed. Brewster was in rare form—cranky, belligerent, trying to provoke an argument, but Bartley refused to be baited. He had vowed not to argue with Brewster since the day he moved into Pierson. In his first months at Kensington, Bartley considered Brewster the embodiment of the mindless and obstinate traditionalism of Kensington at its worst. Brewster, a French and Spanish teacher of European tastes and demeanor, had dubbed Bartley "El Pinko, the Prairie Radical." Bartley was still bewildered, when he thought about it, how he had become in a few short years the admiring colleague of the one person whom he had held in open contempt in his first months at Kensington.

"You have to admit Hal sings beautifully and that we get a fair share of hymns."

They took the fire escape entrance to Howe. Brewster's second floor apartment was on the east end of Howe. They walked down the darkened hallway. Bartley felt the quiet. Most of the boys were already on the way to the gym or the last period class.

"That may be so, but I'm really getting tired of 'Amazing Grace,' which is not a negro spiritual. It was composed by a white man, a slave ship captain who got born again. There was no excuse for last Easter. I didn't mind the Black preacher. Actually he was very good and spoke about God for a change as I remember. He was as embarrassed as anyone, however, by our chaplain's performance, when Hal started jumping all over the place and racing up and down the main aisle waving his arms in imitation of Cab Calloway, leading us all in an antiphonal round of 'Dese Bones, dese bones, Day gonna walk around.' I don't care if the boys loved it. That's not my tradition or my style, and, Jack, I was here first before anyone else presently at the school, including Woody. I've put up with a lot of changes and am about to have coeducation shoved down my throat, but I reserve the right to protest if only to you in private."

"Annie and Rachel loved it. They went around the house all day Easter Sunday raising their arms and shaking their hands, singing 'Dese bones, dese bones. Day gonna rise again.' Charles, like it or not, they learned more about the meaning of Easter with that song than I did in twelve years of Catholic indoctrination in the meaning of Good Friday—that I had personally pounded the nails into Christ's wrists and ankles. It never occurred to me that Christ's Resurrection could possibly make up for the horror of what I had done. My problem was, of course, I never believed that any evil that I had done could possibly have warranted the descent of a perfect being in this world to endure the agony of crucifixion."

They reached the door of Brewster's apartment and stopped as Brewster shifted his books and papers from one arm to the other and withdrew his key. Bartley could hear the echo of their footsteps dying down the hallway.

Entering Brewster's apartment was like re-entering the Nineteenth Century through the portals of a Parisian salon. The apartment was like a crowded antique shop of highboys and lowboys, Chippendale chairs, Empire desks and divans, layers of oriental rugs, two gilt framed portraits of ancestors, dark and foreboding, and ornate silver service and crystal. Brewster himself was something of a relic or artifact, a living monument of a bygone era.

He was a tall, handsome man with brown, slightly greying hair that he tinted occasionally into a sandy blend. His profile was impressive, suggesting to Bartley the likeness of General MacArthur. Brewster dressed with elegant taste, preferring ascots and decorative brocade vests and silk shirts. The students called him the Count or Monsieur Le Comte if they were in his French class, and he had assumed over the years the role of Dean of Decorum. His main extra-curricular duty was as Le Grand Maitre'D of the dining hall committee. Twelve fifth and sixth formers served under him as headwaiters. Each student in the school took turns waiting on tables under the jurisdiction of the headwaiters. The dining hall committee managed the rotation of waiters and students to the huge, round, white oak tables hosted by faculty families. There was a fierce competition among students to be selected headwaiter and to enter Brewster's inner circle.

Once Bartley entered the apartment, he began to unfold the chairs stacked just inside the door by the janitor and then settled into his favorite leather chair against the back wall of the room. To the front of the room was Brewster's throne from which he would sit and deliver his review of the timetable and dormitory procedures for the rest of the year through the graduation luncheon. Brewster disappeared into the kitchen for several minutes while Bartley opened his briefcase and extracted some student essays that he began reading. Brewster returned to the living room, carrying a tray with two cups of coffee and the divided turnover. The two men drank their coffee and ate their pastry, then turned to their papers and read without speaking as they waited for the other dorm heads and the prefects to arrive. Except for the wrinkling sounds of turning pages and the ticking of a clock, they read in absolute quiet.

Brewster began the meeting punctually. Peter sat in the front row and came prepared to take notes. Brewster would type everything up sooner or later but he did not trust anyone to read any handout. In two or three weeks he would follow up with a printed and detailed outline. Bartley would wait for the outline. He pretended to scribble in his notebook every so often but since his very unsatisfactory meeting with Bill Henry that morning, his thoughts turned to a review of his years of improbable association with Charles Brewster.

Brewster was a stickler for consistency. He enforced the rules, and the bed hours. He believed in order, habit, neatness, and punctuality and he taught those precepts by his own example and his ubiquitous presence in the dormitory. Each night he left the door of his apartment open and sat reading or grading papers, clearly visible to students. He insisted that a dorm master in a boarding school was always on duty.

Although Brewster was an educational reactionary who was constitutionally opposed to change, there was always a certain wisdom or elegance of style that softened what he said. He rarely debated issues on the faculty floor, but he had a set speech that he delivered just before the vote on any major piece of liberal legislation. "When we begin to suffer the adverse consequences of this ill-advised course of action," he spoke in his monumental voice, "remember these words of Beaudelaire that I now paraphrase for you: Life is like a hospital in which the patients think they will get better by changing beds."

On one occasion, in his first year, Bartley had been pleasantly surprised when Brewster had won the day for a motion to change the dress code. The student council passed on to the faculty a recommendation that either turtlenecks or ascots with open collars be considered as acceptable substitutes for neckties at evening meals. During the debate, Bartley had spoken enthusiastically for a "liberalized" dress code. He was certain that Brewster would oppose him, but when Brewster was recognized, he delivered a wonderfully sarcastic repudiation of the necktie, proclaiming it to be as sartorially useful as the codpiece and moved that reasonable modification of the dress code by approved by acclamation.

Much later, after Bartley had moved into Pierson and they met frequently in Brewster's apartment over drinks, Brewster tried to convert Bartley to the wisdom of his ways, indirectly competing, Bartley suspected, with Bill Henry for Bartley's allegiance. The curriculum according to Brewster was divided into two kinds of courses—solids and gases. Math, science, and languages were solids—subjects in which student progress could be measured objectively and concretely. English, history, and religion were gases—amorphous and unwieldy bodies of opinion producing confusion among the students and apprehensions in their parents. "Teach them skills and information, Bartley," he warned. "They don't need ideas. They already have too many, the little bastards. They're already brighter than we'll ever be. The only thing I have on them is about forty years and my knowledge of French and Spanish. The only thing you have on them is that you've read more books. But the little buggers will pass us both up in a few years." Bartley learned to just smile and nod agreement.

Perhaps, because of the happiness of their own marriage, he and Karen had been moved by the loneliness of Brewster's life as they came to know of it piecemeal over the years. He had been married twice and divorced twice. His first marriage to an artist was doomed. She lived mainly to paint. She was moody, irregular, sloppy. She hated boarding schools, the degraded role of faculty wives, the gossip and intrigue and community volunteerism, the competition of silver service at teas. He changed schools three times trying to find a place where she felt comfortable, ending up in a day school near Los Angeles, but finally it was clear she hated even the confines of a childless marriage and they were divorced just before he returned east to Kensington.

He left the dorm for five years when he married a second time to a widow with teenaged sons. The sons attended Kensington and were academic and disciplinarian embarrassments for Brewster throughout their mediocre careers. Those who remembered his second wife disliked her; some faculty hated her sons. She left him upon the graduation of her youngest son and moved to the Boston area where her sons were attending college. Brewster returned to the dormitory the following fall.

The Bartleys included him in their family outings, Annie and Rachael called him "Uncle Charles" and he was a standard presence at whatever dinner parties they gave. So they got along for a variety of personal and practical reasons that overcame the profound differences that might have separated them. But for Bartley his willingness to tolerate almost anything Charles Brewster might say or do could be traced to an episode in his second year at Kensington when Bartley was having his first trouble in the dormitory and in classes.

Bartley owed his survival at Kensington to Charles Brewster.

Brewster invited him for a drink one evening about the time Bartley noticed that more and more students were challenging his grading, quibbling about his corrections, bitching about his assignments. And he also noticed that unsigned notices objecting to dorm policies and scatological graffiti were beginning to appear on bulletin boards—a sure sign of widespread discontent. After a few drinks as he began to relax in a large, comfortable leather chair in Brewster's apartment, Brewster stood above him and spoke.

"Well, Bartley, I think it's about time someone graded you now that you're finishing your second year, now that your value as a curiosity around here is beginning to dull. If you don't think I'm being presumptuous, I'd be happy to offer my unbiased evaluation."

Brewster poured Bartley another drink and handed it to him. He walked back and forth slowly as he spoke.

"First of all, you get good grades for some of your classroom work. I check on that sort of thing with your students in my dorm. You prepare your lessons, you get papers and tests back quickly. That's good because the authority we establish in the classroom carries over when we have to enforce the dormitory rules and regulations, that is if we have the will to enforce the rules without worrying about our popularity. The boys will accept discipline from a teacher who has established credibility in the classroom.

"Last year you were popular because the boys perceived you as a new point of view. Even the faculty appreciated your candid and original ideas, but, Bartley, you are beginning to wear thin. You talk too much. In fact, you talk all the time. You have been repeating yourself since Thanksgiving. You don't have to make a comment on every issue in faculty meeting. Your opinion is now painfully predictable on every issue. You harangue the students everywhere. In the dormitory you spend most of your time trying to convert students to your peculiar brand of neo-populist radicalism. You argue with them all the time, everywhere, on the path, in the halls, even in athletics. They perceive you as an Enthusiast, Jack, and around here that's about the same thing as being a Methodist or Baptist however intellectual you may pretend to be. At present your constituency has shrunk to a handful of disaffected sixth formers and a coterie of fifth form malcontents who look upon you as some kind of anti-establishment guru. Your support in the faculty is vanishing rapidly. You are reaching for universal popularity and achieving universal contempt.

"You cannot make everyone love you or agree with you, Jack. Over the years a teacher develops a natural constituency of students and colleagues that is considerably smaller than the school. Right now your influence is diminishing. Some students even think you are a joke, a kind of prairie preacher still haranguing about being crucified upon a Cross of Gold. Some of your colleagues think worse.

"I have my own personal objections. You are often discourteous. You break in on others' conversations, you talk so fast no one can understand you, you can be rude and inconsiderate, and a social clod. Above all, Bartley, you dress abominably and conspicuously. It's time you looked around at what others are wearing and stop trying to define your individuality through your vulgarity of taste."

Bartley was silently raging when Brewster paused and smiled, sipping from his glass and continued.

"You may not believe me, Bartley, but I like you. You're a good man. You care about ideas and kids. You're too full of shit right now to make it. The first thing you have to get over to become a teacher is graduate school—all the hot air they fill you up with there, the notion that you're some kind of anointed prophet of the divine order of things. Once you get over that, Bartley, you'll be a good teacher. Shut up for a year except in class. Narrow the range of your relationships. Let me guide you in the purchase of a new wardrobe. The first thing you'll do is go out and buy some goddamn polyester suit from Montgomery Wards."

Bartley stood up and walked to the door without a word. He looked at Brewster for a moment with hatred and then stepped into the dormitory hall and slammed the door.

He walked for an hour from one end of the campus to the other raging at Brewster's snobbery, his arrogance, and the truth of his observations. At nine o'clock he returned to Brewster's apartment. When Brewster answered the door, Bartley stared for a moment and then laughed.

"When do we go shopping?"

They began the next day with a visit to the Christ Church Nearly New Thrift Shoppe and a trip to Brewster's tailor in Kensington Center. Within a week, quietly and unobtrusively like a chameleon, Bartley took on the color and texture and tone of the school. Holding his tongue while listening to the outrageous, atavistic cant of his colleagues was much more difficult than changing clothes, however. And he often smiled inwardly, remembering the struggle to keep his mouth shut until he had established his credentials in the classroom and in the dorm before he once again presumed to instruct his colleagues in the obvious wisdom of his prejudices.

Now, fourteen years later, as the dorm committee meeting ended and its members folded and restacked their chairs, Bartley acknowledged to himself that his friendship with Brewster stood as objective evidence that though Bill Henry had overstated his case, he was not far off from the truth: the greatest change in twenty-five years at Kensington School might very well be the mellowing of Jack Bartley.

*   *   *   *

He did not invite Annie to join the third form team. She did not ask in any explicitly formal way. She simply showed up that afternoon after school. She appeared beyond the right fielder during an infield-outfield drill and spent that first day retrieving balls that his outfielders misjudged often intentionally though they made the appearance of trying. She roamed the outer outfield, chasing balls until they died of inertia in the deep grass. Then she relayed the balls underhanded to players who in turn threw to the cut off man.

She did that for two days, chasing errant throws, missed flies, "hot" grounders. When he saw her hurrying across the field from the dorm after school on Thursday, arriving at the end of infield drills, he threw her his glove and a Kensington baseball cap which became the symbol of her belonging. The next day he delayed the beginning of practice by extending the length of cals so that she could warm up with the team. She found a partner for throwing and catching—the most inept of the several second basemen who didn't mind playing catch with a girl. Soon she was staking base bags, handing out balls at the beginning of practice and collecting them at the end, arranging the catcher's equipment, the bats and hauling everything back to the equipment room after practice.

She quickly sensed the order and rhythm of the practices. She had bats and helmets arranged in rows to one side of the bench for batting practice. She pulled out the safety net for batting practice, and when the varsity let them use the pitching machine, she fed it balls. She ran bases when Bartley needed runners for situation practice. When she had nothing to do, she practiced herself, throwing to anyone who would play catch with her, joining small groups of players in games of pepper, swinging a bat to one side, working on timing as she made dry swings at balls thrown during batting practice.

Bartley was surprised at the players ready acceptance of her, her need to learn the game, her incessant questions, her quickness at grasping fundamentals, but for all her hard work and devotion, she was hopelessly awkward and inept at throwing and catching and when Bartley let her take a turn batting, she swung with a terrible fierceness at where the ball had been or was yet to arrive. She did everything with fierce intensity: her arrangement of equipment and her attempts to learn the skills of the game, trying in a few weeks to catch up on a lifetime of neglect.

After practice they stayed behind and he worked with her repeating basic drills that the team had worked on during practice. In the evening after dinner and before he began his class preparation, he explained the rules of the game, the rationale and strategy of the situational drills, and how to keep the score book.

On Saturday when they didn't have a practice, she watched the varsity game, scouting Bobby Bennett and making mental notes of the bat boy's duties. While distributing equipment on the last practice before the first game, Bartley gave her a game jersey and a pair of cleated sneakers. That evening after dinner in the Commons, he saw her talking and laughing with three of his players. She had become in a little over a week one of them.

Later, before bed, he went to her room and tried gently to cool her enthusiasm and unrealistic expectations, but she was sure this would be a special season, and he went away to his study. He had been hardened over the years. He felt already the disillusionment and humiliation she was sure to feel after the first game. He had never won an opening game, had never even come close.

*   *   *   *

Peter sent his letter on Monday. He received Mrs. Powell's response Saturday morning. He was waiting outside of Bartley's classroom at the end of his last class before lunch.

"No luck, Mr. Bartley." He held the letter in one hand and gave a thumbs down with his other hand.

"Any sign of hope? Anything personal or friendly or forgiving?"

"Nothing. Actually it's a strange letter. Very formal like a general statement she might send out to a hundred people. She said that Jennifer had family commitments on the weekend of the dance and that it would be in her best interests to finish the academic year as strongly as possible since her second semester grades would be the basis of her college applications next fall. It wasn't an answer to anything in my letter. Do you want to read it? She even sent a carbon copy to Jennifer. There was a cc at the bottom of the page."

"No thanks, Peter. She's sent you a boiler plate letter."

"What's that?"

"Like a rejection slip from a college or university such as—after reviewing your application carefully the committee regrets to inform you that we will be unable to offer you a place in the freshman class of 19 something or other."

"Pretty hopeless, I suppose. Not even on the waiting list."

"I'm afraid so, Peter."

"Everything seems to be going to hell."

"How so?"

"Oh, everything was going great in crew until Andy Paine, the power oar in my boat, sprained his ankle in a get-up softball game right after Coach Dennison absolutely forbid us to do anything that might result in an injury. Well, he's gone for most of the season. The doctor said he might as well have broken it the sprain is so bad. The coaches have been juggling personnel all week. We're just not ready in any of the boats for our meet this afternoon."

"I'm sorry to hear that. I wish I could do something, but I don't know what."

"That's O.K. Thanks for helping with the letter."

"Good luck today anyhow. Maybe you'll do better than you think."

"The way things are going maybe we'll do worse than we think."

Late Sunday morning, Jennifer Powell called Bartley's apartment looking for Peter. She couldn't reach him on the dorm phone. She had left Randall Hall without permission and taken a bus as far as Hartford but missed the only bus that connected to Kensington Center. Bartley found Peter and the two of them drove in a developing light rain to pick her up. Then he spent an hour listening to their anger and frustration. Jennifer was determined not to return to school, but once at Bartley's apartment over tea, Bartley and Karen convinced her that she was hurting herself more than her mother by jeopardizing her diploma and college. The young lovers were pathetic and forlorn, walking hand in hand distractedly around campus in what had become a steady downpour.

Peter accompanied Bartley when he drove Jennifer back to Randall Hall. By the time they reached Hartford it was dark and the rain was still falling heavily. The slow, twisting fifteen miles of secondary roads after he turned off the Interstate west of Hartford seemed endless.

Jennifer had acquiesced to their persuasion. When she got in the car, there seemed to be a reserve, if not a smoldering resentment, in her manner and voice as though Bartley and Karen had been her mother's accomplices. But she fell asleep under Peter's arm against his chest before Hartford and by the time they pulled up in front of her dorm, she had awakened to a new hopefulness and talked quietly with Peter. She would take her chances—leave Randall Hall for the dance without permission and hope she would get a lenient judgement because of her good record—a possibility that three hours ago she had rejected as impossible. She thanked Bartley profusely, and then he waited almost ten minutes as the lovers said goodbye inside the entrance to her dorm.

He drove back to Kensington more directly, taking an alternate route through New Britain and Middletown. Peter didn't speak for almost half an hour. He sat staring at the flapping windshield wipers and the oncoming headlights with a grim and unflinching persistence. Bartley stopped for gas outside of New Britain, and when he resumed driving, Peter spoke.

"What are we going to do, Mr. Bartley? What in God's world are we going to do?"

"I don't think you are going to do anything, Peter, because you don't have a problem. You've already done all you can do with Mrs. Powell. You've written and apologized as honorably as you can. It's Jennifer who has a problem, not you. Actually, Peter, it's Mrs. Powell who has a problem even more serious than Jennifer's."

"Mrs. Powell! What problem does she have unless she's some kind of psychopathic sadist who needs a shrink?"

"Mrs. Bartley and I have done what we can to get Jennifer back to school so she won't hurt herself to spite her mother, but that solution is only temporary. The problem is not what you and Jennifer have done, but Mrs. Powell's reaction to it—a reaction that seems headed toward the destruction of her relationship with Jennifer. I don't think Mrs. Powell is at all sensitive to what she is doing. I've listened to Jennifer today, and I am convinced that if her mother doesn't relent, Jennifer will defy her and never forgive her."

"Maybe that's what Mrs. Powell deserves."

"Maybe, but does Jennifer deserve to hate her mother for the rest of her life? What ultimately hurts Mrs. Powell will hurt Jennifer equally."

"How?"

"Whether she means to or not, the effect of her punishment will be seen by Jennifer as an attempt to humiliate her. Jennifer won't take that, Peter. Not the girl I listened to today. When Mrs. Powell finally realizes what she has done, it may be too late."

Peter leaned his head back on the seat and stared at the ceiling.

"I guess you're right. I really don't have a problem. You're also right that Jennifer may never forgive her mother."

The intensity of the rain had diminished. Bartley increased the speed of the car on the now virtually empty highway.

"We should get back in time for one of us to handle early check-in. Who has the duty? I didn't check the board."

"You have, sir. But I'll take it. You've already done more than your duty today."

They rode in silence for several minutes. Bartley glanced at Peter when he slowed for a red blinking light and then he spoke.

"There's something you can do, Peter, to help Jennifer. It's very simple if both of you are willing to do it."

"I'll do anything, Mr. Bartley," Peter answered, but his voice sounded hopeless and mechanical. He continued to stare down the tunnel of light ahead of them.

"You and Jennifer have made much of the spring dance as a kind of culmination of your relationship. I know you will have to separate in June, but, frankly Peter, you have overdramatized the importance of the dance. There is no reason you won't see each other again. It's not the end of the world. You'll find a way to meet again—this summer, next fall, sometime."

"I don't follow you. What should we do?"

"Back off from the dance. Let Mrs. Powell have her way, but if you can convince Jennifer that it's no longer important, you can take the sting out of Mrs. Powell's punishment and you can avoid the confrontation that will hurt Jennifer as much as her mother."

"But I won't see her again, Mr. Bartley. I'll never see her again if we don't think of some way to change Mrs. Powell's mind. I don't think I can take that—not seeing her again."

"You're over-reacting again, Peter. Why can't you say to hell with the spring dance? Go visit Jennifer that weekend. You can stay at a nearby hotel for Saturday night."

"But I have to row the afternoon of the dance."

"Leave after the race. You can get to Randall Hall by six o'clock. Take Jennifer to dinner. Spend the evening with her. What time is Saturday night check-in at Randall Hall?"

"Eleven."

"You'll have until eleven and then all day Sunday. You don't have to be back here until nine o'clock for Sunday night check-in. If the transportation doesn't work out, I'll pick you up at Randall Hall or Hartford or wherever so you can stay as late as possible on Sunday."

"She'll still win, Mr. Bartley. She'll have punished us, made her point that we've done something wrong."

"At least, you'll have a choice, something to think about and talk over with Jennifer. If you defy Mrs. Powell and Jennifer leaves Randall Hall without permission to attend the dance, she may be fired and then everyone loses, especially Jennifer. Are you prepared to spend the rest of your life knowing you were a party to that? And how will it affect you in the long run? Do you really want her to throw away three years of school and alienate herself from her mother and father so that she can attend a dance with you. Peter, you have to think objectively about what you're doing."

"Yes, sir, I'm thinking about it—not very objectively, but I'm thinking."

After a few minutes Bartley tried to change the subject, hoping to pick Peter's spirits up.

"How's crew going?"

"Worse than my relationship with Mrs. Powell. We finished last yesterday." Bartley detected a hint of ironic humor in Peter's voice.

"Nothing, Peter, could be worse than your relationship with Mrs. Powell."

"That's true, but almost as bad. Since Andy Paine hurt his ankle, nothing has gone right. Coach Dennison has tried every combination possible, but when you lose the power oar in fours it trickles down to the other boats. It's not like in eights where one man out doesn't disrupt everything. Mr. Dennison is sick about it. We have the money this year already raised to go to Henley if we do well at Worcester. Last year our first and second boats were undefeated and we were invited, but we fell short of raising the money and Mr. Woodbridge would not let the Friends of Kensington Crew solicit money from normal endowment sources."

Bartley felt instant compassion for Bob Dennison, the diminutive former coxswain of a Cornell crew shell, who suffered agonizing arthritis of the hands from the years of steering shells with his hands on ropes immersed in icy waters. He had also suffered from diabetes from youth, lost his sight once but had it miraculously restored with laser surgery. Though he still had to wear thick glasses to see what little he could see, he taught boring and deliberate math classes that students tried to avoid, but they flocked to row for him, awed by his knowledge of the sport and his example of uncomplaining suffering and quiet, uncompromising pursuit of perfection, without hype or hysteria. Bartley had contempt for all the coaching cliches about "having heart" and "character" and an "indomitable spirit" and he was opposed on principle to post-season athletic contests, but he too was awed by Coach Dennison's "indomitable spirit" and had contributed modestly to the Henley fund.

"Will you row fours or eights if you go to Henley?"

"We were going to put the first two boats together. We've already been practicing and we've done well even without Andy, but if the individual boats don't do well at Worcester, we won't be invited again this year. Kensington may never be invited again. The kind of crews we've had the past few years may never happen again or not for a long time."

"I suppose you're right. It does run in cycles."

Peter became conspicuously silent for some time. He spoke after a few minutes, asking a question rhetorically, knowing the answer already but hoping Bartley would disagree.

"Do you think I've peaked too early, Mr. Bartley—in my crew, my going with Jennifer? We won everything in my fifth form year. Even football and wrestling were better a year ago. And going with Jennifer was perfect last spring. We made promises and just touching her hand was exciting as anything I'd every done in my life. And now, sir, everything's gone to hell."

They rode the rest of the way in silence. Bartley parked behind the dorm and they entered through the back hallway. When they were about to part at the stairwell, Peter spoke again.

"I'll call Jennifer tonight. We'll talk over what you've suggested. If she agrees, I'll make plans to visit Randall Hall at least on the Sunday of Dance Weekend."

"It's your decision, Peter. Let me know in a few days what you're going to do."

"Good night, sir. Thanks for everything."

Peter turned and bounded up the stairs.

*   *   *   *

For two days the image of Peter and Jennifer, walking disconsolately about the campus in the dreary rain, persisted, and for two days his anger mounted. He knew he had no business interfering. Jennifer's problem with her mother was not even remotely connected to his authority as Peter's *in loco parentis* adviser, but he could not dismiss the memory of the two young lovers, forlorn and confused, alternating between despair and rebellion. He remembered their anger and sense of injustice in the car. He believed that whatever Mrs. Powell had interrupted had been for them a natural expression of a sacred feeling that had grown slowly over two years. She had humiliated them with her judgment, and her unwillingness to relent had magnified their guilt. She had been unfair, and he owed so much to Peter, who had virtually run the dorm for him. It was Peter who enforced the rules strictly, permitting Bartley to be the benign and sympathetic court of appeal, thus enhancing his reputation for forgiveness and his popularity. He never overruled Peter, but he often lessened the punishment for a rule infraction that he had threatened would be automatic at the beginning of the year, and Peter's own popularity and reputation for fairness permitted him to manage the good order of the dormitory firmly and consistently without a challenge to his authority.

But for all his sympathy, he did not at first feel compelled to interfere though he could not get rid of the feeling that he was letting Peter down on the one occasion he had asked for help. He did not write Mrs. Powell or call her, not yet. For two days he held off, struggled to control his temper and when he had it under control, he began to feel guilty for failing Peter in his hour of need. Gradually, memories of his own youth began to rise into his consciousness, memories he had successfully repressed for several years. They began in sadness and ended in bitterness and propelled him finally to action.

He recalled how the cold and contemptuous stares of the nuns for the most trivial of misdemeanors had taught him before he had ever really sinned that he was probably beyond the reach of grace. As he grew older the dread of a bad confession for which he would be held in double jeopardy haunted him. The broken vows of his often imperfect contrition and the not very firm purposes of amendment had kept him from the confessional box, and his fear of sacrilege kept him from communion. He broke his fast with water whenever his parents had expected him to receive and he began attending early masses alone and lying to them later that he had taken communion.

In his heart he had never forgiven the Church for that: to have revealed in the Gospels the loving and forgiving spirit of the child in the manger Who later died on the cross for the redemption of mankind, while at the same time to have created and magnified in the minds of credulous children an agonizing sense of shame and guilt for the most ordinary of human weaknesses so much so that in Bartley's case he felt unworthy of the Eucharist out of terror of the desecration he would surely commit whenever he received communion. It was easy to believe in the Real Presence and the profound mysteries of the church. It was impossible for him to accept those teachings that seemed patently unfair and irrational. As he grew older, he became convinced that the attitudes of that education were heretical, de facto Jansenism, as well as immoral, sins against love and justice, in the harshness and cruelty of their effects on the minds and souls and sense of self-worth of children.

It was no better at Christian Brothers High School where he was not convinced in four years of religion classes that the God of mercy and love could be perfectly reconciled, when properly understood, with the God of judgment and punishment, a divinity compelled by the inexorable logic of His own being and the absolute nature of his laws (as though he had no choice in the matter) to condemn to eternal separation and loss those who ate meat on Friday, attended protestant services thus becoming de facto heretics, or those who willfully indulged in sexual fantasies for a second longer than permissible though their bodies urged their minds compulsively toward the opposite sex. It wasn't just that he was taught principles of an unrelenting absolute morality in which trivial actions, natural impulses, and violent and cruel abominations all seemed as one in the pantheon of mortal sins. No, it was more the deliberate and careful elaborations of distinctions between mortal and venial sin that his teachers belabored in almost every sphere of human action, which distinctions they, in turn, ran roughshod over by insisting that any transgression however inconsequential was an act of disobedience if not defiance or rebellion against a perfect God and that each act he committed would reverberate forever in the memory of a disappointed God.

Sadly and despairingly Bartley slowly realized that the good brothers began taking away even the venial sins that he had begun to enjoy as a kind of reprieve from the awfulness of his own damnation. By the time he graduated from high school Bartley knew himself to be full of pride and lust and envy and disobedience and sloth. He didn't need an external authority to tell him what he knew to be true in his own heart. He tried to develop self-discipline, the uncomplaining acceptance of pain, and self-sacrifice. He tried prayer and campaigns of deliberate kindness to those he disliked or resented, but nothing seemed to be effective in extinguishing the fires of his lust, in diminishing his self-lacerating envy especially of athletes coddled and beatified by teachers and adults, in tempering his arrogant pride of intellect, or in staying his often cruel disdain of authorities that he frequently mocked mercilessly. He felt himself beyond forgiveness, hopelessly damned so he gave up. When he entered the navy soon after graduation, he simply fell away from what had already become at best a nominal Catholicism and he engaged in four years of mildly riotous and relatively guiltless self-indulgence and rebellion.

Later he experienced two brief periods of reconciliation with the Church, but neither was sufficiently strong to bring Bartley back to the communion rail. At the end of his sophomore year at Northwestern, Bartley decided to major in history, a decision that was the climax of three years of radicalization he had been undergoing. He had become a closet socialist of sorts unwilling to openly join any of the public social-ist groups on campus because he was offended by the strident and mil-itant rhetoric of their pamphlets and the humorlessness of the bearded prophets and their emaciated and conscientiously asexual, almost nun-like, female compatriots. He was also tentative and cautious. He didn't want to be officially labeled a Red and risk being forever excluded from teaching at public institutions. He knew that Mc Carthyism might be dead but its spirit would probably linger for years in the FBI.

A course in European history led him to a paper on the worker priest, which in turn led him to Hans Kung and Simone Weil and Teilhard de Chardin, none of whom he could really understand, but his paper also brought him to *Commonweal*, and he began reading it regularly in the library. And then as though the Holy Spirit had been orchestrating his spiritual growth he came across Dorothy Day and the *Catholic Worker*, and he began reading her books and all the articles he could find on her movement. He had found what he needed: pacifism,

Christian socialism and a concrete way to express one's faith daily; soup kitchens and demonstrations and ordinary kindness, something he could do and feel close once again to the Church, at least its social teachings, without an ideological compromise. For a whole winter, the writings of Dorothy Day became his Bible and the *Catholic Worker* became his manifesto. He volunteered his time on weekends to help in soup kitchens at poor parishes in Chicago, sometimes in shelters for the homeless where he helped scour the side-streets and alleys on bitterly cold nights for those who had drunk themselves into helplessness.

And then it seemed as though God gave him a personal shove toward some kind of commitment. He saw the flyer on a bulletin board outside the office of the history department. Dorothy Day was to speak on the upcoming Wednesday evening at the University of Chicago. Late Wednesday afternoon he took the El south out of the loop in a developing snow storm. He got off on 63rd Street and walked back across the Midway to campus and found the small amphitheater where she was to appear. It wasn't that he was disappointed. He still felt that for once in his life he was in the presence of a saint, but she seemed so ordinary, actually kind of dumpy. Her face was bland and plump and her hair graying. She wore a nondescript dress, and she spoke sitting to one side of the lectern at a table that faced the audience—almost apologetically and laconically with little enthusiasm or focus. Her fingers clenched and fumbled her rosary as she rambled along, at times incoherently, about her demonstrations against the air raid drills in New York, about her time in jail, her communist friends whom she prayed for frequently, about Archbishop Spellman, a dear friend though they openly disagreed, about how all social workers were immoral for taking a salary for helping the victims of the corrupt capitalistic system that needed to be destroyed.

The audience was small and asked the predictable questions and Bartley departed without making an effort to speak to her. He decided later that there was no-one to meet, that Dorothy Day was speaking from some spiritual plateau, that she was already half way to God. But the words though delivered flatly were daring and revolutionary and he had sat in the presence of one of the great moral visionaries of the time. The snow storm was so furious when he was leaving that he slept on one of the couches in the Reynolds Club and took the El back to Northwestern the next morning.

He signed up that summer as a volunteer in a program for disadvantaged boys in Evanston, but soon after beginning work with the eight twelve-year olds he had been assigned to shepherd for six weeks, he came down with tonsilitis. He ran a high fever for several days and finally went to a doctor. His throat was almost closed and his tonsils were covered with white spots and patches. He went home to his family doctor. He received daily shots of antibiotics for over a week and then had his tonsils removed and spent the rest of the summer recuperating under his mother's care. By the time he returned to Evanston to resume classes in fall, his moral and social fervor had diminished, and his workload in classes became all consuming. His sympathies with the radical left in the Church persisted, however, though they remained academic rather than activist.

His second brief reconciliation began with a knock at his apartment door and the entry into his life of Father Bill Shea, the newly appointed pastor at St. Joseph's who brought the reforms and renewal of Vatican II to Bartley's small corner of the world. What he discovered when he began attending mass again was a church swept clean by a Jeffersonian spirit of most of what had alienated him. Most of all it was the positive enthusiasm of Father Bill who pursued Bartley with ardor, wooing him to begin again, to give the Church a second chance to point a new direction with a Gospel of love and the Good News of Grace and Redemption and a theology of liberation. So caught up in the spirit and energy of his new mentor, Bartley agreed to serve on the education commission of the Parish Council and to teach a small group of young men and women who had dropped out of high school for the diploma equivalency test. He began regular attendance at mass—especially the guitar mass where he participated with a joy he never felt before. After several months he went to Father Bill and told him that he and Karen had not been married in the Church and that she was willing to have the marriage blessed and to take some instructions if necessary. He believed he could be a communicant again without qualms of conscience.

But on the eve of renewing their marriage vows with the blessing of a priest, Father Shea was seduced into a nervous breakdown by the divorcing wife of a local disc jockey. She had come to Father Bill for spiritual consolation and had left him a broken man. The bishop decided that the renewing spirit at St Joseph's had gone far enough. He replaced Father Shea with a priest of decidedly conservative and authoritarian disposition. Within a month Bartley and the new priest had argued about everything—cremation, birth control, women in the priesthood—until Bartley disappointed and almost embittered stopped attending mass and Council meetings, and the new priest made no effort to pursue him. Since then he had drifted away. Though he continued to live outside the sacraments, he still believed in the social and moral teachings of the Gospels of love and he still believed in a forgiving God who would permit his wife and children to live forever.

After recalling his lover's quarrel with the Church, he felt he was ready to act. There was the "old law" and the "new law." The "old law" persisted in the minds of people like Mrs. Powell. She needed to be reminded that there was a "new law." She had punished them enough. She needed to be reminded that only those without faults had rights to cast stones. She needed to be reminded that without faith in the soul's self-correcting powers, all are lost after the first transgression.

By the time he worked himself up to a sufficient pitch of anger to write the letter he had no business to write, he had managed to transmogrify Mrs. Powell's intellectual and moral identity and attribute to her all of the spiritual embarrassments it had been his misfortune to endure as a sometime Catholic in the rational humanist world of academia. He attributed to her the conversion by sword, the suppression of Galileo, the Inquisition, the Index List and the Legion of Decency.

Finally, in his mind's eye, she became a disciple of Father Coughlan and a witch hunting supporter of Joseph McCarthy. When he finished the letter, he believed that win or lose he had struck a blow for liberal Christianity and Democracy.

$$*\qquad*\qquad*\qquad*$$

The morning of April 15th college acceptances and rejections literally exploded in the post office lobby. The faculty wives and children avoided the area all morning. Bartley would keep the door to his study open all evening to celebrate and mourn with his senior advisees. He heard rumors that Harvard had dumped all over Kensington's Sixth Formers but that Yale, where Kensington was a traditional feeder, had compensated for the vast cloud of ignorance that had settled over Cambridge.

The piecemeal results of college placement seemed grim. It was probably that he had met a non-representative cross section of disgruntled sixth formers. More than half the sixth form had applied to Harvard and Yale. The College Counselors had discouraged most of them. Though they knew they would be rejected, deep in their hearts they harbored the secret hope that they would make it against the odds, that colleges would overlook mediocre boards and grades and a lousy interview. They still believed in the power of a legacy or of athletic prowess or school leadership or wealth or just plain luck.

So when they received the letters of rejection, they were disappointed. By supper, they would be reconciled to second or third choices. By the next day they would be enthusiastically planning new destinies at their backup choices now that their fantasies had been dashed forever. But the rumors that this year's sixth form had begun Kensington's Great Slide into mediocrity persisted.

After lunch, while Bartley was drinking coffee in the faculty corner of the Common Room, Peter approached him and asked if they could talk alone for a few minutes. They walked back into the dining area, now occupied only by student waiters clearing off the tables.

"You made up your mind yet about next year, Peter?"

"Yes, sir. I made it up a long time ago. Grinnell, but that's what I wanted to talk to you about. Not Grinnell or next year, but the year after."

"The year after?"

"Yes, sir." Peter seemed hesitant and embarrassed. "You won't get pissed at me will you, Mr. Bartley. I have another favor to ask you. I know I've been a pain lately, but, well…nothing seems to be working out with Mrs. Powell and now I wish I were coming back East to college next year and I'm angry at myself for not applying to at least one or two colleges back here so I would at least have a choice."

"How can I help?"

"Could you talk to Mr. Macrakis for me? I want to apply for transfer back East next year and I want to know what I should do."

"Why can't you talk to him?"

"I couldn't do that, Mr. Bartley. He'd kill me. Last fall he begged me to apply to Harvard or Cornell or Penn, somewhere I could row if I wanted to continue crew, and I refused. I just didn't want to come back to New England again. I liked Jennifer a lot then, but I didn't feel the way I do now."

"Why, Peter, have you saved all your problems until the last two months of your four years at Kensington?"

"Sorry. Actually, sir, I have only one problem with different ramifications."

Bartley laughed.

"O.K., Peter. I have to talk to Mr. Macrakis anyhow about the college results of the rest of my senior advisees. If I can find him, that is. He's hiding. Every year he disappears about the 15th of April until the heat dies down. But I'll find him. I know his hang-outs."

"Thanks, sir. Tell him I'm sorry and that I know he told me this might happen, that I might change my mind by spring."

Later that afternoon he found George Macrakis, assistant college counselor and wild man of the English department in the faculty room. He was sitting in an old, worn, leather chair in a far corner, his feet up on a desk, reading a set of essays.

"Are the rumors true, George? I hear that nobody made Harvard, that Yale cut us in half, all of the Princeton acceptances were the same students accepted by Yale. I also hear that Brown and Dartmouth, paranoid about being second choice to H-Y-P, put every one of our candidates on the waiting list."

Macrakis removed his feet from the desk, placed the set of papers on the floor, and stretched. He grinned at Bartley and twirled the tip of his handle-bar mustache.

"Worse than that, Jack. That's why I'm hiding in here. It's a disaster, the end of Kensington as a competitive school. Harvard wrote and said that not only were they not taking anyone from Kensington this year, they decided to kick two of our kids out who were admitted last year. Yale called and told us not to present any candidates in the future who could not play Division I hockey or football. Princeton said they don't want to see anything except alumni sons from families who have donated more than a million dollars to Princeton. You want my job? I'll trade you even up for the Discipline Committee."

"No deal. I wouldn't take your job for anything. I already turned it down before they offered it to you full-time. When do you take over from Harding?" He lied in a vain attempt to dash Macrakis' good spirits.

"Next year. I'll be college counselor the first time we have Fems to offer. The sooner the better, Jack. We've almost waited too long. All the Biggies are co-ed now. We're trying to compete with a traditional student body in a world with completely new quota guidelines."

It was a mystery that Macrakis had survived at Kensington. If Bartley had been considered a risk by the old guard when he arrived fresh and innocent from the Midwest, Macrakis was considered Woody's "experiment" in testing the outer limits of the faculty's spirit of toleration.

The son of a Greek immigrant who ran a coffee shop in the West Nineties, Macrakis had rarely been out of New York City when he came for his interview at Kensington. He had attended public schools and Columbia, taught in a high school in the Bronx for two years and was discovered and recommended by an alumnus whose children had come under Macrakis' mesmerizing influence.

He was more a preacher than a teacher, rhapsodic and evangelical who taught his own moral passion. In the twelve years he had been at Kensington he had gone through eschatological, apocalyptic, existential, and incarnational stages of spiritual development. In his first years, everything was existential. He taught Camus and Hemingway, Conrad, Dostoyevski and Sartre. Then he got caught up in the Black movement and taught Wright and Malcolm X in all of his courses. Then he became anti-war and anti-establishment and taught Vonnegut and grew a beard and led the students in their protest march to Washington after Kent State. Bill Henry gave up expecting Macrakis to follow the syllabus or the course descriptions. Henry simply re-wrote the course description to include whatever Macrakis was doing that year. Woody never faltered in his support of Macrakis, turning away curtly a faculty petition that he be censured and an ad hoc delegation requesting he be fired. Woody told the delegation that Macrakis was one of the few genuinely Christian people he had ever met and that he was actually considering appointing Macrakis chaplain rather than firing him, a thought that he had never entertained until that moment.

The students believed he was one of their own, that he was their voice in the moral wilderness of the faculty meeting. He became the unofficial adviser and friend of every student in academic trouble. He spent hours of extra time in conferences over failed papers, helping with revisions. He taught vocabulary review in highly popular voluntary sessions on Saturday morning. He held grammar review sessions for third and fourth formers having trouble in foreign languages. He was a kind of cheerleader with an inexhaustible capacity for encouragement despite the score. He graded students on effort and improvement. He was famous for inflating the grades of pluggers and deflating the egos of bright careless prima donnas.

Over the years Macrakis had mellowed or perhaps the times had mellowed and he reflected that easing of tension. He shaved his beard and grew a handle-bar mustache. He was almost thirty when he married. Now he had two children and his family had become the passionate center of his life along with his students and the varsity soccer team whose winning record had become almost legendary in Macrakis' ten years as head coach. Now he had broad respect among his colleagues. Only Charles Brewster had reservations. He had never been able to understand how anyone who dressed as well as Macrakis could have so many crackpot ideas.

"Seriously, George, are the results as bad as I've been hearing?"

"No. In fact, we did very well considering we didn't have any Fems. The scholarship kids—the blacks and ethnics and Midwestern kids did well. The bright boys from New York always do well. We got some breaks on geographical distribution—southern and California kids that eastern colleges like so they can claim they're national institutions. And the legacies scored well. Your boy Forester is going to get in to Daddy's college even though the school's recommendation was tentative and unenthusiastic.

"All in all, as good as last year, better than the year before, but we got to get the Fems, Jack, or we won't make it over the next five years. Inflation is eroding the scholarship money, tuition is going up. Our source of Black students is dwindling. We simply can't offer the kind of scholarship we used to. We need the Fems to improve the quality of our pool."

"You sound like a pimp, George."

"Me a pimp! You're the biggest advocate of co-education, not me. I'm just being practical. Did you know if we do it right we can replace a bottom twenty-five percent of boys with a top twenty-five percent of girls? The quality of the whole school will go up and the anxiety of the college counselor will go down."

"If we go coed, the trustees are going to insist that the number of boys here remain the same. We're going to expand, my friend. Rumor has it that they're already receiving bids for three dormitory additions on three faculty houses. I've also heard we're going to increase in size to keep tuition costs down."

"How will that keep tuition costs down? The costs of educating more students will increase."

"Not if they keep the size of the faculty down, and increase the size of classes. Food is not a big item in the budget, but faculty salaries are."

"So that's why the bastards have been so secretive. That's why your student-faculty committee on co-education has been defunct since you made your recommendation."

"We have not been consulted for a year, and when I asked Woody why, he just shrugged. He said the matter was out of our hands, even out of his hands. It's strictly a trustee matter, but I think we'll know in a month."

"You think it'll be that soon? I bet they drag their asses for another year. The good old boys will pressure them."

"I don't. The good old boys have daughters and granddaughters. They know we're in a strong enough position to attract first-rate female candidates and that the reputation of Kensington depends on continued good results in college admissions. Actually, George, I believe revisionist historians of the future, if they bother at all, will look back and discover that the present deliberation of our Board of Trustees is not an enlightened gathering of progressive and broad-minded men of vision committed to a better tomorrow but is in fact a conspiracy of Good Old Boys and Male Chauvinists determined to maintain at least a fifty percent quota for males at Kensington. It's a rear guard action to prevent the whole school—students, faculty, and trustees from going all female."

Macrakis stared at Bartley with a sudden look of wonder. Bartley knew Macrakis was a sucker for any conspiratorial explanation of events.

"You know, you're probably right." He began to shake his head. "Screwed again. We're nothing but a bunch of puppets, Jack, even when we do what we think is right, especially when we think we have freely chosen a fair and responsible course of action."

"We must be content to mind our own gardens, George. How's yours coming?"

"Only got the peas in so far. This college business has had us straight out for the past month. Thank God, I'm not coaching this spring."

"Can you tell me how my advisees have done or probably will do so that I can face them this afternoon and tonight? I'd also like to know who really got screwed and will need some convincing that the world has not come to an end."

"We haven't heard from everyone. Harding's putting in some calls now. I left the office to hide here. Not all the letters are in. Some of the kids won't hear until tomorrow so they're trying to find out what we know. By the way, what's your boy, Peter Colby, going to do?"

"He's leaning toward Grinnell."

"It's a shame to waste all that talent on some piddling, obscure Midwestern college. He could have gotten in anywhere he wanted—Harvard, Stanford, if he really wanted to go out West. We could have fattened our acceptance figures even if he matriculated out there in the corn fields."

"He wasn't interested in staying East until recently."

"Why the sudden interest?"

"A girl friend who will probably go to Smith next year."

"He should have thought of that last fall. He could be rowing at Harvard next fall and visiting his girl on weekends. A terrible waste of talent. It's too late now. No offense to you now, Jack. I've never been west of Yonkers. How should I know what's out there? Probably got a library bigger than Widener and Sterling put together out in some abandoned silo for all I know. Just the word hasn't got back here yet."

"Jesus, George. I can't believe what I'm hearing from you. You sound like a car salesman."

"I can't help it. I know in my heart that college placement is a crock. We peddle for prestige conscious social climbers and snobs. But I can't help it. I'm competitive. I want to win."

"Listen, George, I didn't just come here for a general discussion. Peter asked me to talk to you."

"Colby?" He began to grin.

"Yes. He wants me to ask you what he has to do to transfer next year to any college or university within a few hours of Smith. He's afraid to talk to you."

"I knew it. I told him, Jack. I told him last fall he might change his mind and that he should have kept some options open."

"Gloat some other time, George. Just tell me what he has to do."

"Notify me in writing next fall. Before he leaves in June, he should have all of his second semester teachers write an evaluation. We don't ask for them from teachers of seniors unless they don't get into college. He shouldn't wait until next year to ask for them. The reports are sharper when teachers write them fresh—right after teaching a student. Reports written after several months are flat and lack revealing detail."

"Thanks, George. I'll tell him."

"Send him in. I won't bite his head off. In a week or two when things settle down here."

"If he isn't still too embarrassed to face you."

"He shouldn't be. If he makes a strong academic record at Grinnell next year, and I'm sure he will, I can use him to fatten my placement record in my first year as head honcho around here. Actually, the Fifth Form SAT's are a little flat. I may need a little help from transfer students to keep the prestige college acceptances up to snuff."

Whenever Bartley experienced an anxiety crisis over his creeping conservatism he took solace in considering Macrakis' case of galloping pragmatism.

PART II

▼

YE OLDE MORALITY

CHAPTER 3

▼

He didn't know why he over-responded when he talked to Ned Phillips, the Dean of Students. He didn't like Phillips but that wasn't the reason. He was edgy, irritated that he had so much to do, he wasn't doing anything very well. He raced from class to committee appointment to baseball practice to dinner. He skimmed reading assignments, used old lecture notes without re-reading sources. After two weeks with the team and the first two games, Annie had disappeared and he hadn't the courage to confront her. He regretted the letter he had written to Mrs. Powell. As soon as he had mailed it, he wanted it back. He was certain that it had sealed Peter's doom.

Before dinner he found Phillips in the faculty mail room stuffing faculty boxes with his weekly disciplinary summary sheets. Phillips handed Bartley a copy of the charge sheet he was about to put into the boxes of members of the Discipline Committee. As Bartley began to read the charge sheet, Phillips began to leave.

"Hey, Ned. Don't go away so quickly. I may have a few questions." Bartley read the sheet quickly. A sixth former, Tim Atkins, had been caught around midnight Sunday by a security guard in the faculty room with the ditto carbon of a math examination he had apparently retrieved from a wastebasket.

"I've got to run, Jack. Why don't you see me before the meeting tonight if you have any questions?"

"Because I won't have time between now and then to see you. I have a dorm committee meeting before this D.C. meeting special you just sprung on me."

Phillips stood reluctantly in the doorway holding the door half open.

"Shut the door a minute while I read this again. You don't have anything urgent to do. You can give me a minute now."

He read the paper through a second time.

"Why have you listed three charges here when the one charge stealing testing materials is enough to fire just about anyone. Why clutter the issue with the charges 'absent from the dormitory after check-in and unauthorized presence in a restricted area.' How the hell could he be stealing at midnight in the faculty room if he wasn't out of his dormitory?"

"It's my job to prepare a complete statement of the charges. Any lapse in procedure and we can be sued." Kensington had actually been sued in a pot case three years before and settled out of court.

"You're trying to stack things against the kid. One major charge would be enough."

"It's the job of the D.C. to formulate the language of the final charge."

"All right. I just want you to know that I intend to move that the two minor charges be dropped."

"That's your privilege, Jack."

"I wouldn't have to do it at all if you hadn't listed them."

"You do your job and I'll do mine. I try to be thorough in preparing the case."

Bartley realized the futility of arguing with Phillips and turned away as Phillips left. It was difficult for Bartley to think of Ned Phillips as a Dean or to call him by his title. He was appointed five years before. Actually there had not been an official Dean of Students before Phillips. Headmaster Woodbridge created the position for Phillips who was about to be let go after fifteen years on the faculty because the enrollment in Latin, which he taught without imagination or enthusiasm, had fallen off so much that there were not enough students for Mr. Hawkins, the senior Latin master.

Bartley groaned to himself when he thought about what was about to happen. Why couldn't it have been simple? Why couldn't the culprit have been some arrogant, insolent malcontent on probation for drinking—hated by students and faculty alike—caught in an unequivocal act of plagiarism. But it never happened that way. Now they were faced with an unambiguous act of dishonesty, one that usually called for *pro forma* dismissal, by a young man of such widespread popularity and good will that even those members of the faculty who believed that the Kensington honor code was the last moral fortress still standing in defense of Western Christian Civilization might hesitate before recommending firing.

Though Bartley had never taught the boy, he knew him informally and his career at Kensington was a matter of public knowledge. Tim Atkins was the senior sixth former at Kensington, having repeated his fourth form year after failing two courses. He had since then been on perennial academic warning or probation because of his inability to pass math. Twice he had been advised to withdraw. He spent three summers taking math courses or being tutored only to return to Kensington and fail a subsequent course. Now he was in his last semester of the math requirement—and failing miserably.

Through all his difficulties he had maintained outwardly at least a remarkable equanimity. He actually studied math consistently and persistently. He was a good English and history student but the center of his life was his art courses and the studio where he could be found almost any hour of the day or evening, sketching, drawing, painting. He conducted unofficial drawing lessons for faculty children. He made watercolors and pastels of scenes on campus that faculty members offered to buy, but which Tim bartered for home-cooked meals for himself and a friend or two. He designed and painted most of the sets for dramatic productions, did all the art work and sketches for the year-book, and was in charge of dance weekend decorations.

He had a square face and jaw. A shock of dark hair fell across his face which he continually brushed back with a quick, nervous thrust of his arm and hand. He was famous for his lack of ability and interest in athletics. The PE department had finally given up trying to teach him skills in its developmental program. He sat on the bench for two years in soccer and baseball, the coaches believing it was too dangerous for Atkins to be put in a game, and then, to accommodate his special needs and to give him more time to paint, someone invented an aerobics pro-gram for him. Four days a week he had to walk or jog a three mile course around campus or two miles in the gym when the weather was bad.

His room was a disaster. Prefects and dorm masters had given up urging him to keep it clean. Once every two weeks he had to put every-thing in order, but it was a mess by nightfall. But his temperament was absolutely placid. He was shy and respectful. He smiled continuously. He was witty without being cruel.

He had survived five years at Kensington during which time his identity had undergone a gradual transformation. At first he was a loner and a loser, a pitiful failure in everything important at Kensing-ton. By the sixth form year, his classmates cherished him as a symbol of the individuality and originality of their class and in February had organized a surprise retrospective showing of his works in the dining hall and common room. They borrowed sketches, watercolors, and pastels from faculty apartments; his parents brought up two years of his paintings. They worked all night hanging and labeling the pieces, which the school discovered at breakfast. It remained by popular demand until the spring break.

That evening it took the Committee a half hour to finally agree upon the language of the charge. It was clear that the students on the committee sympathized with Atkins. They quibbled about "stealing," insisting perversely that since the ditto carbon had been thrown away,

Atkins didn't really steal anything. They settled upon "illegal appropriation of testing materials before an announced examination."

Atkins appeared with his adviser and admitted his guilt and that he had been driven to dishonesty because he knew he no longer had a chance to pass. He admitted that he hadn't understood much of anything in class for over three weeks. It might as well have been Greek. His math teacher, Mr. Warner, appeared before the Committee briefly and confirmed that Atkins' average was thirty-seven and the probability that he could pass the final was virtually nil. He had flunked a test that very morning, the one he tried to appropriate ahead of time.

Then the students learned for the first time that in the fall the faculty had rejected Atkins' petition to substitute a philosophy course with emphasis on logic for math, and one student, already angry at one of the faculty members for lecturing the group about the serious nature of the crime and by attempting to humiliate Atkins, suddenly attacked the faculty as inflexible, which produced an instant polarization of the Committee and two hours of wrangling. Bartley's head began to ache soon after Atkins left the room and continued past midnight. Later in bed, waiting for the aspirin to work, he tried to explain to Karen why he voted the way he did.

"Everything seemed to be going all right. The boy made a good impression, answered questions directly and respectfully. Then that goddamn Skinner gave everyone a lecture about how cheating was the most serious crime in an academic community and began grilling Atkins about whether he knew the difference between right and wrong and whether he was defying the faculty and the rules of the school and how his cheating on the test deprived the other students of a fair grade. He cheated his fellow students and himself, not the school. Then that stupid Phillips tried to suppress the psychologist's report that accompanied Atkins' petition last fall, arguing that it was restricted to the faculty and not for student consumption. Then I suggested the general nature of Atkins' problem could be characterized without invading the boy's privacy, since it was obviously relevant and the student members of the committee could not vote intelligently or fairly unless they knew about possible extenuating circumstances. It was the only thing I said all night. Then the students got angry when they realized Atkins had been tested and had some kind of clinically documented learning disability in math and that the faculty had backed the math department last fall in rejecting the petition. Then that smartass Harrison charged the faculty with 'academic neanderthalism,' that we had driven Atkins to dishonesty, but I had to agree with him since I voted last fall to substitute the logic course for the math requirement. Then my head began to ache and I began to think of the assignment I hadn't read for class tomorrow and the lecture I have to prepare and I tuned out until the vote because I had already decided not to vote for any motion to fire."

"And now you're in the middle of another disciplinary case?" she asked.

"And now I'm in the middle of another disciplinary case at exactly the worst time possible," he affirmed gloomily. "I should have voted for firing and then I'd be off the hook."

"Did you vote for the boy or against Skinner and Phillips?"

He hesitated but then answered firmly.

"It was an ideological issue. I voted against Skinner and Phillips. The kid's guilty and probably ought to be to be fired for his own good, but now I'm going to have to defend my vote on the faculty floor. The vote was 5-3 for probation. I was the only faculty member to vote against firing."

"Oh, Jack, you're your own worst enemy."

"I know. Sometimes, I can't help myself."

"It seems mostly all the time you can't help yourself."

"I know. But if you could have heard that pair of inquisitors going after poor Atkins. They made the case a contest of values, not me. They refused to see Atkins as a person, not me. They argued that if we let the boy off with probation, the school would probably fall apart."

"Well, I'm glad you voted for probation. I just wished you'd voted for the right reason."

"What other right reason is there?"

"Oh, just because Tim is a sensitive, kind young man who was driven to do a terrible thing for someone else and that he is suffering and condemns himself and will probably never do it again."

"How do you know?"

"He sat next to me in concert choir. We talked."

"That's all. No other evidence?"

"That's all, and my instinctive feeling that most young people are not incorrigibly cruel or selfish or dishonest."

"I suppose you're right again as usual. Hey, my headache's gone away."

"That's because now you know the true reason why you voted the way you did."

"Most likely it was the aspirin, but wouldn't it be nice if just knowing what is right would clear everything up and eliminate everyone's pain!"

"Isn't that some kind of fallacy, pathetic or something like that?" she yawned.

"No. But you're close. That's the Socratic fallacy."

"Whatever. What's the pathetic fallacy?"

"That there is an intimate interconnection between what humans do and the order of nature and history, or something like that. I don't know exactly. I wasn't a philosophy major."

"Why is it?" she asked sleepily, "that most of what I believe is some kind of fallacy?"

She turned over and soon fell asleep. He lay on his back brooding for an hour before he dozed off.

*   *   *   *

He didn't sense any tension yet about the Atkins case. The faculty meeting was not until Friday when the case would be presented for the full faculty decision, three days away. Annie didn't show up again at practice on Tuesday. He decided they really should stop avoiding each other and talk matters over. That evening she was asleep when he entered her room at nine o'clock, but the light by her bedside was still on. On the floor beside her bed were two books and across her stomach opened face down was a handbook on strategies and techniques of base running. She had not been to practice for three days. In the two weeks since she joined the team, they had lost their first two games by scores of 17-3 and 22-0. In the first game, they had played even for three innings. They were behind by only two runs when a combination of walks, errors, and hits produced ten runs before four pitchers finally produced three outs.

During that nightmare of ineptitude, and in stark contrast to it, was Annie's professional performance as bat girl and equipment manager. He would never forget her look of stunned disappointment after the disastrous fourth inning. He could tell that she struggled not to cry. Though she had cheered and shouted to the bitter end, he knew that she knew then and forever more that her father was, indeed, a pathetic coach of pathetic teams and that for some strange reason, it didn't seem to make any difference to him. He didn't know whether she was disappointed more by the truth of the situation or by his own virtual immunity to defeat. He knew his hopefulness must have been incomprehensible to her. He shouted encouragement after all was lost and was already optimistic about the next game as they gathered equipment and bases after the last out. But the second game, 22-0, was apparently too much for her. After seven runs in the second inning, she handed the score book back to him; she had neatly marked the symbols, blackened the diamonds for runs scored. The other team had batted around once and a half. Two of the outs were the gifts of a merciful umpire. It must have struck her that there was little connection between the third form team and its opponent—as if each team were playing a different game. The sad part was that she would probably never understand the necessity of his enthusiasm. The 17-3 loss was a decided improvement over the opening score of the previous year.

He slipped the book gently out of her hands, closed it and placed it on the floor. Then he sat down on a bed side chair and watched her sleep. She lay on her back; her arms outside the covers were folded across her chest and her head was propped at an angle by double pillows. The sleeves of her pajamas were puffed and bore a tight pattern of tiny red flowers each inter-connected by a complex network of delicate, fragile green vines.

He picked the books from the floor and smiled as he examined the covers. They were books on baseball from the public library. He had withdrawn them himself in his first years of coaching. They had been hopelessly complicated then and only made sense when he read them again after several years of coaching. The black and white photographic illustrations were of players wearing old-fashioned uniforms, but he knew that for all the changes in baseball—of training methods, playing surfaces, trendy and splashy uniforms—the hard facts of the game remained consistent. Over the years the major league batting averages remained a constant .260, and the pitchers ERA reflected the same consistency. The more baseball seemed to change, the more it was the same. Once a season was over, it joined every other season. As each season became history after the World Series, it diminished the importance of previous seasons. Only the current season really meant anything just as only his current classes meant anything to him. Who he was teaching or coaching now was important. Once his students and players moved along or graduated, they became irrelevant, diminishing each other from year to year, joining the ever growing throng of faces he could no longer associate with names. He didn't know why he coached baseball and had become a student of the game. He had accepted in his radical years in college, the intellectual contempt of all athletics, but he had become something of an expert since coaching at Kensington. He understood the strategy of the game and he had garnered an encyclopedic knowledge of Red Sox batting averages, ERA's, slugging percentages. His father had taken him to games at Wrigley Field before he died—in a car accident returning from Milwaukee on a snowy night when Bartley was fourteen years old. Perhaps he had continued his father's interest as a fan as the token acknowledgment of a heritage or a debt of gratitude, the only debt he could repay him, could remember owing him, his memory of his father had faded so quickly.

As he stood up to reach for the light switch, she opened her eyes, then closed them quickly.

"Hey, Pal, you asleep or only faking?" he asked and sat down again. She opened her eyes and smiled weakly.

"Hi, Daddy. What time is it?"

"A little after nine."

"I must have dozed off for a few minutes."

"I can't read in bed either. Two minutes at the most and then out like a light."

They were silent for several moments, each conspicuously avoiding the other's eyes.

"Haven't seen you lately. Came to see if you have an infirmary excuse from sports. If not, I'll have to put you in for three unexcused absences."

"I've got an excuse. I have a bad case of despair."

"But, we've only had two games. We're hardly organized. I've got lots of changes planned."

"Oh, Daddy, there's nothing you can do. Only three or four players know how to play. We don't have anyone who can catch. Every time the other team gets someone on base, we might as well send them to third base right away instead of waiting for the player to steal. Everyone you've tried at catch is awful. Our pitching is almost as bad as the catching…most of the boys are afraid of getting hurt. Some have never played before. I just don't understand why they even try. Why can't they do some other sport?"

"Well, the school requires at least two seasons of team sports the first two years and the boys only have a few choices. Besides, they're learning. Many of them have never played any sport in their lives. Some have never even exercised. You have to admit that with the jogging and the cals, they're getting exercise."

"I suppose so. Some practices go O.K., but the games are so…"

"Pathetic?"

"Yes, pathetic."

He tried to laugh.

"I'm sorry, Annie. I'm a pathetic coach and most of the players are pathetic misfits, but we get exercise and the non-athletic kids learn from the better players and get the feeling of being on a team."

"You're not a pathetic coach, Daddy. I've been watching the varsity and J.V. practices the past few days, and you do everything Mr. Bennett and Mr. Arnold do. And I've tried to read these books and you do a lot of these drills and you try to do what you're supposed to do, but losing 22-0 is just too much. You might as well not play games, just have practices."

"You're telling me you're quitting, is that it? I still need a bat girl and manager. We'll win a few games, we always do. The first two games are always tough. It gets better."

She turned away from him.

"That's not really why I want to quit. I don't mind being a manager. I don't even mind losing though that's depressing. It's just…I know this is going to sound dumb, but I only joined because I thought I could learn to play. I had this stupid fantasy that I'd turn out to be a good player and that I'd be good enough to make a boys' team and you and Mom could come and watch me play."

"But you just started to learn. It takes a few years. You've already improved on throwing and catching.

She sat up and implored him with her arms.

"Daddy, I'm pathetic. I have absolutely no ability. I'm afraid of the ball when I bat and even sometimes when I'm just playing catch. I haven't even come close to hitting a ball yet even when you pitch underhanded."

"You hit the ball off the batting tee pretty well and you're developing good form. You have to have patience, Annie. You stick with the team and we'll practice a lot this summer and if you haven't improved, then you can forget all about it."

"Daddy, I'm no good. I'll never be any good. It was just a dumb dream." She was almost shouting. He spoke quietly.

"I just don't want you to feel bad some day because you quit. And I can use a bat girl and manager. You've done a super job and the players accept you as one of the team."

"I know. I feel terrible about that. It's just that it hurts to see us lose. I don't mean just to lose—I mean to be so bad, everyone thinks we're a joke."

"Well, I won't argue with you. It was your choice to join the team and it's your choice to leave. I just kind of liked us doing something together here at the school. You do lots of things with Mom, but we've never really done anything together here at school. We're together during summer vacation but during the school year, we live almost separate lives except for some things like dorm feeds."

"I don't think I'm ready yet. I think maybe we're a few years off from doing things together."

He could sense the seriousness in her voice. He could tell she had already thought things out. He stood up, preparing to leave.

"Hey, Pal, you're probably right. Maybe the time isn't ripe for us yet. Should I shut the light off?"

"No. It's early yet. I think I'll read a while. Would you get me my social studies text over on my desk."

He walked across the room and returned to her bedside with the book.

"This book is monstrous. I hope it's more interesting than it looks."

She took the book from him and opened it on her lap. He kissed her on the forehead quickly and turned away.

"Daddy, is everyone on the team a third former? I was talking to two boys after practice the other day and they talked about biology and geometry, which I though were fourth form courses."

"Well, most of the players are third formers, but technically we're a coefficient team. We have some fourth formers every year who can't make the J.V. As long as they qualify with certain coefficients—height, weight, age, they can play with us. The teams that we schedule know what our range of coefficients is. It wouldn't be fair to use fifth and sixth formers against the public junior high schools we play. Against private schools we match up pretty closely over the years."

"You ought to include ability to play baseball in your coefficients."

"Then we wouldn't have a team."

"I was wondering. I don't know. Do you ever trade with the J.V. or anything."

"Sometimes, I send a really good third former up to them to play in their games. They play on Wednesday and Saturdays when we're off. Why?"

"Well, I've been hanging around the J.V. the past few days. I thought I could learn something to help you with. I am dumb sometimes, really dumb. I thought I could help you by reading the books. Isn't that a joke? Anyhow, there's a fourth former new this year named Mitchell Morgan whose a really good catcher but he's small and Mr. Arnold doesn't let him play much and I heard him complaining to some of his friends. He may quit baseball and try out for track. You could really use him, Daddy. He's a super player. He could practice and play with us and if the J.V. needed a substitute catcher for their games, he could still play for them."

"That's not a bad idea, Annie. I'll check out his coefficients and talk to Mr. Arnold, and if he agrees, I'll talk to the boy. Maybe he won't want to play with us, though, might be too humiliating. If he doesn't want to play on our level, it wouldn't be fair to him or the team. Things could get worse if he's sour and ruins our morale."

"Things can't get worse, Daddy."

"I suppose you're right," he laughed. "Hey, if he wants to play with us, if he works out, I'll give you a job in the front office. Director of player personnel or chief scout."

"He'll want to play. Even with us. He can't stand not playing."

She opened the book on her lap and began turning pages.

"Will we see you at practice tomorrow, Pal?"

"Maybe. Maybe not," she muttered without looking up from her book.

✳   ✳   ✳   ✳

The next day after lunch Bartley was reading in the library in the Main School Building when he became aware of someone standing by his elbow. He removed his reading glasses and looked up into the taut white face of Tim Atkins.

"May I speak to you, Mr. Bartley?" he whispered.

Bartley looked at his watch. "I have baseball practice at 2:30."

"That leaves plenty of time, sir."

"Let's find an empty classroom."

The boy followed Bartley out of the library down the hall past rooms with classes in session until they found an empty room. Bartley shut the door and pulled a chair with a study arm out from a row and spun it around. He sat down and motioned to Tim to sit in another chair.

"What can I do for you, Tim?"

"I really shouldn't be talking to you, Mr. Bartley. You're not my adviser, but Mr. Henry asked me to. He promised to do something for me at the faculty meeting on Friday if I could talk you into backing him up."

"Why Mr. Henry? He's not your adviser either."

"He's my English teacher, sir." He waited a few moments, brushed the shock of his hair back, and went on. "He has lots of respect on the faculty and so do you."

"Why me? There are lots of other faculty who can support Mr. Henry. I've already had enough of your case, Tim. I've listened and I've voted on the Discipline Committee. I don't plan to say anything at the faculty meeting."

"It's because you're on the Discipline Committee, sir. It's because of the way you voted."

"How do you know how I voted?"

"The vote was 5-3 in favor of probation. I know how the students voted—one of the faculty had to have voted in favor of probation. It was either you or Mr. Le Clair.

"All right. I voted for probation. Skinner made me angry. It was your first major offense. I accepted the extenuating circumstances. Mr. Haskell argued your case forcefully after you left. You made a good impression, but I've done all I can do for you. I'm way behind in my work. I've got problems in my own dorm. If Morrison or Forester get busted, I might as well give up teaching for the rest of the year. I really don't want any further involvement. Why don't you talk to one of the other faculty on the D.C. who voted to fire you? I'll probably vote for a probation motion again in the faculty meeting."

"Mr. Bartley, I've asked Mr. Henry to argue against probation and to support a firing motion. He said he wouldn't do it unless you changed your vote. He said he respected your judgment and that unless you changed your mind, he doesn't want to interfere because he's really out of the loop. He said you must have had a good reason to vote for probation on the D.C."

"You've asked Mr. Henry to make a statement on the floor in support of a motion for firing! And you want me to support that statement and announce that I've changed my mind and support it too?"

"Yes, sir."

"Has Mr. Henry lost his mind?"

"No, sir. If you'll listen to me, I'll explain why I asked him."

"What made you change your mind? You seemed pretty desperate to stay at Kensington last night."

"That's because Mr. Haskell was all excited about getting me off and the students were all hyped up. It's his first big case and he wants to prove he's on the student's side. It's his first year teaching, sir, and he identifies still with being a student and he wants to be liberal and popular. I kind of got caught up in his enthusiasm to save me, but I've been thinking a lot since last night and I've changed my mind."

"You're going to have to enlighten me, Tim. I am confused. I think you have a decent chance tomorrow. Any kind of narrow faculty vote either way will be good for you. Mr. Woodbridge won't fire anybody unless the faculty recommendation is decisive especially since the D.C. recommendation would contradict it."

"I know that. That's why it's got to be decisive and that's why I've come to ask you to change your position and announce during the faculty meeting that you have changed your mind and are going to vote to fire me."

"All right. I'll listen." He looked at his watch. "I've got about twenty minutes. Will that be enough time? I'm going to need a lot of convincing." The bell rang. Bartley paused as doors opened and the corridors filled with sounds of footsteps hurrying down the halls.

"I think so, sir." He brushed his hair back once again and licked his lips. He spoke calmly, deliberately as though he had rehearsed his presentation carefully. "When I got caught the other night, when the security guard surprised me, he almost ran into me as I was leaving the faculty room, I jumped. I was so startled and scared, I felt my world had come to an end. I've never cheated on anything at Kensington, never, and I was ashamed and thought of my parents and how hurt they were going to be, but by the time the guard had brought me to Mr. Phillips' apartment and woke him up, I felt totally relaxed. No, I felt relieved, almost happy. It was all over, sir, all over. I would be fired for cheating and never have to flunk another goddamn math test for the rest of my life. I can't express to you what that meant. It was all over. No more bullshit. No more grinding or praying. No more looking hopelessly at a page of letters and numbers and problems that didn't mean a thing to me, sir, not a fucking thing. I was crying when Dean Phillips took me into his study for a preliminary interrogation. I was crying tears of relief not tears of grief or shame." Atkins' eyes began to water as he spoke, but he didn't cry. He paused and licked his lips again.

"I couldn't take it anymore, Mr. Bartley. I think I committed academic suicide. I think I wanted to get caught and get kicked out and go back to high school where I will probably graduate in June or after summer school at the latest anyhow because I have so many credits from five years at Kensington."

"But Tim, if you waited a few more months you'd finish here and if you flunked math, you could still get a Kensington diploma if you passed a math course of the same level in college or simply study some more next summer and take the final again. Besides, You can make up a failed course simply by passing the final."

"I've already spent three summers preparing to come back here and take another make-up exam. I'll spend the rest of my life trying to pass that math final. I've tried and I've tried and I've tried. The only reason I've gotten through two years is because I did well enough in geometry. Somehow I could see the geometry but I can't see algebra. I can't understand anything. I don't know how I got a D-in the first semester. It was a gift from Mr. Warner. I guess he counted my daily work or something. I wish he had flunked me at Christmas and then it would have been all over. But if I get kicked out for cheating everything will be over for good. You can't make up a disciplinary dismissal."

"I'm sorry, Tim. None of us sensed it bothered you so much. We didn't know you hated it here so much. We advised you to withdraw, but when you came back last September, we thought you wanted to be here."

"Wanted to be here? Of course, I wanted to be here, Mr. Bartley. I love Kensington. It was tough the first two years, but the last three I've been able to work at my art all the time and I've got some good friends and great classes. I just like being here, drawing, sketching the school, it's so beautiful, the buildings and the grounds and the fields and the trees. I'd like to spend the rest of my life here, be an artist in residence or get a job on the kitchen staff or grounds crew or something, but always hanging over my head has been that goddamn, fucking impossible math requirement. I can't do it, Mr. Bartley. I don't have it up here." He pointed to his head. "My math aptitude has always been low, but my parents sent me to be tested last summer when the faculty advised me to withdraw, and the results of the tests suggested I've only got one hemisphere in my brain or something like that. The psychologist said the symptoms were evident in my SAT's. There's a four hundred point difference between my verbal and math scores. I'm all visual and verbal. I've got a learning disability. It's got nothing to do with how much work I do. Some people just can't do some things and the Kensington math requirement for all students is college level. For five years now, except the year I repeated when I dropped math for a year so that I could pass French, I've been on the verge of flunking math every semester and I worked at it and worked at it. Half the guys in my dorm have tutored me. I just wish you'd kicked me out three years ago or let me take another course this year similar to math like Mr. Le Clair's philosophy course. I've just quit, Mr. Bartley. I refuse to spend the rest of my life trying to pass the Kensington math requirement. I don't care if I don't get into college, but if you don't fire me for cheating, I'll have the possibility for getting my Kensington diploma if I pass the third year math final. It'll haunt me for the rest of my life. I don't want another chance to fail. I just don't want it. I've failed enough."

The hallways were now absolutely quiet. Bartley could hear the hand on the clock click off another minute.

"Why didn't your parents take the faculty's advice last summer? I don't understand. The math department stated very clearly that your chances were slim. Your parents apparently must have understood the results of the tests last summer, that your learning disability had nothing to do with your general intelligence. Why did they let you come back in September?"

Atkins' forehead wrinkled. "They wanted me to come back even more than I wanted to come back. There is nothing more they want in life than for me to graduate from Kensington. For four years now, my Dad has been giving me lectures before I came back. 'Work a little harder, Tim,' he says. 'Hang in there, old man. It'll come. I had troubles in math too. I almost flunked for two years and then all of a sudden, I understood and became a whiz.'

"And my Mom thinks of Kensington as a second home. We live only about an hour and a half from here, near Stamford, and they come up whenever they can. They find any excuse. They've never missed a parent's weekend and they're on the parents' fund-raising committee. They love to stay at the Kensington Inn and take me and my friends to dinner there on Saturday night or to Sunday brunch. And they tramp all over campus on Saturday to see games. They've come to every play when I've worked on the set. They were so proud of my art show. They think Kensington is some kind of Camelot. They're so proud I got in to start with. They don't care what college I go to. In fact, I've talked them into letting me go to an art institute if I don't go to Tufts. I'm in two already. Art schools don't care about math. They want to see my portfolio."

"But if you get kicked out, you may not get in anywhere. Acceptance at Tufts depends upon the successful completion of the senior year. I don't know about the art schools. We don't send many students to them."

"I'll have to take my chances. From what I know of sixth formers who have been kicked out since I've been here, mostly for booze, some were deferred for a year, a few were rejected, and some were accepted without a diploma from Kensington. They finished the year at their public high schools and still got in even to Harvard and Princeton."

"You mean Lesie and Goodhue three years ago, but each had a legacy a yard long and high grades and boards."

"I know my circumstances are different, but right now college isn't very important."

Bartley sat quietly for some time.

"What's your Dad do?"

"He's a lawyer. My Mom works, too. She sells real estate and she's really good. She probably makes as much as my Dad. My sister goes to Hotchkiss—she's in the tenth grade, and they visit her on weekends when they're not visiting me. Sometimes they visit her on Saturday and me on Sunday."

"I assume they know what's happened."

"Yes, sir. They wanted to come up today, but I told them there was nothing they could do. I told them about the D.C.'s recommendation for probation, and they were so happy my Mom was crying on the phone. They're coming up Friday morning and if the faculty votes probation, we'll go to the Inn for dinner to celebrate and they'll give me pep talks about working harder at math and that things will work out in the end, and I'll have the math final hanging over my head for the rest of my life."

"I suppose they'll take it pretty hard if you get fired?"

"It's better for me to get out of here now and get it all over with and done. For the rest of my life I'd look in their eyes and I'd see this pleading look, 'Try a little harder at the math, Tim. It'll come. You'll get your Kensington diploma yet.' I can see myself thirty-five years old, and every time I see them, their eyes will say 'Have you studied for the math test, Tim? You can still get your diploma from Kensington.' Mr. Bartley, I cannot pass that test. I want to kill all of their hope and my hope, now, so I can get on with the rest of my life."

"It'll be tough for them, knowing you got booted for cheating."

"They'll get over it in a week. Right now they really don't care that I cheated. They just don't want me to get kicked out. If I get probation, they won't say a thing to me about the dishonesty."

"Will it bother them that they may have driven you to cheating by deciding that you should return last fall?"

"I suppose so, but they can learn to live with that. All they wanted was the best for me. They'll rationalize their way out of the guilt."

"Either you're terribly cynical about them or terribly realistic."

"I'm not cynical. It's what they're like. I don't want to hurt them, but I can't go on living with their illusion, this false hope that I can pass. I can not pass math. I have my own life to live even if it means they're disappointed. I've had almost five good years here. So have they. Well, it's over. I've learned a lot. The school has let me develop as an artist, working alongside my teachers. They've let me out of athletics. I've been happy here except for the math. What the hell difference does it make if I don't get the diploma. I've had the education and the opportunity."

They sat in silence for a minute or two. Finally Bartley said, "I'll talk to Mr. Henry after practice. I can't promise you anything."

"Thanks, Mr. Bartley. I'm sorry to be such a pain. I'm not in your dorm and I've never had you in class." He paused for a while and then added. "If I do get kicked out Friday, would you talk to my parents—if Mr. Henry can't explain to them that it's not the end of the world?"

"What about Mr. Haslett?"

"I'll have to keep them away from him as much as I can. He'll be angry and make them think I'm some kind of martyr and then they'll really feel terrible."

Bartley smiled. "You may be a poor math student, but you are not without dialectical skills."

"I'd have done great in Mr. Le Clair's philosophy course. I'm a great hair splitter and a rationalizer and quibbler like Mr. Le Clair."

"You have thought this out carefully, Tim?"

"Yes, sir."

"I guess that will have to do. I'll talk to Mr. Henry."

"Thank's again, sir."

"For now, thank Mr. Henry."

*   *   *   *

After practice Bartley found Bill Henry in his classroom. He pulled up a chair and sat down across from Henry, who did not look up. Bartley tried to sense Henry's mood. He could be amiable, hostile, cantankerous, sullen, indifferent, playful, ironic—all strategies of classroom persona he used to keep his students off balance or to keep a colleague at a distance. Since Bartley knew the moods would change, he never felt offended by Henry's facades of brusqueness or sarcasm or indifference. Sooner or later, there would be moments of brotherly affection and fatherly solicitude.

"What the hell do you want, Bartley?" Henry asked without looking up from what he was reading. "Can't you see I'm trying to finish this assignment before dinner?"

Bartley smiled. The mood was cantankerous. Henry had dark, short-cropped slightly greying hair. His eyes were narrowly spaced and deep set and the rimless glasses set high on the bridge of his nose gave his face a thin, sharp angularity. How often had Bartley's advisees come to him after two weeks of sixth form English with Bill Henry? Was he for real? Was he always that sarcastic? Did he believe the outrageous statements he passed off as commonplace truisms. What did he believe? He argued opposite positions or interpretations within the space of ten minutes? Sometimes he didn't say anything for long stretches of time, sitting at his desk like a disgruntled Buddha while the students argued among themselves.

"I just dropped by to find out what you're going to do about Tim Atkins."

"I'm not going to do anything until I know whether you're willing to change your position openly on the faculty floor." He looked at Bartley for the first time.

"I'm half convinced by the boy right now. I'm curious, however, why you're willing to support firing, aside from the fact he asked you to."

"I did a little research to refresh my memory. I read the minutes of the meeting last fall when we rejected Atkin's petition to substitute logic for math. I also read the psychologist's report on the boy. No wonder we didn't pass the petition. Besides, his petition was lost in the business of starting a new year."

"What's the no wonder of it all?"

"That I couldn't understand the report then and that I can't understand it now. It is full of the goddamnest gobbledegook that I have ever read. I read it three times yesterday morning and I still have no idea what the sonovabitch was trying to say. So I called him yesterday afternoon. I didn't let him say a thing but yes or no. I asked him two questions. Number one, according to the results of the test, could the boy expect to pass math on the level of difficulty we require in the last year here?"

"His answer?"

"No. Absolutely not. Not unless he underwent a special re-training regimen and even then the possibilities of handling our math curriculum were slim. We, of course, have no one on the faculty to handle that kind of problem."

"The second question?"

"Did the boy's parents understand the implications of the testing results? That is, did he tell them in plain English and did he make a recommendation about our advice to withdraw him?"

"The answer?"

"Categorically yes. After looking over the text Tim would use this year and representative tests our math department sent home with him to study over the summer, he told the parents that the boy didn't have a chance."

"So they sent him back here anyway."

"Unfortunately, yes. Now, since they were unable or unwilling to make a responsible decision, we must make it for them. Once he was caught, we must act. If we place him on probation, he'll finish the year flunking math, fail to get a diploma, and be required to return to high school next year. If we fire him now, he can return to high school and graduate in June or after some summer courses at the latest. I called the guidance counselor at his home high school already and he did an unofficial assessment of Tim's transcript that I read to him over the phone. But most importantly the boy doesn't want probation. He wants out and you're going to have to talk to him to find out exactly why."

"I have talked to him. Now an entire faculty is going to spend a few hundred man-hours deliberating and debating a decision that whatever way it goes is going to be a losing proposition for the boy, his family, and the faculty. The moral absolutists will have a field day reminding us that they are against sin and evil and that if we at Kensington don't take a stand we'll disintegrate and the boy himself will someday end up robbing a bank or murdering his wife and children."

"They always take that stand, Bartley, even in trivial matters like playing the stereo too loud, which they see as disobedience or rebellion. The problem is that whenever we have cases of plagiarism, stealing, cheating, hazing or dishonesty, the credibility of the moral reactionaries is intimidating. Neither you nor I believe that there is anything morally wrong with a seventeen year old kid having a few cans of beer, so we can argue effectively that the school can tolerate those kinds of occasional lapses, but when a kid cheats, we are back to the bedrock of the old morality and we believe in it."

"Why do we keep doing it, Bill? Why do we make our lives miserable by spending hours sentencing this poor kid when nobody else in the world seems to care about these judgments. Our work schedule is disrupted, the faculty divided. All of our repressed guilt re-emerges. We sense our own culpability and our unworthiness to judge. Each of us has been dishonest or cheated in some way or other. If we decide to fire the boy, we will once again produce a schism in the school—between faculty and students, and we will have to return to the dormitories and try to justify a decision we don't even believe in. Why don't we just give the whole matter of discipline back to Woody?"

Henry put his book down and faced Bartley for the first time across the desk. Light from his reading lamp glinted off his glasses.

"Well, Bartley, if you're losing your nerve, why don't you go teach in some university where they don't give a damn or where all the power is wielded by some Iron Dean or worse yet where the professors are out there screwing coeds and offering higher grades for a great lay. Go teach in a public high school where most teachers are powerless to do anything at all. The poor bastards can't even decide what to teach in many cases, let alone have any power to change the values of the system that constantly humiliates them. It's painful to make these collective decisions. It's myopic overkill. Why should the son of selfish social-climbing parents have lavished on him all the personal and moral concern of thirty-five adults, when many of the adolescents of our society suffer from either neglect or abuse or both.

"Any amateur Marxist could tell you that what we are doing is nothing more nor less than the manifestation of the inequities of the capitalistic system. But since neither of us, Bartley, is going to go to the barricades to replace our system of economic injustice with an equally unfair as well as deadening totalitarian socialism, we have to come up with some other reason for making ourselves miserable over the trivial matter of one young man who tried to steal the carbon ditto of a math test so that he might have a chance to pass the test if we could figure out the answers ahead of time, which he probably couldn't do. And we know the kid wouldn't ask a fellow student to help because we both know he has too much personal honor."

Henry looked at his watch and stood up. "It's time for a drink before dinner."

"You haven't answered my question. All you've done is convince me that my questions are valid. Why do we continue to do it? Why are you going in there Friday and argue that Tim Atkins should be fired for reasons of compassion—to put him out of his misery and give him a new beginning? Why do you want me to confess I've made a sentimental mistake out of misdirected compassion and that you've persuaded me of the error of my ways when both of us would rather put the kid on probation and exempt him from the last semester math requirement, which we cannot do any more?"

Bartley preceded Henry out the door into the darkened hallway. Henry snapped out the light and they walked toward the red exit signs at the end of the hall.

"We do it because it goes with the territory. Making judgments is our business. If you don't want to make judgments, Jack, then you better quit grading papers and tests, nodding approval or disappointment, cheering our players or raging at their bonehead plays, turning down stereos, discouraging or encouraging students to apply to Harvard or Podunk U., smiling at kids we like, turning away from those we don't like, admonishing the discourteous, humiliating the arrogant, encouraging the dispirited. In everything we do we are telling the students what we stand for. You don't teach just in the classroom, Jack, when you're peddling that neo-Jeffersonian prairie populist cant you pass off as American history.

"As painful and frustrating and emotionally exhausting the process may be, we have an opportunity realized by few teachers anywhere: we can monitor the direction or drift of our values. We do it more for ourselves than for the students. We are what we decide. On Friday we will say to the student body and to each other that sometimes we must be cruel to be kind. Other times we will say that such and such a student can grow only if we forgive, soften the harshness of our judgment and each of those disciplinary judgments is a reflection of the values we bring to bear in every class, every discussion, every paper, every test, every dormitory incident, every baseball game."

They had emerged from the basement door of the Main School Building into the fading light of the setting sun slanting across a football field. The grass was brilliantly green, but the trees along the path had yet to leave and stood starkly bare, their branches scoring the sky. Already it had begun to cool off. They walked between the Fine Arts Gallery with its skylights and the old Victorian infirmary with its tall curtained windows. At the end of the science building they entered the quadrangle outside Camden Commons. Students in dark suits were beginning to enter the quad from all directions and stream toward the dining hall. Boys late to their duties as waiters rushed past them half dressed, ties and shirt tails flapping behind them.

"We will meet as a body and deliberate for an hour or two, as you have already done with your committee that includes students, and we will be telling the students, the parents, the world or whatever little bit of it has ever heard of Kensington School that we believe in the importance as well as the rights of each student at this school, in the open and free and democratic process of discussion and voting that results in our muddled version of justice, and we will proclaim in our decision that we disapprove of cheating and lying and hazing and racism and bigotry, however liberal and understanding and fair minded and compassionate we may be in arriving at our conclusion. Each of us will vote. We won't duck our responsibility and hand everything over to some Grand Inquisitor or totalitarian tribunal.

"And tomorrow we will hear Haskell, one year out of Swarthmore, lecture us how difficult it is to be an adolescent. He will harangue us with youthful idealism and faith in the essential goodness of human nature just as you did fifteen years ago, and we need to hear that point of view. Nothing is more important to those of us entering our anecdotage than to be reminded of what it means to be young and to make mistakes. It's the process that keeps us honest, not whether some kid is kept or fired."

At one time or another Bartley had heard everything Henry had just told him. He was impressed by the passion that continued to give force and authority to Henry's articulation of the credo of the Kensington system; much of what Bartley had just heard had found its way into the

catalogue. The headmaster had assigned a section at a time of the catalogue to Bill Henry to re-write. Now after twenty years, it was entirely
Woodbridge's document. Year by year it seemed to grow younger, it's
language more confidently idealistic. The format of the catalogue had
also changed, the traditional grey cover with only the name of the
school on the front in simple, elegant dark maroon print, had been
replaced by a collage of color photographs depicting the chapel, the
Main School Building, the Bancroft Gym, and the Munson Science
Building. The school's name, its founding date, and the year of the catalogue appeared on the lower half of the front cover in white letters.
The back cover was an aerial photograph of the school, its buildings
obscured by trees, its playing fields occupying most of the picture.

The buildings of the school were ageless. Most of them were copies
of styles already a few hundred years old. The natural pastoral setting
of the school repeated its cycle of life each year, beginning with the
dying leaves of fall and ending in the flowers of spring.

Only over in the gym in the gallery of varsity team pictures was
there any proof of the passage of time. There in the black framed photographs of varsity baseball teams Bartley could observe Bill Henry
grow old. As his players remained perennially young and the uniforms
changed in imitation of the new styles and colors of the major leagues,
Bill Henry grew thin and tired, the creases of his face deepening, the
fatuous incongruity of an aging man in boy's clothes more apparent.
Bartley always missed team pictures for the yearbook. He didn't want
to leave behind a record of his mortality as a legacy to future Kensington students.

Henry stopped in the path suddenly and turned to Bartley. "What
are you going to do Friday?"

"You have convinced me that I should continue to support the recommendation of the Discipline Committee."

"You had decided that before you came to my classroom, hadn't
you?"

"No. You changed my mind. The boy had me convinced. Now, I guess I'd better talk to him again, give him a chance to change my mind again."

"Why did you provoke me into an oration? I get sick of hearing myself talk."

"My questions were rhetorical. I knew what your answer would be. I just wanted to hear what you had to say."

"You wasted my time."

"I'm sorry about that, Bill, but you've convinced me that so far as our disciplinary process is concerned, the boy doesn't deserve to be fired. We and the parents drove him to it. We have no right to fire him for a single desperate act."

"All right. I won't say a thing one way or other until I hear what you have to say on the faculty floor. You're so feckless, Jack. Who knows how many times you'll change your mind before Friday? I'll just wait. You know where I stand."

Henry turned away abruptly and began walking.

"I'm sorry about that, Bill, but you've convinced me that so far as our disciplinary processes are concerned, the boy doesn't deserve to be fired. You have just convinced me once again of the legitimacy of our process and I shall vote my mind and accept responsibility for my decision. We have no right to fire an essentially good kid for a single desperate act committed under extreme stress."

"All right, Jack. If that's what you think is right."

"I think it's right."

"Well then, I'll either go it alone or just say nothing and hope there's a coalition of moral absolutists who will kick Atkins out on general principles. Maybe I wont need you at all."

CHAPTER 4

▼

Disciplinary case or no disciplinary case, life went on, gloomily, for third form baseball. The team had suffered its fourth loss, by twelve unearned runs. The prognosis was dismal. He needed a catcher. He had to train someone to throw strikes. He didn't care if he lost to hits, but he couldn't stand losing by walks and passed balls. He would negotiate first, but if that didn't work he would beg.

He called off practice fifteen minutes early and hurried to the J.V. field and sat on the bench watching Sam Arnold finish pitching batting practice to his last three players. When practice was over, he joined Arnold walking back to the gym.

"Can I talk to you a few minutes, Sam. I've got some problems I thought you could help me with. Actually I think we can help each other out, me in the short run, you in the long run."

"Sure, Jack, you can talk to me, but I don't know that I can help you. Actually, I was expecting you. Bill Henry said you'd be by about this time trying to trade me out of a winning season without materially improving your own team."

"Sam, Henry is no longer part of the program. The nucleus of the J.V. comes from the previous third form team. The rest of the players you pick up from new fourth formers. But the core, the nucleus comes from me. It's a farm system, Sam, and your success depends to a great extent on my success. I don't mean my won and lost record. I mean it's important that players get useful game experience on the third form level. Right now we're not competitive. We're not playing baseball yet. I need some help. I'm willing to give up something to get that help. In the end you'll get all the best players next year. You know, Sam, it's not just your record this year that counts. We have a developmental sequence here, moving the boys along to a full realization of their potential. I know you're new and you want to do well your first year, but it's how well you do with the boys over several years that demonstrates you can become more than a coach. You can become an educator."

"Bill told me you'd try to con me too. He said you'd manipulate me personally, professionally, and ideologically."

"I wish you'd forget about Henry. He's retired, over the hill. You and I have to work together as colleagues in a continuing program for years to come."

Arnold stopped and started to laugh.

"All right, Jack. I'll listen, but I already think I know what you want and the answer is no. I need Morgan disgruntled or not. If I get an injury to Fleming, I'm all through. Right now I've got a good team, but if I lose my catcher, I might as well cancel the rest of the season unless I have Morgan ready to fill in."

"You're not going to lose a catcher, Sam, you're going to gain an experienced back up catcher with a positive attitude and real game experience."

"How's that?"

"Our teams don't play games the same day or at the same hours. I play Tuesday and Thursday or Friday. The two times we play on Saturday my game is over before you begin. Morgan just needs to change uniforms on those two days and then report to you. You can have him every Wednesday and Saturday. He'll be playing and practicing regularly with us on the other days."

"He'll lose our sense of rhythm and timing."

"He doesn't have it now, Sam. He's sitting on the bench. Works out a little at the end of your drills. My sources tell me that he thinks you haven't given him a fair chance because Fleming's so strong. I hear Morgan's going to quit and then neither of us will have him. Besides I have a ball player who can play regularly for you-infield or outfield. I'm willing to give him up for Morgan because I simply can't play ball without a catcher."

"Morgan's a fourth former. I thought he had to play J.V. I cut only the third formers to you that tried out for the J.V. I kept the fourth formers."

"We're a coefficient team-not really a third form team. Morgan won't be sixteen until summer and he fits my categories of height and weight."

"You've done your homework, I see." They stopped outside the lower corridor entrance to the gym.

"I've also found a kid who can throw the ball," Bartley went on not wanting to lose the initiative. "He's awkward—never played much before, but he's strong as an ox and can throw the ball a mile. He needs to learn form and technique and control. I thought he could work with your pitchers, then pitch for me. Next year, you'll inherit a battery that has worked together."

"Who's your good ball player you're willing to give up?"

"Ricky Thomas. I'll send him for you to take a look at tomorrow. He can field and hit. Good arm."

"Not tomorrow. I have a game."

"Thursday."

"O.K."

"And you'll send Morgan down to me on Thursday. And I'll send my budding pitcher up to you during pitching drills. Actually he needs to learn everything, fielding off the mound, pick-off motion. You send him back to me for everything else."

"Somehow I feel I'm being hustled. Should I have listened to Henry who told me that you'd make a damn fool out of me."

"Listen, this is all tentative anyhow. We'll try it out for a week. You're not a damn fool, Sam. You're an educator, a teacher who cares more about the individual growth of the student than about winning seasons or college placement or any of those other Skinnerian measurements of success. You're already an educator in your second year of teaching. It took me ten years to get to be even a beginning educator."

"What took you so long, Jack?"

"Naivete, inexperience. Came from the Midwest. Takes three or four more years when you're from the Midwest. Mostly though I made a mistake. I floundered under the ideological influence of Bill Henry for several years. I suffered from arrested professional development because he had become my Svengali, my mentor. Once I quit listening to him, I began to grow."

Bartley patted Arnold on the back in farewell.

"Sam, you're already well on the way to being an educator. You've made an independent judgment in defiance of Henry's advice. You've got a promising future."

"I've been conned."

"Wait until the end of the season. Wait until the end of next year and then tell me you've been conned and if you think so then, well…it won't be the first or last time, Sam."

Just before leaving for dinner, he called Bob Dennison, the head crew coach. As he dialed the number, he knew this would be tougher, requiring greater skills of manipulation than were necessary with Sam Arnold, who, by virtue of his youth, lack of seniority on the baseball pecking ladder, was more vulnerable. Besides, Bartley knew Arnold needed Bartley more than Bartley needed him. But Bob Dennison was another matter. He was afraid he had worn out his welcome with Dennison.

"Denny, I have a problem on third form baseball I thought you might be able to help me with."

The pause that followed was long, even for Bob Dennison who was as slow and deliberate in speech as he was in physical movement, the systemic arthritis making each physical movement an episode of often excruciating pain.

"Don't we have a conversation like this every year about this time, Jack?"

"I suppose so. It's time for adjustments in the spring athletic program, Denny. That's all."

"Why me, every year, Jack. Crew isn't a dumping ground. We've already got too many kids and we're three weeks into the beginning program both for oarsmen and coxes. I assume you want to send over a candidate for cox. You've never sent me anyone who was six-three and 195 pounds."

"They don't come that big in the third form, Denny. This young man is a little small, but he might grow."

"I'd rather you could guarantee he won't grow, Jack. Every kid you've ever sent me grew just enough by the fifth form to be too big for cox and too small to be an oarsman. I can think of Everson, DeMerit, Koerner. I wasted two years with them as coxes and then they became too big, but it was too late to train them as oarsmen."

"Everson and Koerner became first-rate managers. You admitted that yourself."

"All right. So you've sent me a couple of managers. I still resent you think crew is a dumping ground for your athletic misfits and incompetents."

"You know very well why I want the boy to go to you. He'll learn something with you, Denny. They always do. You'll encourage him without creating illusions, you'll correct him without diminishing his sense of self worth. You won't scream at him and humiliate him in public."

"If my memory serves me right, this is the time you flatter me, tell me what a great coach I am, call me an educator. That's right, it's time you called me an educator."

"Well, you are, Denny, you care about the individual development of the student and not about your won and lost record."

This time there was a long pause—longer than he expected even from Bob Dennison. He imagined Dennison on the other end of the phone—the scrunched diminutive build, the high forehead and white crew cut, the thick glasses that made blue saucers of his irises, and the twisted, knotted joints of his hands, swollen and gnarled from the years in icy waters as the cox of the heavyweight 8 at Cornell, and afterwards for rowing clubs during his first years coaching on the university level before his health forced him to private schools and a less competitive and more balanced life as math teacher.

"Why do I listen to you? You're just going to con me with some sob story and I'll give in and take the kid off your hands."

"Denny, I'm faced with what may be the worst team I've every coached and, well, the kid is a cut below the usual level of incompetence I get in baseball, but this case is special for other reasons. He simply has to get out of baseball."

"All right, I'm listening."

"I knew you would, Denny. I just couldn't bring this to anyone else."

"Because I'm an educator, right?"

"You are, Denny. I know you think I'm just hustling you, but you are an educator."

"I'm a damn fool, that's what I am."

"Wait until you hear the problem, O.K.? Sam Arnold thought the same thing about some trades I wanted to make until I explained everything and he agreed."

"All right. I'm listening, but make it short. I've got some problems to work out and grading to do before I go to bed. I'm skipping supper to get at them. Math isn't like American history where you can just go in there and wing it every day. I have to have some answers—can't just sling the bull and pretend I'm earning my pay."

"I understand your problems, Denny. You've got higher standards than I do. Actually, I feel guilty every time I get my check. I asked for a cut in salary last year and told Woody to give the cut to you. I begged him. But he couldn't do it. Said he had to keep everyone's salary competitive even though some of us weren't doing our share. I just want you to know I appreciate your carrying me along."

"Would you cut the bullshit, Jack, and get on with the sob story?"

"Right, Denny, right. The kid's name is Bobby Hunter. I noticed a developing problem about two weeks ago."

"Tell me before you go on. Is this a case of extraordinary incompetence or did you screw up?"

"Something of both, I guess. My mistake was putting him into a game too early. He wasn't ready yet. Actually I don't think he'll ever be ready but it's too late now. Anyhow, he made two or three errors in the outfield trying to get out of the way of the ball while pretending to catch it. He struck out twice with men on base and then he got beaned trying to get out of the way of a pitch that was already three feet behind him. I guess he had made up his mind to get out of there before the ball was pitched. I admit the pitcher was wild but the ball was coming so slow it hardly made it to the batter's box. We could have won that ball game just standing up to the plate and letting the ball hit us. It would have been impossible to get hurt."

"Now tell me, Jack. What the hell did you put the poor kid into the game for if he wasn't ready and never would be?"

Bartley paused a long time before answering.

"To be absolutely honest with you, Denny, I got sick and tired of him, sitting next to me on the bench in every game and second guessing every move I made, yelling at his teammates for making mistakes with the most grating, squealing voice you have ever heard. Then he started nagging me about getting into the game and when I didn't let him in, he started nagging about keeping the score book, which is the one thing I do well and the one thing that I truly enjoy because it's the only thing I can really control. So when I wouldn't put him in the game, he started looking over the score book and complaining that I didn't do it like in the major league score books, and godammit, Denny, I have some of my own symbols for scoring and nobody ever sees those books but me, so I put him in a game and now he's got headaches from a ball that grazed his batting helmet and he's got to get out of baseball and start somewhere else fresh."

"Where'd he learn all the baseball if he's as awful as you say?"

"Oh, he's one of those textbook fans, an armchair manager. He's been going to White Sox games with his grandfather in Sarasota every spring. Knows all of the game and player statistics since 1880 or so. He studies the moves of all the major league managers. Reads books and sports columnists, I guess. A real aficionado but he's never played before. He can't catch or throw. Hitting the ball even off a batting tee is on the moon for him. Now he's humiliated because he cried when the ball hit him. He lay there as though he were dead. I thought he was for a few moments until I leaned over and heard him sobbing. Now he's got psychosomatic headaches. He checks into the infirmary each day before practice and every evening before lights out. He follows the poor night nurse around until about midnight, talking her arm off until he nods off. He's kind of a lonely kid, Denny. I've been checking around on him. Bright as hell. High grades in math, science, and French. No real friends. Short and chubby. Prissy in speech and manner. Parents are divorced and each has remarried. Manhattan. He's a hot shot architect and she's an interior decorator. Mother has custody but she's off traveling in Europe with her new husband. Actually the new husband is a Kensington alumnus. Mother sent the boy here to stick it in the ear of her first husband who wanted the kid to go to Exeter where he went. Admissions beat Exeter for once on the kid. Must have hurt them. They only care about brains up there and this kid has the scores."

"Jack, would you cut the bull and get to the point."

"Sure, Denny, I'm almost there. Where was I? Oh, yes. Grandparents are *de facto* parents. Typical case of upper class child neglect. Father feels guilty now and wants a CAT scan. Threatening to sue the school for negligence, the old trickle down ploy, but he's just bluffing to cover his own guilt. Doc Bates has covered everything, all the right tests and they're negative. There's no injury except to the ego and no serious damage except to his fantasies as a baseball player."

"Let me see now if I have this straight. You want me to take the Hunter boy into crew so that we can cure him of the symptoms of his shame, the psychosomatic headaches, which in turn will get his old man off the school's back, the kid off the night nurse's back, and the guilt off your back."

"Something like that though I'm not really feeling that guilty."

"I know you, Jack, and I know you wouldn't be calling me if you hadn't screwed up."

"O.K. I screwed up."

"You don't have practice Wednesday. Bring him over to watch crew. Let's see if he's interested first. I'll take him if he makes the choice to come over."

"Thanks, Denny. I knew you'd help. The kid needs a second chance, a new beginning. He might make it with crew."

"I repeat—if he makes the choice himself, I'll take him."

"He will. I'll drive him over Wednesday afternoon, maybe get Peter to talk to him. How about letting him ride in the power launch with you in the time trials. He might like that. Maybe you could let him steer the launch for you."

"That's all I need. I can see it all now. The bow of the power launch slicing the first boat in two, putting an end to the season when we've just begun."

"That's a pretty grim scenario. How do you know, Denny, he might be a natural. Some day he might be a world class speedboat champion and you will be able to say you gave him his start."

There was a long pause on the other end of the line. Then he heard Dennison's voice again.

"Are you all done with the bullshit, Bartley?"

"Yes, I'm all done...all done for another day...more or less...if something else doesn't come up."

*   *   *   *

A warm spring rain began shortly after midnight and continued as a steady downpour throughout the morning and into the early afternoon, turning the playing fields into mud. Team practices outdoors were canceled and each team was rescheduled by the athletic director into a designated time slot and space in the gym. The lower level teams were given thirty minutes at the beginning of the early sports period. Bartley led his team in calisthenics and then dismissed them for the afternoon.

He spent twenty minutes in the sauna and after a leisurely shower he dressed, and climbed the stairs from the faculty locker room to the main floor of the gym where the varsity baseball players were working out. Pitchers were loosening up, one group was playing pepper, another fielding grounders and throwing across the gym to the first baseman. Above him he could hear the pounding of footsteps of the varsity track team running laps on the wooden track suspended from the walls and ceiling around the periphery of the building. He crossed the floor to a side entrance which led to the crew room. Even before entering he could hear the sharp, high pitched voice of a cox chanting the cadence "Stroke...stroke...stroke."

To his left in the first rowing machine he saw Peter's arms and back leading his crew, sliding back and forth in unison, as they stroked the truncated oars attached to tension sprockets. Across the room he saw several oarsmen working the ergometers, an exercise he loved to watch: the long graceful pull, the whirl of the fan, and the sliding release and return forward to the ready position. He could never quite get the leg and arm timing right when he tried it himself. He crossed the room and climbed the stairs to the upper level lobby and found his rain gear where he had hung it an hour before, then opened the glass door and stepped outside.

The rain which had tapered off before lunch had resumed the heavier, steady tempo of early morning leaving the football practice fields, between which he walked toward dorm row, a quagmire of mud and puddles. The early grass glowed a luminous green. At the far end of the field adjacent to the infirmary, a small group of mostly third and fourth formers had begun to throw a frisbee in gradually widening arcs toward midfield. Dismissed from practice early, some still wore the gray sweats or shorts from the cals. They pursued the flight of the platter, splashing through puddles, diving to catch it before it hit the ground and then sliding headlong into the mud. Bartley could hear the shouts and laughter as he approached the dormitory side of the field.

The rain suddenly intensified into a torrent when he reached the service road that ran along the back of dorm row. He sprinted the last twenty yards to the porch of a connecting passageway between dorms. Once safely sheltered he removed his raincoat and hat and shook them. He stood resting and watching with admiration the flight of the frisbee arching sometimes across the width of the entire field. The circle of participants grew as several fifth and sixth formers joined in and began to push and shove the younger boys as they competed for possession, and within a few minutes teams emerged along form lines into a game of keep-away.

From behind him, Bartley heard the dorm door open and the quiet swish of the hydraulic arm gradually collapsing. He turned to greet Bill Henry, who was wearing a yellow slicker and a floppy golf hat.

"I thought it was you ducking in here, Jack. I was looking out the window of the faculty room trying to decide what was the best way home in the rain. I was watching the frisbee players when I saw someone leave the gym and walk toward dorm row. I couldn't tell for sure if it were you, but then there was a heavy burst of rain and the person began to run toward the arcade shelter and I knew it was you."

"How could you tell?" Bartley asked with a shrug, knowing that he was setting Henry up for one of his jibes.

"Well, your walk does not have a distinctive style, but you have an unmistakable awkwardness or flailing in your sprint."

Bartley looked back toward the practice field where more students from the gym and the dorm joined the unfolding fray.

"I looked for you after lunch, but George told me you were having a department meeting." Bartley paused deliberately. "Do you have a few minutes? I've been thinking a lot about what you said yesterday. You've had your say and I appreciate your reminding me of some very important matters about teaching, with which I mostly agree. Now I want you to hear my side."

"I didn't come by this way for my health. I know it's your turn."

"You finished by evoking the moral absolutists who might win the day for Atkins. I am troubled by them. I know you were joking, but they are not joking matters to me. Since my first years teaching here at Kensington whenever they win everyone loses. There's always a coalition of moral absolutists who have their minds made up about firing kids for major offenses before they even know the facts of the case. They meet over a cup of coffee or in the locker room and try every serious disciplinary case on hearsay evidence or something Phillips has leaked to them before it comes before the faculty. The old cronyism. They gather after practice, Bill, sitting naked on the benches in front of their lockers before heading for the showers. They flip their genitals as they shake their heads collectively and wisely and bemoan the pervasive corruption of young people who without the vigilance, judgment, and punishment of proper adult authority would tear the school and society asunder. Then as they throw towels over their shoulders, they march into the shower, sharing their indignation about their unenlightened colleagues—all wimps, perverts, cowards, or fags, their words, not mine, who will listen to the evidence of the disciplinary case thoughtfully and make a fair minded educational decision that will help the offender learn from his mistake and hopefully mend his ways through modest punishment, counseling, community support, and a determined effort at self-correction."

"Christ, Jack, I was just thinking of a few of the Old Guard like Brewster taking Olympian moral postures and accidently influencing everyone for a change. Who are you talking about? You sound almost paranoid."

"You want names? You know damn well who I mean. What difference does it make if I list names? The names change over the years but the moral pretense doesn't. They're here. They're out there in the real world and always have been. They've always been here despite common sense, fairness, compassion. They are obsessed with judgment and punishment, especially if some kid rocks the boat a little or is different or original or independent or non-athletic or imaginative. To them every disciplinary infraction is an act of rebellion against authority. They caucus informally before the faculty hears the case and they vote as a block to kick the kid out so they can prove to themselves that they are tough and responsible and macho and that they are doing God's own work. I simply won't join them by voting with them just because the boy wants me to."

"What would you do without the moral absolutists, Jack? You wouldn't know who you are, ideologically speaking, of course. Actually I think you have invented them, created a mythical enemy to give yourself some kind of moral legitimacy."

From above they heard a loud, rhythmic vibration for several seconds and then a crashing blare of musical chords bouncing off the facade of the gym across the field. Bartley stepped out into the rain and looked upward to the third floor where he saw two black rectangles balancing on the sill of a dorm window. Out on the field he heard the roar of a crowd, now swollen by varsity players still in sweats who had emerged from the gym after practice, cheering the music and wild melee in the mud. Several non-varsity sixth formers entered the field and seized the frisbee, passing it back and forth, taunting and intimidating the younger boys with excremental epithets,—shitbird, pee-brain, turdball—and threats of physical violence. From further down along dorm row another stereo began pounding out a counter rhythm. Bartley stepped back out of the rain.

"I suppose you're right. I acknowledge I have a tendency to over-simplification and abstraction, but I know the moral absolutists exist, not just in my imagination but out there in the real world. I have heard them all my life, pre-emptive voices of order, orthodoxy and authority, suspicious of everyone, demanding rules and obedience and mindless conformity, full of self-righteous exhortations for punishment and pain and restrictions and humiliation. In my childhood they wore habits and collars and convinced me that every natural impulse was a sin. Later, they were clothed in uniforms and patriotic fervor or wrapped themselves in the Stars and Stripes and told me that thinking too was a sin—the worst of all because it leads to heresy and treason. They don't wear cowls or Sam Brown belts, but they're here too on our faculty and we're in two different worlds, morally and educationally, when it comes to the young people we're teaching."

Suddenly a stream of screaming weanies from the 3rd form dorm came charging down the service road past Bartley and Henry to join and reinforce their classmates in what had become a humiliating domination by the older boys, who had begun catching victims and washing their faces in the mud. The weanies swarmed onto the field, outnumbering and surrounding the enemy and isolating individuals whom they forced to the ground and pinned there in pig piles. In a short time they trapped the 6th former with the frisbee, recovered it, and broke free across the field tossing it back and forth. The older boys gathered their forces and pursued the frisbee, which had become transformed into a trophy. Suddenly the two groups merged into a huge scrum that flowed randomly about the field, with the frisbee popping into the air at short intervals.

"You know who they are." Bartley paused to watch the action and then continued. "You taught me all about them in my first years here. Now you want me to profess their morality when you know precisely the gulf that separates us. Where they see simplicity, I see complexity.

Where they see absolutes, I see relatives. Where they find corruption, I find the power of grace. Where they see wimpiness, I see fear and loneliness. Where they see weakness, I see confusion and helplessness. Where they see evil, I see ignorance. They idealize conformity, I cherish diversity and idiosyncracy. They insist upon order in everything, I insist upon freedom and flexibility. Where they see sin and the need for punishment, I see immaturity and the need for counseling and understanding. Do you want me to go on?"

"I'd love to hear you go on and on polarizing the rest of the universe into two neat camps of good and evil. You have a remarkable facility for endless bifurcation, almost Manichean, but you have made your case and there is no point in being redundant."

"Bill, I know that what I say or don't say or how I vote at the faculty meeting Friday doesn't count for a tinker's damn in the great or small scale of things. I just want you to know why I won't join the Draconians by repudiating everything I've come to believe about fairness. I voted on the DC to put the boy on probation because it's right and proper according to the circumstances of Atkins' case."

Henry remained silent for a while, watching the melee in the mud. When he turned at last toward Bartley, he removed his glasses that had steamed up and wiped them with a handkerchief he withdrew from beneath his slicker. Bartley noticed that the skin around Henry's eyes seemed tender and white and his briefly unfocused eyes seemed weak and vulnerable. When he put his glasses back on, it became apparent that the lenses were tinted a pale gray.

"Will you speak to Tim again?"

"I suppose so. I don't know that it will make any difference."

"Give yourself twenty-four hours and then give him a second chance."

"All right. I'll put a note in his box to meet me sometime tomorrow."

"I've been enjoying the free play in the mud and I've been thinking how this kind of student activity must be especially important to someone like you."

"Why me? The boys have some fun letting steam off. It's kind of therapeutic, but not especially important."

"Well, as I see it what we are witnessing is a kind of existential scrum, which ought to appeal to your obsession with process over product. There are no goals, no scores, no rules, just an *ad hoc* spontaneous wandering about in circles. There are no winners or losers, and no adult interference or control. In fact, as you remember we voted this field as one of those places where the students can just about do as they like so long as none of their projectiles hit any buildings, and we wisely amended that piece of legislation to the effect that all faculty, their wives, children, cars and dogs were to be defined as buildings.

"Most of all, however, there are no moral absolutists out there blowing whistles, signaling with waving arms, meting out penalties, punishments or banishments. No one will be elected most valuable player. There are no silly codes of good sportsmanship and no-one will be awarded a letter or any other athletic behavioristic incentive that you are always railing against as the result of the deification of jocks you experienced in a Midwestern Catholic high school."

"You forgot some very important other advantages of this spontaneous free play, Bill. The faculty will not be asked to abandon their classes so that the students can enter post season playoffs against teams that have already destroyed us in the regular season. And there will be no athletic awards banquets with their sentimental and sappy speeches about character and manhood and standing ovations and weepy acceptance speeches quoting or paraphrasing Lou Gehrig's final words in Yankee Stadium—without an echo."

"I'm not done yet, Jack. But I appreciate your observations. Yes, the existential scrum like the dorm snowball fights may very well be one of the finest examples of pure, unadulterated individual expression short of total anarchy left to young people today. And we have no responsibility to break it up, their rights legitimatized by faculty vote."

The hammering drive of the stereos stopped abruptly and a few moments later in the sudden stillness the scrum seemed to hesitate and freeze before it fell apart. On the sidelines the cheering varsity players quietly turned slowly and began drifting toward the gym to shower and change. The scrum players formed two large huddles, the weanies in one and the upper formers in the of other, and each group chanted, in turn, a final cheer of appreciation for the other. Within a few minutes the field was almost empty except for a few stragglers throwing the frisbee. The mud spattered weanies, with laughter and shouts of victory, hurried past Bartley and Henry on their way to their dorm.

"Well, I guess it's time to head home." Henry looked at his watch. "I suppose Phillips got to the loud music, though even he knows better than to stop the mud bowl. Besides, these things end themselves, run out of energy. A kind of entropy sets in." He paused briefly, his voice and tone now serious.

"Talk to the boy again, Jack."

"I will. Tomorrow."

$$* \qquad * \qquad * \qquad *$$

By ten o'clock that evening Bartley had given up trying to re-read the assignment for the next day's discussion. He would have to depend upon his memory and what he called his ad hoc talents, his ability to wing it spontaneously as ideas and interpretations of the material emerged. Besides, he could always steer the discussion to safer grounds, where he felt more comfortable or where he was more certain of his grasp of detail.

He mixed a drink and joined Karen in the living room where she sat, legs drawn up sideways in a stuffed chair reading. He collapsed in the middle of the sofa. Gradually, over the next few minutes, he began to feel a sense of absolute fatigue settling over him.

He heard the doorbell in his study ring, but he didn't move. He decided to out wait Karen or whoever was calling. At this time of night, most of the students would give up after a few rings, deciding he was asleep or unavailable, but Karen got up to answer the third ring and returned with Peter, who handed him the duty board.

"Everyone present or accounted for, sir." He gave Bartley a mock salute and grinned. "Thought I'd bring you the duty board now rather than tomorrow morning."

"You could have left it outside the door."

"I know. I just thought you might have time to talk for a few minutes."

"About Tim Atkins?"

"Not really though I am supposed to let you know that the Sixth Form feels very strongly that he should get probation."

"Have you had a meeting?"

"Yes, sir. A regular meeting and his case came up. It's no big deal. We all kind of agreed to say something in his favor to faculty members we thought might be sympathetic before you vote tomorrow rather than bitch later."

"That's a dangerous strategy that may hurt more than it helps. Most faculty members want to make up their own minds. Some resent students attempts to influence them."

"That's all I've said." Peter raised his arms in surrender." I won't say another word. Make up your own mind, sir. Besides, that's not why I really came to talk to you."

Bartley smiled to let Peter know he wasn't really angry.

"Would you care for a cup of tea or instant coffee, Peter?" Karen asked.

"I'd love a cup of strong coffee, black, Mrs. Bartley. I'm expecting to be up half the night on a paper."

"If you didn't seem to be in such a good mood, I'd kick you out of here. But since I'm half relaxed, you can stay. Have a chair."

Peter sat down heavily in Bartley's favorite wicker rocker. Bartley gritted his teeth, expecting the chair to explode in splinters. Karen went to the kitchen to put some water on to heat and returned to her chair and book before Peter spoke again. It seemed to Bartley that Peter had waited on purpose, that he wanted Karen to hear what he had to say.

"I feel so great. I've just finished talking to Jennifer on the phone and we've agreed to everything you and I talked about Sunday in the car coming back from Randall Hall. Actually, we've gone even further than what you suggested."

"What did Mr. Bartley suggest?" Karen asked. "I hope it was sensible."

"He suggested that we back off from the dance. Just forget about it and avoid a confrontation with Mrs. Powell."

"That's certainly sensible," she nodded.

"Thanks for your approval," Bartley said. "I acted unilaterally, without your advice and consent. I meant to tell you but I just forgot."

"You did very well on your own. I would have advised the same thing."

"We, Jennifer and I, talked a lot on the phone the past few nights. It took almost a half hour Monday night to convince her just to think about what you suggested, but she came around by Wednesday and then she came up with the idea of going home dance weekend rather than staying at Randall Hall."

"What about your going over to see her that weekend? You assured me you would probably pine away of a broken heart if you didn't see her once more before you go home."

"I will probably pine away this summer anyhow, but I will see her again—before graduation—the weekend before the dance. We're rowing at South Kent that Saturday. I'll take a weekend and get off the bus just a few miles from Randall Hall on the way back. I don't know how I'll get back here on Sunday, but I can figure that out later."

"Maybe we'll find an excuse to go to Hartford that Sunday," Karen said, "and you can meet us there late Sunday afternoon." She got up and went to the kitchen to make Peter his coffee.

"I couldn't ask you to do that, Mrs. Bartley. I'm sure there's probably a bus from Hartford to Providence on Sunday afternoon."

"Well, if there isn't," she spoke from the kitchen, "we'll figure something out." She returned with a steaming mug and handed it to Peter.

"I've never felt so good about anything in my life. It really bothered me what you said, Mr. Bartley, about what Jennifer might do and what might happen. I really couldn't live with that, her getting kicked out of Randall Hall and defying her mother just to go to a dance with me. It wasn't worth it."

"We're proud of you, Peter," she said, "and I'm proud of Mr. Bartley for being so sensible in his advice."

Bartley drained his glass and began to laugh.

"Well, I'm too tired to be proud of anything tonight, so please excuse me from this mutual admiration society. I need another drink." He extended his empty glass toward Karen. "How about getting me a reward for being such a sensible adviser?"

"I saw you pour the first drink. One double bourbon is enough—a sensible reward for a sensible adviser who gets violent headaches from more than one sensible drink."

"You made Peter a cup of coffee."

"Would you like a cup of coffee?"

"Forget it. I'd be up all night. I'll be sensible. I'll just sit here and relax and pretend it's the day after graduation."

"We were thinking, Jennifer and I, that maybe doing what we're doing about the dance and if Jennifer goes home instead and smiles all weekend, maybe Mrs. Powell will let Jennifer come to my graduation. Mrs. Powell obviously doesn't trust us here dance weekend, but maybe she'll trust us at graduation with about a thousand people around in broad daylight. We might even see each other twice before I leave."

"Your cheerful hopefulness is depressing, Peter."

"Why not be cheerful, sir? I spent over two weeks in despair and that didn't change anything. How you feel about something has nothing to do with how things turn out. It's what you do that makes a difference."

"You're getting to be a genuine philosopher, Peter. In later years, when you achieve some kind of cosmic serenity, write me your secret of success."

"Mr. Bartley doesn't learn much from his own experience, Peter," Karen explained, "but he is always willing to learn from books, newspapers, magazines, documents, letters, even nature. Sometimes he learns from other human beings, any person who doesn't talk back or disagree."

"When I find the secret of cosmic serenity, I'll call you up. You'll be the first person I'll pass it along to."

Peter began drinking from his mug in larger swallows now that his coffee had cooled. He rocked slowly, tipping backwards as far as he could and then easing himself forward. Bartley was certain the thin, curved railings would crack under the stress of Peter's poised weight.

"You know, Mr. Bartley, I've been thinking a lot about Mrs. Powell, lately, trying to figure her out. I was listening in on a bull session the other night. Some Fifth Formers, Carter and Whiteside, they have Mr. Mackrakis in English and they're reading fairy stories and interpreting them psychologically. It was really fascinating. They were talking about Snow White and Cinderella. Now I know this is kind of far out, but some of the things they were saying, if I understand them right, seemed to apply to Mrs. Powell at least theoretically."

"What in the world has Mrs. Powell to do with Snow White?" Bartley asked.

"I sense some bad Bruno Bettleheim coming?" Karen laughed.

"Don't laugh now, Mrs. Bartley. I'm serious. I think what they were saying really explains everything," Peter protested.

"What everything?" Bartley asked.

"Her attitude toward Jennifer, us, her over-response."

"All right, Peter. Go ahead and tell us your theory. I'm relaxed enough now to listen to almost anything."

Peter rocked forward and placed his elbows on his knees. As he talked, he opened and closed his hands by way of illustration and explanation.

"The theory is based upon the assumption that all mothers or adult females are really in competition with all young women, including their daughters, when they begin to grow up and become sexually attractive. I guess as women grow older they worry about losing their beauty and thus their power and importance in a male dominated society. They fear being replaced by younger women and so they try to control them by moral codes and sexual taboos. In Snow White, for example, the wicked stepmother is an extreme example of this jealousy. If you remember the story, the stepmother looks into the magic mirror, a symbol of narcissism, and asks, 'Mirror, mirror on the wall, who is the fairest maid of all,' or something like that. And for years, so long as Snow White is real young or sexually latent, the mirror tells the stepmother that she, the stepmother, is the fairest maid of all. Then one day, the mirror tells her that Snow White is the fairest, that is, now that she has grown up, she, Snow White is sexually more attractive than the stepmother. That's when the stepmother gets the hunter to kill Snow White."

Peter beamed when he had finished. Bartley waited for several moments after Peter had stopped talking.

"So. What are you saying?" he asked.

"That mothers are jealous of their daughters' emerging sexuality," Karen interrupted, "and want to control it for their own purposes, or in the extreme cases of women like the stepmother, destroy all the competition. But tell me, Peter," she went on, "isn't the stepmother competing with Snow White for the affections of the male power figure, who is actually Snow White's father?"

Peter flushed and laughed embarrassedly.

"I left that part out. I don't want to get into Freud and all that. Besides, it wouldn't work with Mrs. Powell—Jennifer loves me. Besides, I don't understand everything. I just borrowed what I thought fit Mrs. Powell."

"What's that?" Bartley persisted in his guise of obtuseness, forcing Peter to repeat his explanation again.

"That some women," Peter spoke slowly and with some exasperation, "as they grow older become resentful of the younger women who are replacing them and try to control them or put them down because they're jealous. They don't want to admit they're growing old and that another generation of women is taking over."

"What about all the mothers who can't wait to marry their daughters off to just about anybody just to get rid of them. Surely they aren't jealous of their daughters' sexual powers?" Karen asked.

"Well, it doesn't apply to every woman, Mrs. Bartley. Just those women with a *Hedda Gabbler* power complex or something like that. I don't know. Maybe the theory doesn't work. Maybe I'm just fishing in a dead lake. The other night when I was listening to the guys talk, it all seemed to fit perfectly. Maybe I didn't get it all. All I know is that something is wrong with Mrs. Powell. The way she has treated Jennifer is strictly abnormal, maybe even pathological."

"I hate to disagree, Peter," Bartley said gently, "but I find Mrs. Powell's behavior to be perfectly normal given her heritage, her upbringing and education in what was essentially for most American Catholics an Irish Immigrant Church that fostered a heavily puritanical enclave mentality."

"Well, Lah-Dee-Dah," Karen laughed out loud. "Did you hear that, Peter? A heavily puritanical enclave mentality. Sounds impressive if slightly pedantic. I wonder what Mr. Bartley means. What do you mean, Jack?"

"I'm glad you asked. I've been thinking about Mrs. Powell for some time now," he smiled at her benignly, then turned away from Karen to Peter, "and have been trying to understand her historically in terms of our common background and heritage. You see, Peter, one has to understand the history of the Catholic Church in America and the history of the Church in Ireland in order to understand Mrs. Powell. In the Nineteenth Century, the English did not permit Roman Catholic seminaries in Ireland. As a consequence, many of the young men who wanted to be priests went to French seminaries for their training for Holy Orders. Many of those French seminaries were heavily influenced by Jansenist thought. Jansenism is essentially the Calvinist or Puritan theological wing of the Catholic Church in Europe. The Jansenist influence was transferred to Ireland via the young priests trained there and in turn to America.

"Once in America, the Irish priests dominated the hierarchy. American Catholics developed, because they were primarily a minority in a society dominated by Protestants, an enclave mentality, that is, a claustrophobic, defensive, ethnocentric mentality. Relating to Protestants under any circumstances was discouraged. It was everyone's responsibility to insure that Catholics stick together, that young people be indoctrinated in the principles of Catholicism in Catholic schools and that ultimately young Catholic women marry young Catholic men and produce loyal, indoctrinated Catholic children.

"I remember once a girl I knew, Protestant, in my neighborhood died of leukemia, and I caused great turmoil in my family because I wanted to go to her funeral. At first I was told that I should go to my parish church during the time of her funeral service and burial, and pray for her soul. When I rejected that and pigheadedly insisted upon attending the service, I was permitted to attend providing I did not participate in the service, stand up with everyone or sing or say any of the Protestant prayers. I was cautioned particularly not to say 'For thine is the kingdom, the power, and the glory, for ever and ever,' at the end of the Lord's prayer because that was tantamount to acknowledging the Protestant version."

"You're kidding," Peter interrupted.

"I am not kidding," Bartley answered with a touch of remembered anger in his voice.

"What does all this historical background have to do with Mrs. Powell?" Karen interrupted sharply, apparently impatient of what she felt was a pointless digression.

"I assume Mrs. Powell was indoctrinated, as I was, by the same obsessively puritanical sexual morality and the defensive enclave mentality. Whether she inherited wealth or married into it or is one of the nouveau riche, I don't know, but for whatever reason—probably social—the Powells decided to educate Jennifer in non-Catholic, independent schools—outside of the enclave. She has been seriously remiss in her duties as a Catholic mother. Her extreme reaction to your recent relationship with Jennifer, Peter, is probably one of personal guilt for failing to do her duty. She has exaggerated your guilt in order to minimize her own failure and has made the two of you the scapegoats of her own irresponsibility. In brief, she is probably more angry at you for being Protestant, Peter, than for anything you might have done."

There was a long silence after he finished. Peter stared at him with a dumbfounded expression. Karen shook her head slowly in a kind of stunned disbelief.

"Did you say 'in brief?!'" she finally asked.

"For me, yes, that was a relatively brief explanation."

"Would you like to hear my opinion, in brief?" she asked.

"Why not?" Bartley laughed. "As long as we're speculating, you might as well add your two cents worth."

"I say pooh on both your theories. All I know about this is from overheard conversations, but my opinion is that poor Mrs. Powell came home with a dreadful headache from a perfectly terrible evening at some awful country club full of smoke and loud music and people she didn't like to find her daughter and her boyfriend, a guest in her home, engaged in some sort of activity she considered a breach of trust. She overreacted in her anger that night and now can't relent without losing face or undermining her own authority. She has trapped herself and is probably secretly yearning for almost any excuse to retract her position."

"God, I hope you're right, Mrs. Bartley. If you are, it's possible she might change her mind when she finds out we aren't going to defy her." Peter stood up and stretched. "Now that we've figured Mrs. Powell out, I guess I better get to work on my paper. Could I have a refill on the coffee, Mrs. Bartley."

He followed Karen into the kitchen. Bartley could hear Karen pour the water and then Peter's footsteps as he left the kitchen through his study. "See you tomorrow, Mr. Bartley," he spoke from the dormitory door in Bartley's study. "I'll leave the cup outside the door in the morning, Mrs. B."

"Goodnight, Peter. Keep the natives quiet tonight."

"Yes, sir. You know I will. If there's one thing I can do well, that is to intimidate restless underformers with my size. Good night, Mrs. Bartley. Thanks for the coffee and the hopeful explanation of Mrs. Powell."

"Good night, Peter."

Bartley heard the door close as Karen re-entered the living room. She picked up Bartley's glass on the coffee table and turned toward the kitchen.

"You certainly gave Peter a hard time tonight, Jack, pretending you couldn't understand anything he was saying and making him to repeat himself."

"I gave him a hard time! You demolished every argument he presented."

"I was just asking critical questions so he could rethink his position."

She stood facing him, framed by the kitchen doorway.

"I hope you're right about Mrs. Powell though," he said. "You may very well be and if you are and I'm only half right, she may relent."

"What have you done, Jack?"

"I'm not saying, but she has an excuse to save face, change her mind, and have a scapegoat to boot."

*   *   *   *

Early Thursday morning he checked Tim's schedule in the Dean's Office and then placed a note in his P.O. box, asking him to come to his classroom during the fourth period when both of them were free. He waited several minutes after his students had left, then he gathered the text and his notes and the primary source book, a passage from which the class had been discussing, and inserted the material carefully into compartments in his valise. He sat for a few more minutes, and then impatient to get on with preparation for his next class in the library, he moved toward the door. As he reached back to switch off the light, he bumped into Tim who was sliding to a stop in the hallway outside.

"Oops. Sorry, sir. Sorry I'm late. I couldn't get away from Mr. Henry's class. He ran over again, carried away by rhapsodic appreciation of 'As Kingfishers Catch Fire, Dragonflies Draw Flame.'"

"What's that?"

"A poem, sir. By Hopkins. Damned obscure, I'll tell you, but Mr. Henry was so excited about it, we just sat there awed by what we thought it was all about."

"Mr. Henry is an Enthusiast. He would have made a good Puritan or Methodist."

"Probably, sir, but he's pretty secular."

"Yes, I didn't mean he was religious. I just meant that he has the spirit." Bartley closed the door as they re-entered the classroom. He sat behind his desk while Tim slid under the writing arm of a front row chair.

"Do you think my case will take very long tomorrow, sir?"

"No. I'm sure there'll be a call for the question within an hour. No one likes to be recalled in the afternoon and taken away from sports.

Unless some other business takes extra time, we should be done in the morning."

"I understand. Will an hour be enough time?"

"I think so. You'll find out from Mr. Woodbridge, of course, later. It's his final decision, but I can't believe that he would veto a faculty recommendation. Are your folks still here?"

"Yes, sir, trying to drum up support among the liberal faculty. Mr. Macrakis has been running from them since last night, but I think they caught up to him sometime this morning."

Bartley paused for a few moments and then spoke directly.

"Tim, I don't think you're going to like what I'm about to say. I want you to understand my point of view and then I have some questions, and then I want you to have the opportunity to convince me that I'm wrong. Right now, for personal reasons and reasons of principle, I'm going to continue to support the D.C. recommendations for probation."

"Yes, sir, I understand. Mr. Henry already explained what it would mean to you before I first came to see you. It wasn't fair of me to ask."

"Tim, it's not the end of the world. You've trapped yourself into thinking that you'll never escape the pressure of earning your Kensington diploma. These things fade, become unimportant in time. You don't need it for many colleges or art institutes. You may find a summer course at your home high school that you'll pass and we'll accept. Maybe a college course in logic or something close to math will be accepted as a substitute by the faculty. Lord knows we change our minds all the time."

As Bartley finished speaking, he looked up and realized he had been looking downward and that Tim had been sitting bolt upright in his chair looking directly in Bartley's face throughout his speech.

"Yes, sir, Mr. Bartley. I understand your position. It was wrong of me to ask. Mr. Henry said that to reverse your vote and call for my firing would be embarrassing to you. I withdraw my request. You do what you have to do." Then he laughed. "Besides, maybe I'll get kicked out anyway."

"Right now, my decision is to say nothing. Just listen to the debate and then vote. You still want out?"

"More than ever, and for more reasons than ever."

"That leads me to one of the questions I wanted to ask you. Why don't you just walk away from here? Pack your suitcase and take off. We'd have fired you for failing to meet school appointments or absence from the dormitory after check-in. Why don't you leave right now? Withdraw and force your parents to accept it. Or why didn't you just quit studying, cut classes, flunk out in every subject not just math, making it impossible to ever get your diploma? You seem to want the school to fire you and that's what troubles me." Tim pushed his chair back, stood up and then walked slowly to the window, looked out across the trees below toward the chapel for several moments. He returned and sat down as Bartley waited.

"I'll try to explain. It's kind of complicated." He paused again and licked his lips."When I realized that I might not get kicked out, I guess I panicked. Since then, I've thought a lot about what's happened and I've asked myself the same questions you've asked. What I did, I did almost unconsciously, instinctively, sir, but it was probably the result of a rational process. I'm beginning to believe that much of what psychologists call irrational or unconscious behavior is at heart rational though we don't go through some consciously deliberate process of decision making. What I'm trying to say is that what I did, Mr. Bartley, I meant to do for lots of good reasons though when I left the dorm to sneak into the faculty room I was conscious only of a desperate need to pass math, to get that terrible goddamn burden off my back. That's what I felt. That's what was in my mind, but that's not why I did it. What I'm saying is that the conscious motivation for stealing was irrational fear, but the unconscious or underlying motivation was absolutely logical. It's taken me all week to sort things out. I think I know now. May I explain myself now even though it's too late?"

"It's not too late, Tim. Never too late for me. I'm famous for changing my mind. I told you I'd give you another chance to convince me. Besides, I'm intrigued."

"First of all," Tim began, "I couldn't just walk away from here or intentionally flunk all my subjects. That would be cowardly and I would be making a statement to the school I don't want to make. I would be saying to hell with everything—with Mr. Henry's English class, to Mr. Le Clair's French course, to all the teachers and courses that have been so great. Especially, I'd be running out on Miss Dunlop's work with me in art—for five years now, I've worked with her, learned from her example, and criticism, everything I care about doing for the rest of my life, she's taught me."

"So what you did in trying to steal the test in some conscious or unconscious way was to make a selective statement."

"Yes, sir. Exactly. And all week I've been trying to figure out what I was saying by doing what I did. Now, I don't want you to laugh, at what I'm about to say. It may sound pretentious or vain or artificially profound as though my life resembles something out of Camus, but I don't think I went into the faculty room just to get caught and kicked out to escape having to take math tests for the rest of my life. That's what I thought at first, but now I see it as a more positive act—an act of rebellion and a statement. I said to the faculty as a whole, live with the guilt of firing me for doing something I absolutely detested, an act of dishonesty when you could just as easily have granted my petition last fall. And to my parents I was saying join me, feel the humiliation and failure I've been feeling for five years. I refuse to graduate ever from Kensington and the only way I can do that is to get kicked out for moral reasons, to become a pariah, a thief and a cheat. How do you like that? I reject you and declare my independence and this is the only way I can do it because I love you and know you love me, but goddamn it I cannot do what you want me to do. I've tried and tried."

He did not cry, but Bartley could tell Tim came, at that moment, as close to crying as he ever would. They sat in silence for what seemed minutes though it probably wasn't more than twenty seconds. The moment for tears passed. Tim grinned suddenly.

"Pretty melodramatic, huh? I sometimes get carried away. Not often. Sorry."

"What you haven't said," Bartley finally spoke, "is that if we put you on probation, we will take away the meaning of your action and leave you dangling once again with an even deeper sense of failure."

"You know something, Mr. Bartley, there's a point when forgiveness and getting a second or third chance is almost destructive. It has been for me. Now I have made the statement that I don't want a second chance. I want to be the one who has made the last statement. Sounds kind of metaphysical, doesn't it?"

"No, but I'm not sure I understand what you are saying."

"I know this is going to sound kind of corny, life imitating art and all that, and I know I'm a rich Wasp with all the advantages of family and education and that I really haven't suffered the way minorities do in our society, but I remember near the end of Native Son when Bigger was talking to Max for the last time, he said something to the effect that the killing he did was good because there's a bottom line to what a human being will take. I think my attempt to steal and cheat was good. If I couldn't do that to free myself, then I'd spend the rest of my life doing what other people want me to do and I'd end up using whatever talent I have designing wall paper or linoleum or making illustrations for beer and cigarette commercials."

They were silent again for several moments when Tim smiled and added, "There's something else. It's personal and maybe isn't really important from your point of view, but I'm so ashamed of myself I can hardly look any of my friends in the eye. I don't know how I can make it until the end of the year knowing that everyone knows I'm a cheater. I want to tell everyone I meet that I'm sorry, even students or faculty I don't know."

"You'll feel like that, Tim, for a long time whether you're here or home at high school."

"Do I still have a chance?"

"Yes, unfortunately."

"Well, if you decide to help me, later you can always say to yourself, if I become famous or something, that you were the one who affirmed my right to existential revolt."

Tim looked at his watch and got up to leave. Bartley laughed.

"Later in life I will always harbor the suspicion that I was conned this week by two very slick sophists."

"It's not sophistry, Mr. Bartley. It's not just my trying to convince you. What I said is true as best as I can understand myself now."

"I know that, Tim. Time is in your favor. I've got lots to do before faculty meeting. I won't have time to think much more about what I'm going to do tomorrow morning. You will have had the last word."

"Whatever," Tim said as a parting comment, "Thanks for listening."

"No need for thanks. It's my job to listen."

He picked up his valise and got up to leave. He remembered a quotation Bill Henry had shared with him once. It was a topic the students had to write on in one of the English achievement tests that Henry graded several years before. "The trouble with being open-minded is that your brains might fall out." Henry thought the question was stupid. He was even more appalled by the hordes of unimaginative students who had taken the statement literally. For the moment Bartley sympathized with them.

CHAPTER 5

▼

He didn't feel any anxiety yet, only the first symptoms that tension would emerge as the morning hours brought him closer to the faculty meeting. His earliest symptom was that he woke at 3:15 a.m. and could not go back to sleep until he had gone to his study and outlined the arguments for probation on one file card and the arguments for firing on another. He reviewed each position carefully before going back to bed.

The next morning after school breakfast and before his first class, he found George Macrakis in the Commons and walked across the quad with him to the Main School Building.

"Did Tim Atkins' parents find you yesterday, George?"

"Unfortunately, yes. I ducked them most of the evening before, but they got my class schedule and waited outside my classroom for the fourth period to end. I saw this elegantly dressed couple in the hallway when the students opened the door and thought I might try a quick escape through the window until I suddenly remembered I was on the second floor. God, I hate that, Jack, when they come lobbying like that. Preying on our vulnerability, our readiness to understand. I can deal with the phone calls, but the personal appearances are dreadful."

"I was lucky. They didn't bother to influence me. I suppose they thought I was already in their pocket, having already voted for probation on the Discipline Committee."

They approached the school building and entered the long, high ceilinged corridor that ended in the distance at the faculty mail room door. On the left was the Headmaster's office and on the right the school office, closed yet until after the first class period began.

"Could we talk a few minutes, George, before class about Atkins?"

"Sure. How about my office? I have some material to file there before my first class."

Bartley followed him down the darkened hallway and to the left at the first corridor and into his suddenly bright and cheery office, its walls decorated with ocean and mountain posters, montages of college brochures, and bookcases of college catalogues. The sun streamed through large windows to the left of Macrakis' desk. Bartley sat in a padded arm-chair near the windows as Macrakis opened his briefcase, unloaded it on his desk and sat back waiting for Bartley to speak.

"I'm afraid I'm about to prevail upon you the way Mr. and Mrs. Atkins did. Worse yet, I'll probably be presuming on our friendship."

"You don't have to influence me, Jack, Tim's parents didn't influence me. I know the boy. Taught him last year. Wonderful kid. I don't care what he did, he doesn't deserve to be fired. I know enough about his case to know I'll support the Discipline Committee recommendation. I knew that before I spoke to his parents." He laughed. "My mind was already made up. They wasted their time. You are wasting your time."

"You know I wouldn't try to influence your vote. I can't explain everything right now. All I ask is that you don't speak on the faculty floor. Just vote your own mind, but don't speak."

"Why?"

"Because I may change my mind and support firing. If I do, don't listen to what I say. I don't want us to end up debating each other. We've been good friends and ideological partners too long to become public adversaries. If I speak, forget what I say and listen to Henry. He will make sense. Vote whatever way you want, but listen to him. If I decide not to speak, I'll let you know, send you a note or a signal some-how, and you can say anything you want."

"Change your mind? You must be out of your mind."

"Maybe. I may say things that will surprise you, that you've never heard me utter before. I'll try to be restrained and moderate, but George, all I ask is that you not come on strongly for probation before I've clarified everything in my mind, or it may be too late for me."

"You're serious, aren't you? I can't believe it."

"Trust me. I can do what is right if I don't have to confront you."

Macrakis smiled. "I trust you. Besides, your bribe is more valuable than the one the Atkins offered."

"My bribe! What bribe?"

"Your respect for my opinion and its influence on the faculty floor. Your wanting our friendship not to be damaged over anything so triv-ial as an ideological or moral dispute."

"I suppose you're right. But what was their bribe?"

"What it always is, Jack. Not money, or gifts, or offers of vacation retreats. Not jewelry for our wives, airline tickets, bicycles for our chil-dren. Nothing crass or commercial, Jack. Just flattery, plain old flat-tery, the ultimate salve for the bruised and diminished egos of vain and vulnerable teachers."

"So they told you that you were the great influence of Tim's life, how he called home every week exuding excitement. Did they mention your brilliance, George? That always gets me—when they rave about my brilliance."

"Precisely."

"I wish someone, sometime would offer me plain old cash for a higher grade or a sympathetic vote in a disciplinary case."

"Why?" Macrakis asked.

"So I could turn it down and feel morally superior."

"How do you know you could turn it down? It might be too much to turn down."

"Then I would know," Bartley laughed "how much my morality is worth. I would know exactly how much I could be bought for."

"I don't think I'd want to find out. The price might be too low." Macrakis spoke seriously.

Bartley stood up and stretched.

"I'm reminded of the sad case of Jeremy Miller—a year or two before you joined the faculty. Ever hear of the case?"

"Vaguely," Macrakis answered. "Something about attempted wholesale bribery of the faculty."

"You got time to listen? It's a confession of sorts."

"Love to hear anything you're willing to confess, Jack."

"It happened during exam week. The boy, Jeremy, a fourth former, got caught cheating on the Latin final. During the disciplinary proceedings that week it turned out that his history and English teachers, already suspicious about the last papers he had written, tracked each paper down and discovered massive plagiarism in both papers. The evidence was presented to the DC, and they made a unanimous recommendation for firing. That meant that even the students felt the cheating was beyond comprehension.

"Anyway, his father arrived at school almost immediately and began a three-day campaign to win the faculty over to probation or suspension—anything but firing. He haunted the hallways and walks, descended on faculty walking to and from their dorms or houses. He was full of flattery, begged for understanding. When that failed because we wouldn't talk to him—I personally walked away from him twice and closed the door to the apartment on him—he resorted to a last ditch campaign of bribery.

"Like a fairy in the night, he stole from doorstep to doorstep delivering gifts to the younger, the influential, the probably liberal faculty members. He had done his research well, knew what we might cherish—bottles of fine Bordeaux, wheels of brie and Camembert, half gallon bottles of Chivas or Johnny Walker, Jack Daniels, Beefeater, huge imported Danish hams, even desserts—pies, tarts, cakes. Karen and I had taken a short vacation trip to France and England the summer before and we were in love with everything French and couldn't afford anything. There on our doorstep in the morning of the faculty meeting were a wheel of brie and four bottles of vintage *cabernet sauvignon*. He had been selective. The Old Guard, the disciplinary conservatives, got nothing. He didn't waste a gesture. Bill Henry, liberal and influential, won the grand prize bribe, a half gallon of bourbon and tins of gourmet smoked turkey and ham.

"No one touched their gifts. There was no note, no indication of the identity of the donor, but we all knew. I remember going to the faculty meeting, scheduled for the whole morning because exams were over and grades were in. We had the disciplinary cases first. Fired the boy by acclamation with a minimum of debate, one of those pathetic, irremedial situations. I suppose we were sending a message to father, who was probably the cause of his son's cheating. We finished the disciplinary cases about mid-morning. During our coffee break, Woody went back to his office to inform the Millers of the faculty decision. He came back in about fifteen minutes, and we resumed to finish the rest of the business—scholastic action, committee reports, et al.

"The meeting was over about noon. I hurried out and made a beeline for the dorm. I had voted to fire the boy. I was clean. George, I confess to you now I wanted those bottles of wine. I wanted to get to them before the good fairy of the night retrieved them. But it was too late. Mr. Miller had made his rounds, collected his bribes, a clean sweep, everything repossessed, and had left campus."

"What's your problem, Jack? You didn't take the bribe."

"But I would have, George. I would have gathered them into my house without a qualm *ex post facto*."

"But it was after you had voted freely and fairly."

"I know, but I'm still ashamed of myself, that I would have taken the bribe after the vote."

"It's the school's fault, Jack. If they'd paid us dignified salaries back then, you wouldn't have been vulnerable."

"I'd like to believe that, but I can't. I regretted at the time that I hadn't run home during the break and beaten Mr. Miller to my door-stop. I wanted those bottles of wine, something I couldn't afford. I wanted them as pseudo-cosmopolitan status symbols that I could serve to the Woodbridges or Henrys at a dinner party sometime. I don't even think I liked red wine then, but I knew their worth. It frightened me. It was as though Mr. Miller knew or guessed my vulnerability, that my secret greed was transparent to the most crass and blatant of manipulators."

They sat for several moments in silence. Then Macrakis smiled.

"I forgive you, Jack."

"Thanks, George." Bartley stood up suddenly embarrassed.

"Hey, anytime. And I'll hear you out today. I won't confront you. If I decide to disagree, I'll wait until there have been a few other speakers after you before I say anything."

"Maybe I won't have to say anything."

"Maybe not. I'll see you third period." Bartley turned around and headed toward the door that opened into the still darkened corridor.

*   *   *   *

The faculty meeting began with the regular business—announce-ments, the reports of the attendance and dorm committees, Dean Phil-lips' presentation of routine disciplinary action accepted by consent, and the explanation of an irregular class schedule Tuesday next to accommodate a visiting speaker at an expanded assembly.

The meetings were held in Camden Commons, which, because it was attached to the dining hall, served as an unofficial meeting room before meals for the whole school. Each Friday morning after breakfast, the custodian re-arranged the stuffed chairs and sofas in a semi-circle around a captain's chair in one corner where the Headmaster sat, his faculty spreading out in irregular arcs around him. The walls were pan-eled with a beige wooden veneer, the backdrop for visiting exhibits the art department provided throughout the year. At that moment, an exhibition of Lautrec posters graced its walls.

Bartley looked across at young Haskell, fidgeting in his seat and reading over a stack of note cards, on which he had probably committed the main points of the defense of Tim Atkins—about to be the main business of the faculty.

The routine business had occupied only fifteen minutes of the meeting. The Headmaster was about to turn the meeting over to the major disciplinary case when a request by the athletic director produced a verbal brawl, an unleashing of resentments that lurked just below the surface of collegial civility. It could happen at any time of the year, but especially in spring when each exhausted faculty member was negotiating with the headmaster his work load for the coming year. It was these debates, erupting suddenly out of nowhere, that reminded Bartley, and he himself was not immune, what the faculty could be like at its worst: a loose collection of competitive prima donnas, each full of self-importance and self-pity, jealous of the success of a colleague, resentful of what each perceived to be another's easier workload, angry that the students considered someone else's hobby-horse more interesting than his own.

The AD's request was innocuous enough. He needed volunteers to transport a lower level track team to a nearby school for a triangular meet. Someone wanted to know why transportation had not been provided from the regular budget, which always managed to have money for the transportation of the varsity and J.V. teams. The AD responded that his budget was low but when he received the offer to participate, he scheduled the meet because he didn't want to deny the youngsters a chance to compete. Then someone else wanted to know why it was always teams with younger or less athletic players who needed "charity" from the faculty to participate in programs already provided for in their tuition money. Then someone wanted to know why these requests were always made for teams that were traditionally not popular with the AD—soccer, or track, or wrestling. Before the AD could answer, Ben Hawkins, the sole surviving classics teacher, wanted to know why most of the athletic budget was spent on football "a brutal and dehumanizing sport that ought to be abolished at any institution that pretended to instill in youngsters a respect for civilized behavior and the life of the mind." Then the varsity football coach came to the defense of the AD and proceeded to lecture the faculty about the moral and intellectual values the students learned on the football field, his thesis replete with anecdotes of the successful careers of Kensington alumni who had played football. Mr. Hawkins countered that perhaps, since *post hoc ergo propter hoc* logic had become the order of the day, he would like to move the restoration of the Latin requirement, abolished twenty years before, because he could cite with the same logic that the success of most of Kensington's alumni could be traced to their taking Latin when it was a requirement.

Judd Hastings, the football coach, responded that he would be willing to vote for the motion to restore Latin if Mr. Hawkins would support a motion to require football for every new boy, as it used to be before the faculty capitulated to the student pressure for soccer—a move that had destroyed Kensington as a traditional football power for over a decade now.

Bartley tried to elevate the discussion by suggesting that the real issue was that each student deserved equal educational consideration in all areas of the curriculum, but that it seemed clear that the non-athlete was discriminated against in an athletic program that clearly favored gifted and motivated athletes. Then the AD argued that the academic faculty did the same thing when they sectioned better students into fast or advanced tracks and covered more material in greater depth. Weren't the poorer students being discriminated against by being excluded from those special sections? Then Bill Henry said that the opposite was true in English where the lower two sections were selected in each form to receive special instruction for problems in reading and writing. The upper sections were normal not privileged. Then someone wanted to know why there was sectioning at all at Kensington, a school with a highly competitive, selective student body. He wondered what the purpose was in distinguishing the learning rates of students with 130 I.Q. from those of 120 I.Q.

Then Le Clair suggested that the discussion had drifted from the real issue. What business had the AD asking faculty members who had already coached their two seasons, or faculty wives, to help in another season? Not only that, but the AD was asking an already overworked and underpaid faculty to give money from their own pockets. He clinched his position by pointing out that academic faculty did not ask for volunteers to grade their papers and didn't think the AD had that right. Someone else suggested that Kensington not schedule any away contests for which transportation could not be provided for by the athletic department budget and that pressure on the faculty to do more than they were already doing was unfair.

Then Bartley heard muffled shouts of "Hear, hear," and the final passionate assertion by Ben Hawkins before Woody closed off the discussion and the meeting: "I have no intention of subsidizing the wealthy parents of my students with my own time or money or my wife's time or money. If the tuition and endowment income cannot pay for our athletic programs, then perhaps we should cut those programs. I would not be adverse to Latin's being considered a sport for building mental muscles to satisfy the physical education requirement. We could save the students and faculty time and the school money as well as help reduce the air pollution resulting from needless bus trips."

The Headmaster announced that the faculty would meet again at two o'clock to hear a case for special consideration, that of Tim Atkins charged with the appropriation of testing materials from the faculty room with the intention to cheat. There were groans from those who had not heard about the case. Then he announced that all members of the faculty were required to attend, especially varsity coaches who could have captains run the first hour of practice. Coaches of lower level teams would have to make individual arrangements. He also announced that practices could run beyond the 5:15 deadline for this one occasion but he didn't want to hear of any students being late to dinner.

Bartley followed Henry out of the meeting. In the foyer he waited for Henry as he put on his trench coat.

"Jesus, Bill, that was one of the worst meetings we've ever had."

"Oh, I don't know," Henry said as they went out the front doors.

"Then therapeutically speaking, it was a good meeting. We got all that resentment of each other off our chests. Besides, Jack, even at their best faculty meetings are dreadful."

"The opposite of sex, right?"

"You remembered, Jack. Good for you. I like a disciple to remember my more profound nuggets of wisdom." He paused, "Yes, I had almost forgotten. The opposite of sex. They're bad even when they're good."

They walked along the path in bright clear sunshine. A light warm breeze had already dried the walkways. The lawns were strewn with students, now putting on shirts from a free hour of sunbathing. Some were already heading for class, books under their arms, when the five minute warning bell tolled.

"Do you have a class?" Henry asked.

"No, just some conferences."

"Have you spoken to the boy again?"

"Yes."

"What do you think now?"

"He's an impressive young man. Honest. Convincing. I'm not sure yet whether his sense of why he did what he did is ex post facto rationalization, but right now I don't think so."

"So you're coming around?"

"No. Leaning, but I've been thinking of other matters I haven't resolved yet, especially after that horrendous meeting this morning when all of our worst qualities were revealed. I wonder sometimes how we ever do anything right. You know, Bill, none of Atkins' problems would have happened at all if we'd granted the kid his petition last fall, and you know goddamn well we would have granted it if Charlie

Wentworth hadn't retired as Chairman of the Math Department last year and if Woody hadn't appointed Chapman as the new chairman. We didn't deny the kid's petition because we couldn't understand that psychologist's gobbledigook. We denied it because Chapman used the occasion of the petition to make his first public stand before his colleagues that he was going to be a hardliner like old man Wentworth— a genuine, one hundred percent academic Darwinist in defending math department territorial rights. And it was easy for Chapman to take a hard line because he can't stand Le Clair and he thinks Le Clair's logic and philosophy courses are little more than scholastic mumbo-jumbo. So the boy was lost between the cracks, his interests denied in the quagmire of faculty politics, and Tim, like the good soldier he is, tried to gut it out until he broke and ended up trying to cheat to pass math so his parents would be proud of him on graduation day.

"Once he entered the mail room and found that ditto copy and was apprehended, there is no turning back for anybody. It's too late to correct our mistakes. We can't just change the math requirement for a diploma after the boy has attempted to cheat. The school year is almost over. We can't put him into another course as we might have last fall. We must follow our disciplinary procedures and confront the consequences of all that he did and his parents did and all that we didn't do. Now you want me to stand up and say I was wrong and the boy should be kicked out when adult authorities—his parents and the faculty are accessories to what he's done. And because I know that and believe that I must make up my mind with that knowledge."

"Why do you have to make everything so complicated, Jack?"

"Because it is complicated, dammit all. I can't speak on the faculty floor and proclaim something I don't believe even if I agree with you and would like to do what the boy wants. I can't do it for an even more important reason, something you taught me when I first came here and a principle you have conspicuously avoided mentioning, which this awful faculty meeting has forced me to reconsider."

"We might as well finish this conversation by my letting you mock me with my own words. Go ahead. My class is required to wait 10 minutes if I'm late."

"During my first years in the dorm you told me that what I did in handling students individually was a personal matter, a matter of style more than substance. You said I should deal with the daily, trivial problems practically, as best as I could on an ad hoc basis with no necessary carryover of principle from situation to situation, from student to student. But when I acted officially by vote or speech in the Discipline Committee or the Faculty meeting, I was not voting for or against a particular boy whom I happened to know more or less, but that I was affirming a set of principles that would apply to every student who ever appeared or would appear for judgment, that I would be making a statement as objectively as I could about what was fair for anyone, anywhere, anytime who might come before any authority or institution that presumed to teach morality."

"Did I say all of that? I can't remember. It sounds more like Kant. Every judgment should be considered as if it were a universal law. Maybe I did say it. I did go through a Kant, Schopenhauer period once, but when they led me to Nietzsche I gave them up. I'm impressed."

"By your own ideas? You hypocrite. You egotistical fraud."

"No, Jack, no." Henry began to laugh. "Not that they're my ideas. I can't even remember holding them. I'm impressed that you still remember them and have tried to practice them all these years. I thought you understood that I was just trying ideas out over the years, sorting things in my mind out loud. I thought you were doing the same."

"Well, I guess I stopped somewhere along the way and I plan to remain committed to the stand I've taken in Atkins case which is consistent with those principles. I will either not say anything or re-affirm my stand. I will not recant."

Bartley looked at Henry in the sunlight and suddenly realized that Henry was smiling, smiling his kind, forgiving, fatherly smile and that he had been smiling for some time while Bartley had been staring at the ground as if deliberating in private.

"You'll come around, Jack. I think I'll just mark you down as voting for expulsion."

"I will not."

"You'll come around. You're full of a lot of bull, but you're a good man. We'll just wait and see."

"I wish I could. It would be a lot easier."

"See you, Jack. I've got to run."

He began to turn away from Bartley and spoke back over his shoulder.

"You'll come around. You're a sucker for trying to be fair."

Bartley watched Henry disappear slowly, leaning to the left and limping slightly from an old athletic injury.

✳   ✳   ✳   ✳

At two that afternoon, the faculty accepted without debate the ordinary disciplinary business presented by Dean Phillips and addressed the case of Tim Atkins immediately. Bartley sat in a row near the rear and in the left quadrant of the arc of chairs that spread out before Headmaster Woodbridge. By turning his head slightly to his right, he could see the anxious face of Jonathan Haskell, Tim's adviser, about to make his first major speech before the faculty. Henry sat two rows over and slightly behind him. Directly across the room George Macrakis sat scribbling in a notebook.

Half the faculty wore athletic gear. The crew coaches sat together in the back few rows ready to escape to their vans, waiting in the parking lot below Camden Commons. Bartley suspected that the motors were probably running. During the forty minutes of debate that followed, Bartley glanced several times back at Bob Dennison surrounded by his assistant coaches. Every time Bartley looked, Dennison was looking at his watch. The shells would not go out on the water without adult supervision. Crew was in danger of losing its last full day of practice before the first important race.

After Phillips presented the facts of the case, he announced the recommendation of the Discipline Committee and summarized the majority and minority arguments. Headmaster Woodbridge then called upon Atkins' adviser for the official motion.

Bartley was surprised at the clarity and authority with which young Jonathan Haskell moved the recommendation of the Discipline Committee and argued the case, though his voice quavered a few times and squeaked embarrassingly once, jumping a full register during a moment of rhetorical emphasis. He cleared his throat, excused himself in a voice rather deliberately *basso profundo*, and carried on with composure though Bartley noticed a pink flush creep up his cheeks and then diminish as suddenly as it had appeared. When he closed his eyes and discounted the distinctive timbre of Haskell's voice, Bartley thought it could very well be he himself who was speaking—all of the liberal principles of disciplinary defense he had formulated in his first years at Kensington seemed to be echoing down the years and into the mind and voice of this first year teacher from Haverford. Haskell presented all of the arguments Bartley himself would have made were he Tim's adviser/lawyer: first major offense; a victimless crime since whether Atkins passed or not had no effect on anyone else's grade, he was so far below the bottom of any grade curve; extenuating circumstances including a clear presentation of the boy's learning disabilities and his almost heroic efforts to do the impossible; a sixth former who had been a respected member of the community for almost five years; the degree to which he had already suffered; his dignity in the face of adversity. Finally, Haskell appealed to his colleagues' sense of compassion, asked them to be generous to a young man who had shared his artistic gifts and good will with students and faculty so generously. He conceded the serious nature of the offense, but he pleaded with his colleagues to do what was best for the boy since his offense posed no threat to the good order of the school.

All of his points, of course, were countered in the first stages of the debate, but it was not the arguments that interested Bartley. He had heard them a hundred times. It was the tone, the mood of his colleagues. Even before the meeting had begun, he sensed a forced joviality around the coffee cart. Opponents who had exchanged bitter words in the morning now spoke to each other confidentially, almost conspiratorially, as though the morning confrontations had never occurred.

As the debate progressed, Bartley sensed an absence of self-righteousness or anger in the voices for punishment and law and order. The speakers for firing prefaced their remarks with a certain regret that the incident had occurred, expressions of sympathy for Atkins, or lamentations that it all might have been prevented, perhaps by locking the door to the faculty room after the day's business was done. Even the demands for firing by hard liners were moderately phrased. Then, suddenly, Bartley knew what was happening.

He shuffled the two three-by-five cards upon which he had outlined alternative arguments—one for firing, one for probation. He worried that perhaps he was too indecisive, too open minded. Since he had spoken to Tim Thursday morning, it seemed he had changed his mind several times. He made up his mind to stick to the decision he had made in the Disciplinary Committee and for a while he would feel relieved and definitive and final in his conclusion. But within the hour his resolve would melt and he would visualize the calm, steady gaze of Tim Atkins and he would hear again the words of the boy's appeal— that the theft had been an act of self-assertion, an affirmation of his right to begin again, an act that could only be validated by his being fired.

He listened to the drift of sentiment back and forth, round and round. Bartley felt no necessity to speak for some time. It was not that he did not know what position he would take. He had to feel the commitment, the necessity to make a statement and that would come only when the deeper urging of the heart rose to his consciousness. As the debate proceeded, shifting the tenor of opinion back and forth, the time of the vote grew closer, and he found himself no longer listening objectively to the arguments of his colleagues. He began to feel anxious when the spirit of the meeting seemed to be moving toward a consensus and he knew how he truly felt and what he must say. He looked over at Bill Henry who returned his gaze briefly and then looked away. Henry would not say anything unless Bartley spoke first.

He almost panicked when he felt he had waited too long to speak. Had he misjudged the ebb and flow of the debate? As long as he had time, he luxuriated in his open-mindedness, weighing pros and cons. But only when time and the current of opinion began to run against his deepest feelings, did he become fully and urgently aware of what he would do.

He folded one of the three-by-five cards in half and placed it in his pocket. He studied the other card carefully and then raised his hand to be recognized by the Headmaster.

*   *   *   *

Bartley had just returned to his apartment after dinner and was reading Peter's comments on the dorm roster sheet before going out into the dorm for the early check-in when Tim Atkins dropped by before leaving campus. Tim had knocked at the front door and was led into his study by Annie. He carried a large rectangular cardboard, wrapped in newspapers under one arm.

"Are your parents with you, Tim?"

"No, well, yes and no. My mom's out in the car. My dad's over at Mr. Woodbridge's."

"Does she want to come in? I'd be happy to talk with her if you want."

"No, sir. That's O.K. They talked to Mr. Henry for about an hour."

"How's it going?"

"Not too good. My dad especially. My mom's O.K., but my dad got in an argument with Mr. Henry when he tried to explain why I was kicked out."

"How about Mr. Haskell? Did they talk to him too?"

"Yes, sir, for a little while, but he didn't have much to say. He felt terrible. He really didn't seem to understand what happened. In fact, he was bewildered at the vote and felt kind of guilty that he didn't do a good job."

"I don't think he knows what really happened."

"You won't tell anybody, will you, Mr. Bartley—Mr. Haskell or my parents or anybody—that I came to you and asked you to change your vote?"

"Only Mr. Henry knows and he certainly won't say anything."

"Good. I don't want anyone to ever know. It was bad enough listening to my dad and Mr. Henry. It got so bad I had to leave. If my dad knew I asked you to get me fired, he'd probably kill me."

"You might have been fired anyway, Tim, regardless of what I might have said." Bartley had said as much as he could though he knew it wasn't exactly true. "Listen, Tim. Why don't you ask your mother to come in for a cup of tea or coffee?"

"She won't come in. She's been crying on and off all afternoon. She just wants to be alone for a while."

"Have you got your stuff moved out yet?"

"Yes, sir." He smiled bleakly for the first time. "It was easy. The room was such a mess, I just stuffed everything into some plastic bags and hauled them out to the car. It was collecting all my art work that took the time. We won't be able to get everything this trip. I'll probably drive back up myself next week sometime and get the rest of it."

"I assume you're going home tonight."

"Yes, sir. It's only a couple of hours' drive. We'll be home by ten o'clock if my dad ever gives up and decides to leave."

"I wish it had worked out better, Tim."

"It's working out just fine. It'll be tough for a week or so, but they'll get over it."

"Is there anything more I can do?"

"No, sir. Not really, but would you give this to Mrs. Bartley?"

He handed Bartley the cardboard rectangle he had been carrying under his arm.

"When I was clearing out my sketches from the art room, I ran into this. It's a charcoal of the chapel. I'd like Mrs. Bartley to have it. She stood next to me in the concert choir last winter when we sang *King David* and she was always friendly and asked me about my painting and sketches."

"Why don't you give it to her yourself? She's in the kitchen or living room. I'll go get her."

"No, sir. Don't bother. I really don't want to see anybody anymore tonight. It's hard enough leaving here. I'll just feel lousy talking to her and remembering the concert last winter. You just say goodbye to her for me and thank her for keeping me in tune."

"I'm sure she'd like to say goodbye to you, Tim."

"Maybe I'll drop by when I come up next week to get the rest of my things."

He offered his hand to Bartley.

"Thanks for firing me, Mr. Bartley. I shouldn't have asked you to get into my mess, but there's no question you helped."

Bartley began to laugh.

"How do you know I helped, Tim? You don't know how I voted or what I said."

"Yes, I do, sir."

"How?"

"Simple deduction. Lousy as I am at math, I can make a simple deduction. When Mr. Woodbridge told me I was fired, he told me the faculty vote—29-4. It's not possible the vote could be such a landslide unless you said you'd changed your mind."

They moved toward the door leading to the dormitory.

"I'll go out this way."

"Good luck, Tim."

Tim hesitated at the door.

"For a while this afternoon my dad was talking about me re-applying for next year, but my mom put her foot down absolutely. Has anyone ever been kicked out twice?"

"Yes. About ten years ago. A young man was fired early in his fourth form year—marginal involvement in drugs. We re-admitted him and then fired him again in the sixth form for plagiarism. He copied an entire article from the Washington Post and turned it in as a history paper. Sad story too. He was already an A minus student. He wanted to be straight A to make sure he would get into Yale."

"What a bummer! Getting kicked out twice. That would be too much for me."

"There's a happy ending to the story, Tim He went to Berkeley and then on to Columbia for graduate work and is now finishing his doctorate at Cornell."

"In history, I assume?" Tim laughed for the first time out loud.

"Of course."

"Why don't you hire him at Kensington when he finishes his Ph.D., and then you'll have a chance to fire him a third time."

"By the third time we would probably expunge him."

"What's expunge?"

"Expunge is the most severe form of punishment in the Harvard disciplinary system. It means to erase completely from all records. When the offense is so serious that probation, or suspension, or firing is not enough, you get expunged from every document that is proof that you attended. I know of only one case when a student hired another student to take his final examination in Spanish. Then, secure in the knowledge that his paid substitute got into the examination room, he went to a coffee shop in the Square and sat down at the counter next to a man who turned out to be his Spanish teacher, who had left the administration of the final to his graduate assistants."

"Hey," Tim laughed. "Getting kicked out isn't so bad after all. At least I won't be expunged. I'll always be a member of my class. In a few years the development office will be hustling me for money, and down the road I might be asked to organize one of our re-unions, maybe even be the class agent, or be elected class president for our 25th re-union." He turned suddenly.

"We'll see you, sir." Tim pulled open the outside door and disappeared. Bartley walked into the connecting hallway to the dorm for check-in.

$$* \qquad * \qquad * \qquad *$$

It was Bill Henry who came to Bartley this time–four days after Atkins had been dismissed. Bartley had avoided the dining hall and the dormitory for the weekend and for the first days of the new week spent all of his free time after classes and baseball practice in his garden, something he had neglected after putting in his early vegetables—peas, lettuce, carrots—two weeks before. The grounds crew plowed the plots in a traditional space beyond the football practice fields and would later surround the plots with snow fences once the crops had come up. He avoided any conversation with colleagues except for immediate matters of daily business. He began to feel a psychological distance from the school and Tim's disciplinary case, so much so that he began to regret he had let himself become so obsessed with the fate of one student. He promised himself not to let it happen again.

Between the last class of the afternoon and athletics Henry found him in his garden. Bartley had caught up on his weeding and with sticks and strings was laying out the rows of flowers on the border of the garden. He had just received the seeds from the Jefferson Foundation in Charlottesville–genuine seeds developed by Jefferson himself in one of his many experiments with cross fertilization. Bartley decided he would reverse their usual roles by feigning anger at being interrupted and then indifference, but he knew he couldn't pull it off. It was enough that Henry was coming to him. He wanted to tell Henry why he had said what he had. He wanted Henry to know that nothing was as it seemed to be. He was on his knees when Henry came across the field and Bartley kept his head down on his work, pretending he didn't see Henry coming.

"I suppose you came by to gloat," Bartley began since all Henry did was to stand and stare at him. "All right. Gloat. You knew what I would do. You predicted it. So, once again you were right. But it was what you said after my speech that won the day, not me."

"I didn't come to gloat, Jack. I came to pay homage. Not for the position I knew you would take. You did what you had to do for whatever reasons. It was the speech you delivered. It was absolutely stunning especially since I don't think you believed a word of it. You touched every base, articulated every argument, appealed to every interest and private agenda and prejudice,—a marvel of sophistry. It was the most convincing and cunning defense of the absolute nature of moral principles and the necessity for authority and punishment that I have ever heard—and all delivered from a liberal perspective—as though you were saddened that you could not maintain your original vote, but that there was a point at which compassion becomes anarchy and pity corruption. Remarkable. A masterpiece. You made my follow up remarks a piece of cake. By the way, are you going to plant those pale, washed out pansies that Jefferson is supposed to have produced back in 1815. It must have taken him years of cross fertilization to ruin the natural, rich blue that God had created?"

"Yes, I am going to plant them again. It's one of my traditions. Would you take the end of this string and this stick and help me line up the furrow I am going dig with my hoe?" He waited until Henry made his way to the end of the row before he continued. "When I was leaving the faculty meeting last Friday, Skinner came up to me and said that it was the first time I had said anything intelligent on the faculty floor since he had come here. He didn't stop and talk to me, of course. He just said it out of the side of his mouth in passing. I don't think he wanted anyone to see that he was talking to me. He was scowling as usual, but I took it as a genuine compliment."

"Did Brewster say anything? I watched his face as you were speaking and I thought he was going to have an apoplectic fit, the look on his face was so incredulous. And Woody kept nodding as he always does when anyone says anything he agrees with, especially about trust and honor and no locks. You must have picked up at least ten votes from those who didn't want to vote openly against what seemed to be the headmaster's position. He can't help himself. I think the nodding is completely unconscious."

"Brewster wrote me a note, congratulating me on my maturity and wisdom. It was sincere. Anyway I feel guilty about deceiving him because he finally thinks he has converted me, but there was no way I was going to feel guiltless no matter what I said, so to hell with it. It's over and done and I think it was the right thing."

"What about George?"

"I don't know, but I prepared him beforehand and asked him to trust me."

After they pressed the sticks in the ground and tied the string, Henry remained standing about twenty feet away, maintaining a distance between them. It was his way of telling Bartley that he didn't want to prolong their conversation, that his visit was meant to be brief. He turned slightly and shifted his weight. He took a step out of the garden toward the school buildings.

"Now that I have paid you proper homage, may I gloat? Just a little?"

"Certainly. You have the right, I suppose. You managed the boy's case very well. You did all the work. It's your victory not mine. You did the research, got me to recant, faced the parents."

"The father was dreadful, but you were the easiest, Jack. You're such an open book, such a soft touch. I knew if you talked to Atkins again, he'd convince you."

"I talked to the boy again, but he didn't convince me. I went in to the meeting prepared to say nothing or re-assert my position for probation. You can gloat. You have the right, but not for the reasons you think. Neither you nor the boy convinced me."

Henry took a step toward Bartley and stopped. "You don't have to be ashamed of agreeing with me, Jack. I understand."

"I didn't change my mind as a gesture of friendship to you. I acted out of anger—for a while I even felt hatred and contempt for almost everyone sitting in that room including myself, especially myself. When I spoke, it was a kind of self-condemnation and self-inflicted punishment as though the only thing I was fit to speak was a lie."

Henry raised his arm and began to rub the back of his neck with his hand as he shook his head slowly more out of bewilderment than denial.

"You're getting too complicated for me again. I guess I just don't follow you. I followed you the other day when you tried to make each subtle refinement of judgment into a Kantian universal. But you've gone beyond me this time."

"Bill, as I sat there listening to the debate, I sensed a certain mood in the room, a kind of groping toward reconciliation after the fiasco in the morning, a kind of forced collegiality. I knew suddenly that the debate was all *pro forma*, just an opportunity for softened rhetoric, to let the hard liners take their stand but gently and mournfully so that they could say they spoke for firing though they would accept probation. Everyone wanted to avoid controversy. The coaches wanted to get to their teams. Quite simply, Bill, we were ready for a consensus to put the boy on probation and so I spoke to stop it."

"Why, for God's sake," Henry snapped, unable to contain his exasperation. "Why did you want to stop it? You just told me you entered the room ready to vote for probation."

"Because I suddenly realized we weren't forgiving the boy, giving him a second chance. We were forgiving ourselves and his parents."

"But what were we forgiving ourselves of?"

"Of the consequences of our arrogance and ignorance, our posturing, and our indifference, of our mistake in asking the boy to do more than we knew he could so that we could affirm or acquiesce to other values that had nothing to do with Tim Atkins."

"Jack, you're being too scrupulous."

"You can never be too scrupulous in making judgments about students. You can never be too vigilant in making sure each student is being treated fairly even if you don't know the student as I didn't know Tim Atkins and thus acquiesced. You can never be too precise in clarifying information about students as you failed to do until last week when you called the psychologist. The clarity of Tim's impossible position should have been understood by each member of the faculty last fall. Goddamn it, Bill, if we're in the business of making judgments, and you were the one who told me that if I was tired of making judgments I'd better get out of teaching, that affect the life and sense of self-worth of our students, then let's do it right with standards and procedures of judgment as high as the standards of behavior we expect from sixteen year old children and with accountability for our own mistakes. We were sloppy, Bill, and we deserved to pay the consequences."

"You're saying we were wrong last fall by omission and commission and that not firing the boy now is just our way of refusing to face the proper consequences of our abuse or misuse of authority."

"That's precisely it. We should all feel the guilt of firing the boy. We forced him into his dishonest act when we could just as easily have substituted another course for the math requirement. We should be forced to fire him and endure the guilt and shame we rightly deserved. I wanted to make sure we did fire him. It was my revenge. No institutional authority should have the procedures and mechanics to forgive its own mistake without paying a price. I wanted to stick it in the ear of every hypocrite in that room and the boy's parents. Probation would exonerate them of their irresponsibility in making the boy come back when they really knew he couldn't do it. I said what I did to punish them and myself. The time to act properly was last fall. Once the boy stepped into that faculty room to steal that test, the time for flexibility and understanding had passed. It was too late to be compassionate or understanding. We and his parents made him a thief and cheat and all the forgiving gestures in the world will not erase in his mind the shame of what he did. I did my best to convince everyone of the necessity to kick Atkins out and I hope everybody in that meeting left feeling like shit."

Bartley picked up his hoe and opened a trench for his seeds.

"Bartley's Revenge?"

"Yes, Bartley's Revenge and I feel embarrassed and ashamed of what I said and I deserve to feel that way. I was indifferent last fall when I should have been vigilant and scrupulous and taken the boy's petition seriously. But I didn't. I let the math department have its way when I knew it was just faculty politics."

"You are too scrupulous for me, Jack."

"I repeat, you can never be too scrupulous, too vigilant, or too precise when you presume to judge. The old Puritans were right about that at least. They may have had an inhumane and unfeeling judgmental morality, but they took it seriously and they worked at it."

"If we all sat around scrutinizing our motives and refining our principles the way you do, Jack, we'd never get anything done. When one of my ball players makes a bone headed play, I tell him it's a boneheaded play in so many words and I don't worry that his psyche is going to be damaged for life because I didn't consider all the principles and consequences of my judgment."

Bartley began to laugh.

"That's a specious analogy and you know it. But I accept that we must act on impulse, spontaneously. That's what I did in the faculty meeting. What I've just tried to explain to you is why I said what I did. At the time I made up my mind I was not thinking either of principles or consequences or Tim Atkins or anything. I was so goddamn angry I could hardly talk."

"I didn't suspect a thing. You spoke with clarity, coherence, and order and with convincing rhetorical strategies. I gave you a flat A."

"Well, my mouth was dry and my heart was thumping, and my knees were trembling and I was saying things I didn't even believe and I spoke them from the depths of moral cynicism without any faith in human nature or benign institutions, blinded as I was by the cowardice and hypocrisy of my colleagues and the certain knowledge of my own complicity."

"Cowardice, cynicism, hypocrisy, complicity?"

"Yes. As I sat trying to make up my mind, trying to do what I thought was right and best for the boy, I listened to all that guilt-ridden sentimental slop about what a good boy everyone thought Atkins was. I remembered that meeting last fall when we denied his petition to substitute another course for the math requirement and I could hear the same voices now lamenting his terrible moral downfall, parading their compassion. I could hear in my mind's ear those voices and they weren't pleading Tim Atkins cause then. Last fall they had stood for high academic standards, grandstanding their toughness as defenders of the integrity of the school's diploma. And I remembered Chapman leading the way and young members of the math department proclaiming their agreement to ingratiate themselves with him and that stupid Phillips trying to read the psychologist's report in such a stumbling way that we all laughed condescendingly at the jargon, and I remember my own acquiescence. I didn't know Atkins very well. I had my own concerns getting the history department organized and moving and I figured it was his adviser's business not mine, but his adviser was new to the school and didn't know his ass from a hole in the ground about our procedures. I realized that we were going to make up for what we had not done in the fall by being conveniently forgiving now that it was too late and I would not now be in complicity with any crocodile compassion by cowards who did not want the guilt of firing a boy we drove to moral failure. So I said to hell with my liberal principles and fairminded procedures which had suddenly become irrelevant.

"But something else happened at that moment that has undermined all that I have believed and will have a lasting effect on everything I will do in the future. I have always believed that mercy, compassion, generosity, forgiveness, toleration—all of the truly profound virtues—spring from something noble in individuals, something almost Godlike—Grace if you will. Now I know their origin can be just as sordid as the conservative demand for punishment which can spring from cruelty and power, even sadism. Now I know that I always suspected but denied: that compassion can spring from selfishness, cowardice, the fear of reprisal, the fear of judgment, the need for popularity, the terrible need to forgive ourselves while forgiving others to avoid the consequences of our own failure."

"I concede the cowardice. That's with us all the time. That's why we have procedures and collective responsibility. Also the hypocrisy and the guilt by omission and the needs for popularity and the fear of reprisal. But why the moral cynicism? Situational and pragmatic, perhaps, but not cynical."

"It was for me, Bill. I think I'll recover but for a brief moment I realized that none of my principles meant a thing. I wanted to be cruel, to deflect to the faculty and Tim's parents some of the guilt and pain and humiliation that he suffered. I wanted to stop them from forgiving themselves and turn back at them some of Neanderthalic cant they've given me over the years."

"Well, cheer up, Jack. Everything turned out right even if it was for the wrong reasons."

"I wish I could believe that, but ever since the meeting I've been thinking about what happened and I've decided that at best all we did was damage control. And I've been haunted ever since that maybe most of what we do is just damage control, like the public school teachers, or policemen or firemen. Even here where teaching conditions are almost perfect, I suspect that we spend most of our time keeping the losses down to acceptable dimensions like my third form baseball team losing a game by only seven runs. I suppose my classes are the same. I probably get through to about twenty or thirty per cent of my students and the rest muddle their way along without much interest or enthusiasm."

"Remember, Jack, it takes only one teacher in the life of each student to make a difference."

"Yes. I'll take consolation from the fact that you made a difference in Tim Atkins' life. Besides all this gloom isn't like me is it, Bill?"

"Quite frankly, I was about to tell you to cut out all this self-pity and pessimistic posturing. There are days when we are damn lucky just to control the damage, so let's thank the Lord for little favors and celebrate even our Pyrrhic victories."

"I never thought the day would come that you would be giving me a pep talk."

"It won't happen too often. I'm just trying to thank you for your help." Suddenly Henry looked at his watch and turned abruptly. Without a word he was gone.

PART III

▼

THE SEASON OF LETTING GO

CHAPTER 6

▼

"If you don't want to tell me why you've been wearing that enigmatic smile since I came home a half hour ago, you don't have to, but I can't stand it and I have a great urge to punch you. I'm buried by paper work, classes, and meetings and if the changes I made at baseball practice don't work, I'll be facing my first winless season. I come home from a terrible practice to find you in some kind of mystical state drifting from room to room smiling or grinning or smirking, I can't quite tell."

They were in the bedroom dressing to go to dinner.

"You? Punch me? Punch anybody? I must be the only person alive who knows the Hemingway side of Mr. Jack Bartley, swaggering threats of violence, false hair on your chest."

"I do not have false hair on my chest. I have little or no hair on my chest."

She continued to smile almost beatifically, he decided, in the bureau mirror as she put her blouse over head and began to shake it down with shrugs and wiggles.

"And if you don't get rid of that complacent grin, you can go to dinner alone. I'll stay here and count the genuine hairs on my chest."

"Oh, Jack, don't be silly. I'm not smug or complacent. It's a smile of serenity, can't you tell? If you didn't feel so sorry for yourself, you'd know I'm smiling out of happiness. And I can't wait to tell you why. At the same time, I don't want to tell you yet. I want to draw it out as long as I can. Besides, you won't let me, you're so busy misinterpreting my happiness through your own misery."

He stopped in the middle of tying his shoe and looked up. He sensed they were talking about something serious. "Should I guess?" he asked.

"Yes. Just to put it off longer. You'll never guess, so that's O.K."

"Should I be serious or can I be flippant?"

"You can be both. Just let me know which you are being first."

"Can you give me some hints, some categories of inquiry, or must I start with vague general questions?"

She stepped into her skirt, pulled it up over her hips and began shaping it to her waist.

"Ask me where I went today?"

"Where did you go today?"

"No, no. Say, 'Did you go to town today?' or something like that."

"O.K. Did you go to town today?"

"No."

"Did you go to the Christ Church Outgrown shop sale today?"

"Well, yes. I did. But that has nothing to do with this. This isn't going to work, is it?"

"If putting me off and driving me crazy with curiosity is what you're trying to do, then it's working."

"I went some place on campus and saw someone important."

"Ah. Now, I know. You went to the basement hallway of the art building and saw the pornographic caricature of Skinner someone painted on the wall there last night."

"No. But did someone really do that? I'd love to see it. That would make me happy too."

"Yes. Someone did it and good old Ned Phillips is going crazy with interrogations of every student with a modicum of talent."

"Let's go see it now, on the way to dinner."

"Can't. Ned declared the hallway off limits until the work crew paints it over."

"Even to faculty?"

"Especially to faculty and faculty children."

"My happiness is doubled."

"We're not getting very far at our original inquiry, are we?" Bartley put on his blazer and sat in the rocker by the bed.

"I'll give you a hint. I received a phone call and was asked to go to the Main School Building to see a person of power and influence."

What she was hinting at was vaguely beginning to take shape in his imagination.

"Woody?"

"Yes."

"Did he want to see you about something to do with the school?"

"Yes."

"For next year—having to do with something that hasn't been announced yet?"

"Yes. And for the year after too and if everything works out after that too."

"I knew the trustees met in secret. I just knew it. They couldn't wait until Trustees' Weekend for the vote and formal announcement. It would be too late to get things going." He stood up and began pacing, talking to himself. "All the rumors are true, the plans for renovations, everything." He had momentarily lost the point of her revelation and he was instantly ashamed. "I'm sorry. I won't guess any more. Now, you tell me. The way you've wanted to for about a half hour."

"Woody asked if I would consider taking a newly created position as Associate Dean of Admissions and half time member of the math department effective July 1st."

"And did you accept it?" He half suspected it was coming, but he thought Woody would have told him about the decision for coeducation first. Perhaps, it was arrogant of him to presume so, but he had steered everything through the committee, taken all the flak from opponents, kept the debate on educational grounds. And now when he should be happy because of Karen's happiness, he felt slighted, hearing about it indirectly.

"I told him I'd talk it over with you first."

"You don't have to talk it over with me. Do you want the job?"

"More than anything I've ever wanted in my life besides you and the children."

He was startled by her answer. In all their discussions about the school, in all their private, intimate revelations of their hopes and dreams, he never sensed she felt so deeply about assuming an "official" status at Kensington. He had assumed she was happy in the life they led, sharing his job as she did, taking care of the children, teaching part time in the middle school and as a substitute in high school.

"I didn't know you felt that way. I never guessed." He could not conceal the disappointment and the bewilderment. Of course, he wanted her to take the job. He was proud she had been asked, but he was hurt that she had hidden from him the depth of her yearning.

"I couldn't tell you how I felt, Jack. I just couldn't. If you knew, your work on the committee would have been compromised. You would have felt you were doing it for me, that there was a personal not professional reason for changing the school."

"Well, whether I knew or not, I'll still be accused of self-interest— free education for my daughters and a job for my wife."

"You really don't care what people will say, do you?"

"No. I don't care about that. I'm just disappointed in myself, Karen. I didn't even begin to sense how you felt for all these years. I complacently assumed you were, like me, completely happy with our life."

"I was, Jack. I am, with us. I didn't care one way or another about changing my role here until two years ago when Woody asked us to host that dinner party for the Trustees so that we could discuss the issue of coeducation in small groups, wives included. That evening was the most humiliating three hours of my life, and I said nothing. I sat there and listened and said nothing and I am so ashamed that I didn't. I didn't want to interfere. I wanted to speak out, but realized to my disgust that, when all was said and done—regardless of how much of my life I had given to the school, I had no right to speak."

"I didn't know. I knew you were angry later that night, but I thought it was because Harlowe had been so discourteous and pompous and ungracious."

"He was condescending and arrogant and disgusting. He never answered one of the women's questions directly. He addressed his answer to the husband. It was as though none of us were there—the women that is—and he was stupid and disgusting and got drunk and urinated all over the wall and floor in the bathroom and I had to clean it up after I served dessert and coffee so others could use it. As I was cleaning up, I realized that that stupid man who knew nothing about education let alone coeducation had the power to determine the nature of the school that I was giving my whole life to."

"He wasn't very informed, was he?"

"Informed? He was the most ignorant and bigoted person I have ever met in my life. Every school I ever attended was coeducational. Ninety percent of Americans attend coeducational schools and have for years and that fool called it a "madness" that was sweeping the nation as though it were some fad or fashion."

"You're still angry, aren't you, and that was two years ago. Well, you can take satisfaction in the fact that Harlowe is no longer a member of the Board. Woody got rid of him last year."

"I'll never forgive that man for patronizing me or myself for not speaking up. I played the role of dutiful housewife. I cleaned the house. I cooked and served the dinner. Oh, Jack, I cleaned the house twice. I even cleaned the oven twice. I don't know why. Did I think he would come into the kitchen and check the oven to see if it were clean? And the oven light doesn't even work. He couldn't see in if he wanted to. And I didn't have the courage to speak up, to tell that dreadful man what I thought, I was so intimidated by the fact that he was a Trustee and a man, in a male school." She was no longer smiling. He tried to cheer her up.

"Hey, smile," he said. "It's all over. You've won, and Woody couldn't have made a better choice."

She would not be consoled. The memory of her night of humiliation had dampened her joy.

"There are still important details. We didn't talk about whether I would do dorm duty or coach or my salary or whether I would be considered administration or faculty and whether I would have voting rights on matters of discipline and curriculum." She had sobered and was suddenly pensive and anxious. She would not be cheered up. They left the house and walked silently to the Commons. It wasn't until after dinner when she was drinking coffee and talking to Maggie Henry that he saw her smile again.

*   *   *   *

But he was not consoled. Later that evening in his study while searching his files for the ditto masters of tests he had once given on the New Deal, Bartley ran across the folder containing one completed chapter and the research data of his now abandoned project to write the history of Kensington School. He withdrew it from the folder and began to re-read it, knowing that it would lead to certain brooding over the failure and disappointment that was at the heart of his victory.

He had been encouraged in the project by Headmaster Woodbridge, who had funded Bartley for two summers of research and travel from the Headmaster's Discretionary Fund and a course reduction for a semester. The project was begun just after the 75th anniversary of the school's founding when they had discovered that no one had ever organized the archives of important periodicals and documents. Much of the school's history was hearsay. The monograph produced for the celebration was thin and shoddy.

When Woody suggested the project, Bartley didn't hesitate in accepting. He knew he would never finish his dissertation. He wasn't really a scholar. His heart might belong to Jefferson, but his will balked at the arduous grind of research and writing. He began by soliciting testimony from the oldest graduates. He interviewed former faculty and trustees and invited the alumni to submit anecdotes of their memories. He established an archives in the library solicited missing yearbooks, catalogues, documents of all sorts that he discovered had been lost or mutilated or stolen or never gathered.

Central to his research was his "oral history," an extensive file of transcriptions of the tapes of his interviews of hundreds of alumni reaching back to the few early graduates still alive and covering all the gaps in public documents as well as representative interviews of members of each class since 1925.

Then he set about writing his first chapter, the Woodbridge years. The book was to be organized in chapters corresponding to the tenures of the school's headmasters. He was excited as he had not been years. The charters of Andover and Exeter were older than the Constitution itself. Harvard was perhaps the oldest continuous institution in the country. Wasn't it possible that Kensington could achieve something of the same permanent status on the American scene someday?

He completed an abbreviated chapter at the end of his second summer and submitted it to Tom Ackerman, editor of the alumni magazine. He was a professional fund raiser brought in by Woody just before the 75th celebration to coordinate all the development and alumni activities—annual giving, capital funds, class news, fund drives, alumni gatherings. He didn't know the school but he knew fund raising. Bartley had hoped that each chapter, as he completed it, would have a large and appreciative alumni audience in the BULLETIN, but the short essay was rejected immediately as "inappropriately subjective."

Ackerman was blunt and honest. The article was too liberal, too progressive, too anecdotal, too much based upon hearsay testimony, contained content more appropriate to a posthumous treatment of Woodbridge. It might double the contributions of recent alumni, amounting to perhaps several thousand dollars, but it would certainly alienate the good old boys in their sixties and seventies prepared to leave millions in their wills to the school. It would be better, he was told, not to remind the older alumni now that the school welcomed Catholics, Blacks, Jews, even atheists, and perhaps some day soon, young women. The old boys preferred to believe that the school was still lily white and Protestant. The less said in print about the changes since World War II the better. The editorial policy of the BULLETIN was to sustain the illusion that Kensington remained the same school they had attended in their youth.

Bartley was crushed by the rejection. He began to feel that the whole project was folly, perhaps even a ruse by Woody to re-direct Bartley's disappointment about deciding against law school into something positive for the school. Bartley abandoned the project immediately and stuffed the folders of evidence and his essay into the back of his file cabinet. The tapes and transcriptions of his oral history he filed away in the archives. Who cared about Kensington School anyway beyond a handful of alumni? It was not a national school, would probably never amount to anything as an important educational institution. It was still primarily a pastoral retreat for the children of the wealthier residents of the fertile crescent: a wonderful place to spend one's adolescent years before entering Yale or Williams and beginning the genuinely serious preparation for the real business of living.

Then several months later in the winter issue of the Kensington BULLETIN appeared an edited selection of excerpts from the oral history, a compilation put together by Ackerman. Most of the contributors were older alumni whose testimony about the good old days at Kensington was like their lives—arrogant, self-indulgent and self-congratulatory. Accompanying the excerpts was a flattering profile of Bartley, "The first historian of Kensington School," by Malcolm Woodbridge. In the profile all of Bartley's work on "Project Past" (a title he had never heard of before) along with a list of his contributions to the school—his participation in curriculum, dormitory, disciplinary, minority students, and scheduling committees; his three awards as best teacher; his service to the school in athletics and the dormitory; his chairmanship of the history department. Woody's remarks were embarrassing, but the excerpts themselves were an outrage, and he could say nothing because he had been compromised by his own vanity and his loyalty to the Headmaster.

What Ackerman had culled from Bartley's interviews was a kind of mosaic of quotes that characterized the old order at Kensington as an often arbitrary, authoritarian, cruel, often brutal atmosphere, but one to be admired for its firmness and disciplinary toughness. The masters were often distant and strict, sticklers for detail, the rules rigid and confining, the food terrible, the grades unfair. Football practice without modern protective equipment was life threatening, and everyone had to play. There were anecdotes about corporal punishment, the mockery and insults by teachers, the viciousness of peer competition, the hazing of new boys by the unofficial Sixth Form "Committee," the humiliation of being called before the Headmaster and faculty if the number of demerits became too high, and of the snow shoveling and leaf raking and floor scrubbing one would have to do to reduce the demerits in order to be eligible for a rare weekend permission. And all of this was portrayed as good for the strength of character it produced. Some of the contributors sentimentalized the harshness as necessary for the development of youth.

There were some memories of kindness, generosity, compassion, fairness, concern,. Lasting friendships. There was nothing about the progressive nature of the school from the very beginning when the first headmaster shared his authority with the faculty and over the years distributed power to students who could through their own council require the faculty to vote on their proposals. Kensington had been their concentration camp, Marine boot training, reform school, and monastic retreat all rolled into one, and it was the school's deliberate harshness that had turned them into men, producing a toughness and discipline that enabled them to compete in the dog-eat-dog world of laissez faire competition. The effect of the article was a kind of shamelessly sentimental eulogy to punitive education.

But what outraged Bartley the most was not the dishonesty of distorted memory. He knew the selections were slanted, that there was ample testimony in his tapes of the fairness and understanding of progressive and humane masters and wives that made the isolation and loneliness of fifteen year olds bearable. No, it wasn't the omissions and selective slanting that desecrated his research the most. It was the editorial implication that punishment and cruelty and brutality had produced lives of success and achievement.

And Bartley knew better, knew that most of those quoted were frauds like most members of their social class. Few of them had made their own money. They had earned their money the old fashioned way; they had inherited it or married into it or acquired it by working their way into the network begun at Kensington and expanded at the likes of Yale or Princeton. They didn't compete in an inclusive, open market of laissez faire competition. They simply took for their own the privileges of power and position and wealth of a closed order of inherited wealth, interconnected families, insider trading, and country club and old school cronyism.

What was actually true was that they luxuriated in the harshness of their Kensington years as evidence of their superiority. The article perpetuated the myth of a generation of privilege and attributed the success of a social class based upon inherited wealth to Draconian educational practices. The article was aimed at the "fat cat" alumni in their sixties and seventies.

It was all lies, lies about the self-made nature of their power, lies about the past, lies about the school's former masters, about its reactionary origins. Bartley was ashamed that his name had been associated with the article. He resented what Ackerman had done. He resented Woodbridge's flattering portrait of him, he resented the lies, and most of all, he was surprised to discover, that he deeply resented not the individual students in his classes but the social class of inherited wealth from which they came and for which Kensington existed from the very beginning. The winter following the publication of the excerpts from the "oral history" were bitter ones for Bartley. He began to feel as estranged from the school and its past as he had in those first few years when he wore a middle class, middle western chip on his shoulder, resenting the East and all the empty formalism it stood for.

Then, within a few months, everything took a quirky turn, or was it as Bartley later suspected, simply the working of one of Woodbridge's stratagems. That spring the issue of coeducation had to be confronted for the good of the school. They were running thin with the kind of students attractive to the top colleges. The competition for high quality students was becoming intense at the third and fourth form levels. They were losing qualified boys who were choosing to attend coeducational schools.

Woodbridge could no longer hold off the pressure to face the issue of coeducation. The students wanted it. Recent alumni wanted it. Woodbridge wanted it. Progressive members of the board stated categorically that the school had a choice—admit girls or become second rate. Inflation and a mediocre performance of the portfolio virtually dictated the need to increase the size of the school but to increase only with males might mean accepting remedial students from the application pool—students who might not even be good athletes.

That winter the Board of Trustees authorized the Headmaster to form a committee to investigate the educational advisability of coeducation and to make a recommendation first to the faculty for its vote and, in turn, if it passed, to the Board for a final decision. Woodbridge formed the committee from all constituent groups—trustees, students, alumni,—but the committee was to be dominated by the faculty, and the chairmanship would be a faculty member. At meetings that winter of trustees and alumni he asked for suggestions. He polled informally the students and faculty. His choice was easy. The trustees and alumni, even the reactionary element already dead set against the move, wanted the "historian," whatever his name was, they couldn't remember, but the one who did the interviewing for the school's oral history. They trusted his objectivity. The students and his colleagues wanted Bartley also because they knew he was for coeducation and they trusted his subjectivity to produce the results they already enthusiastically endorsed.

And so he became the chairman and steered the committee through the research, visited schools that had gone coeducational in recent years, listened to testimony for and against, and with Bill Henry's editorial help wrote the document, overwhelmingly approved by the committee, and then presented it orally to the faculty and later the trustees. He made a tour of regional alumni meetings with Woodbridge, speaking in favor of his report and drumming up support and subsequent pressure on the trustees. He had been the point man and he had taken all the flak, even hate mail. The trustees had been sitting on the recommendation for almost a year now, but since the day his report was forwarded from the faculty to the trustees, he had been out of the loop, and probably didn't figure importantly in the headmaster's plans for implementation.

When Bartley finished re-reading the document, it confirmed in his mind the objective nature of his view of the school. He cringed at some of his sentences and quietly acknowledged that Ackerman's criticism was not unwarranted. But he knew he was right. The school had changed profoundly over the years and during his tenure, broadening the social basis of opportunity for virtually anyone who was qualified to attend Kensington. The school had changed to accommodate Jack Bartley's liberal and reforming values, his Jeffersonian vision, and had encouraged him to be the instrument of that transformation. During his fifteen years he had participated importantly in the dismantling of one of the white, male, Protestant, chauvinist bastions of economic power and social exclusivity, though he knew in his heart that the changes he had supported, trickling down from the private, often prestigious colleges and universities that Kensington served, would have occurred if Jack Bartley had never heard of Kensington School.

*   *   *   *

The next evening after dinner Karen went to choir practice and Bartley stayed home with the girls and later put them to bed. At about 9 o'clock he was alone in his study preparing for classes when the phone rang.

"Pierson," he continued to read the lesson he was preparing.

"Mr. Bartley."

"Speaking."

"This is Elizabeth Powell. Jennifer's mother."

He closed the book and sat at attention in his chair.

"Yes."

"Could you tell me the arrangements and security you make at Kensington for female guests at your spring dance?"

"Well, I don't know exactly what you mean, but the boys clear out of a large dormitory. Some of the younger boys take weekends, others sleep in the common rooms of other dorms or double up with friends in other dorms. The girls are assigned rooms, mostly doubles, in the empty dorm. This year it will be Pierson. My wife and another faculty wife will sleep in the dorm with the girls."

"What must Jennifer do to be officially invited?"

"She has already been invited. If she has your permission, Karen, my wife, will write a note to Randall Hall asking their permission for her to leave on Friday afternoon. Karen will also write to Jennifer. Peter is responsible for her transportation. The Kensington bus is going to pick up a group of girls in Hartford. If she can't make the connection, someone here will pick her up at the train station in New London. We guarantee safe delivery."

He laughed self-consciously. Mrs. Powell did not respond for several moments.

"What kind of activities are planned? Friday to Sunday afternoon is a long time to maintain responsible supervision."

"We simply follow our normal time schedule. Friday night, after a student concert, check-in is 10:30. On Saturday night after the dance, check-in is 12:30. No one may leave the dormitory after check-in until breakfast, and a security guard patrols the dorm area all night. Everyone attends classes on Saturday morning. There are athletics all afternoon, a tea, then dinner, then the dance. If a couple leave the dance before 12:15, they must check out and must check into separate dorms within fifteen minutes. Chapel is optional on Sunday morning. Jennifer can get a ride to mass with Mr. Le Clair or Mr. Delaney."

He literally bit his tongue as he waited for her response. She was about to relent. She had called to give permission for Jennifer, and he had to resist a quarrel with her.

"I've been reading your school catalogue. It says that you, that is the faculty at Kensington, take the responsibility of *in loco parentis* seriously."

"We try to represent in our rules and guidelines the values of the families that have traditionally attended Kensington."

"If I give permission for Jennifer to spend a weekend at Kensington, am I correct in assuming that you as a substitute parent will represent my values, which may very well be different from what passes for values among the parents of Kensington students? I know several Kensington parents and we really don't share the same values. Indeed, I share very little with them. I probably share very little with you even though we had similar educational backgrounds."

"I suspect we have lived very different lives."

"Mr. Bartley, I am having great difficulty controlling myself in this conversation. I find your letter both presumptuous and arrogant. You have no business interfering in my relationship with my daughter. You are not on the faculty of Randall Hall."

The force of her anger had moved her to confrontation quicker than he had expected. He was having difficulty with her voice. He tried to imagine what she looked like. The voice was deliberate and precise, but there seemed to be a note of repressed hysteria below the surface. He tried to think of someone from his own past experience that he could visualize as Mrs. Powell so that he could relate to some form of flesh and blood and not just the abstracted moral posture of a disembodied voice. He could think only of Isobel Broderick, a tall, severe, religious young woman who attended Holy Angels Academy, the sister school of Christian Brothers Academy. She lived in his neighborhood and they had attended parochial school together. In high school they had occasionally commuted together on the bus, separating downtown where each transferred in a different direction. In their senior year, she asked him to attend her senior prom. He didn't want to go, but his mother insisted and he acquiesced. He had chalked it up as an act of charity.

There were four couples in Isobel Broderick's group. Bartley felt uncomfortable. The boys were cordial, painfully polite. He was the only outsider in what apparently was a close knit group, but he had a good time at the dance. There was much humor and much natural, unaffected good will.

Afterwards, in their formals and summer tuxedos they drove to a nearby lake, where someone had reserved four canoes. They paddled to the middle of the moonlit lake, a couple in each canoe, and formed a circle. Bartley held the stern of his canoe to the bow of another. What followed was an awesome exhibition of faith, a faith far more profound than anything he had ever felt. A voice in the darkness began with the sign of the cross and proceeded to lead the group in the rosary. Each person except him (they had delicately sensed that he would be uncomfortable) led the others in a decade until they had gone through two mysteries—joyful and triumphant. Each prefaced his decade with a prayerful reflection about peace in the world or love for the poor or caring for the sick—in fact, they had integrated the mysteries with the corporal works of mercy and the Sermon on the Mount. Later, Isobel thanked him for coming and explained that the group had been together for two years and that they made every social event an occasion of prayer.

Although it probably wasn't fair to the spirit of Isobel Broderick, Bartley decided that he could deal more realistically and more sympathetically with Mrs. Powell if he thought of her as Isobel Broderick grown sternly mature and probably embittered by the changes wrought by Vatican II. At one point in the conversation he almost called her Isobel.

"Mrs. Powell, I didn't want to write that letter, but I felt that you had punished both of them enough. I know Peter Colby to be a fine young man. You have every right to judge an action, but you have no business persisting in magnifying the seriousness of that action beyond what is warranted."

"I don't plan to argue with you now. I have called to grant Jennifer permission to attend Kensington's spring dance under the conditions of security you have described. I shall put it in writing to her dormitory supervisor at Randall Hall."

"You are very kind to do so, Mrs. Powell."

"I am not kind at all. Compassion is not my motive. Some portions of your letter are more to the point, Mr. Bartley. I have often wondered how you professional forgivers can be so cruel when you need to be."

"I did what I felt I had to do. I said what might be true. If it isn't true, then you have no problem."

"How did you express it? Let me find the passage here."

He heard the rumple of paper.

"You really don't have to quote my letter to me. I remember what I wrote."

"Incidentally, I reject your contention that I should have discouraged their relationship or that I provided in my home the unchaperoned occasion of their sin. Oh, I can't find the line I wanted to quote. Your phraseology was effective, however—something about the fact that I was more interested in confirming Jennifer's social class than her Catholicism. It won't make any difference to you, but I gave in to Mr. Powell in the matter of Jennifer's education. She never had formal

Catholic instruction beyond the fourth grade. You were correct in your speculation that I have been remiss. I have failed to do my duty, but what I failed to do or recognize has nothing to do with your letter."

"I'm sorry I wrote that. I was angry. I thought you were being unfair. They have been punished enough."

"Punishment has not been my purpose. I have needed time to sort matters out. I was not ready to answer Peter's letter of apology. I'm afraid I have been guilty of wishful thinking and denial and serious lapses of memory and misjudgment. I wanted to believe that Jennifer's friendship with Peter was innocent and would continue to be so until it would end this spring. They have not seen each other often in the past two years and she was so happy and secure with him that I did not discourage them. Secondly, I have misjudged the importance of this final dance to them. I had forgotten how important these social occasions are to young people, but most importantly I have underestimated Jennifer's growing independence and her resentment of my authority. She has been growing up at school away from home for three years now and has achieved a strong sense of who she is and what she wants. Until this episode, I have been insensitive to her maturity. When she called me last night and informed me that Peter was going to visit her at Randall Hall on the weekend of the spring dance, I sensed her resentment and her resolve to continue the friendship to spite me. I must concede I was proud of her spirit.

"My problem was how to change my mind and save face. I thought of your letter which I had almost burned and decided to negotiate with you and let you take the credit for interceding."

"May I tell Peter that you are sending a letter of consent to Randall Hall so that he can get on with the arrangements for her transportation and a place in the dorm?"

"Yes, but we are not finished with the negotiations. My permission for Jennifer to attend the spring dance at Kensington has a provision, a condition. Since you have chosen to interfere, I feel you have a certain responsibility in the matter. I understand you were raised Catholic and attended parochial schools through high school. I assume you know the church's position on sexual morality."

"More or less. I'm not an expert."

"Since, according to your letter, I have been remiss in providing my daughter with an adequate background in the Church's moral teachings, I would like you as a teacher and a more or less Catholic to provide her with some instruction."

"Me! When? I have no opportunity?"

"When Jennifer arrives on the Friday evening of the dance weekend, I want you to sit down with her and her young man and clarify my beliefs. I want you to represent my values *in loco parentis*."

"That's the condition, the provision you require for your permission for her to attend."

"Yes, Mr. Bartley. That's the provision. It follows logically from your letter."

"I suppose it does. All right. I accept."

"And I want the instruction to be a fair representation of what I believe in tone and content."

"I will do what you ask."

"I guess that's all I have to say. I want to thank you for taking Jennifer back to Randall Hall last Sunday. It was a long trip. I would like to reimburse you for your time and gas if I may."

"You may not."

"Then I have nothing more to say."

He sat silently for several minutes, trying to grasp fully what he had agreed to do. Then he went into the dorm and asked a student to find Peter and ask him to come to the study. Peter appeared in the open door in a few minutes.

"Mrs. Powell called and has given her permission for Jennifer to attend the dance. You better get busy tomorrow arranging transportation and getting her name in to the Dance Committee. It's late in the season."

"Did she say anything more? Why did she change? I can't believe it."

"Well, it's official. I told you she'd come around sooner or later. She just needed time."

*　　*　　*　　*

Dance Weekend began at the noon school meeting when George Macrakis made his traditional announcement.

"As the drunken porter in *Macbeth* instructs us in the matter of too much drink, it provokes and it unprovokes. Like too much drink, I once again must play my role as an equivocator with lechery this weekend. As a member of the dance committee, I have helped provoke the desire (laughter, shouts of approval); as officer of the day, the surrogate of Headmaster Woodbridge in matters of the old morality, I must, alas, take away the performance (boos, hisses, general cacophony). Please turn in all weekend permission slips to me before lunch." (Stomping of feet, rhythmic clapping)

Bartley met the first busload of girls behind Pierson. Karen greeted them in the dorm and showed each girl her room. After they settled in, Karen served tea and cookies in the common room while the girls waited to be picked up by their dates, some of whom were still at sports practice. Bartley took one group of girls on a brief tour. He couldn't believe the beauty of the campus. Everything was perfect: a windless, blue sky, dogwood and apple in bloom, all the trees sprouting tender new leaves, the trimmed grass a rich new green.

Later in his study he delivered his lecture to Peter and Jennifer shortly after she arrived. They didn't pay much attention to him, so absorbed were they in each other, holding hands and smiling at him occasionally. He told them that because he had intervened and supported them, he felt responsible for their behavior. They nodded that they understood.

He felt awkward, uncomfortable. He stood in precisely the same relationship to Peter and Jennifer as Brother Augustine had stood to him and his mocking classmates over twenty years before, but he defended the traditional sexual morality fairly and objectively, for the sake of the spirit of the "new law," he assured himself. He really didn't believe that any sex education was effective except perhaps the frightening VD movies he had witnessed in the service, but the government's purpose had been one of sanitation not morality.

He didn't mention anything about the fires of hell or eternal damnation, about the absolute prohibitions of divine law. He stood before them as an historian and rational humanist, outlining the economic origins of deferred marriage in a society of increasingly complex technological change. The long period of adolescence in America had historical origins in the necessity for a protracted period of educational preparation before young adults could enter the work force and afford to marry. Though many young people were physiologically ready for childbearing, they were not ready psychologically or economically until well into their twenties.

He spoke to them about the terrible psychological price young people must pay for intimacy at too early an age, the stress of separation, the certain change each would undergo, the inevitable rejection that one of the partners must suffer, the guilt of the other. He spoke of the fear of pregnancy, the risks of birth control devices and pills, the disapproval of society, the terrible guilt of abortion, the high risks of divorce if early intimacy led to early marriage.

He didn't tell them of the practical value of prohibitive sexual morality that he had experienced growing up. He remembered how his imagination had endowed each young woman, however plain, with inestimable worth because each possessed an absolute treasure denied until marriage. Each touching of hands at the Catholic Youth Center juke box dances or the slight brushing of bodies on a crowded bus, the trailing scent of perfume, the thrill of approving eyes became sources of exquisite delight, harbingers of an incomprehensible joy that would be his as the pure gift of the matrimonial state.

*   *   *   *

"Hey, stranger, where you been keeping yourself?" he shouted as he approached.

After his last bus run, shuttling students and their dates to the crew lake, he found Karen sitting alone on a blanket about midway along the shore of the finger-shaped lake. From her vantage point, a small wooded knoll that jutted about twenty feet above the water line, she could see the entire race course. To their left about a hundred yards away was the boat house, a red barn on the edge of the water, and the launching docks for the shells. Beyond that was a copse of regularly spaced red pines that served as a parking and picnic area; and beyond that was the open field adjacent to the finish line where clusters of students and dates now sat eating, waiting for the first race.

"Hi. Thought you wouldn't make it. The girls couldn't wait so we ate."

"Where are they?"

"With the Sanders down by the docks watching them launch shells, hanging around poor Peter, I guess, driving him and Jennifer to distraction. I think the first boat is in the water now so they should be coming back soon. Except that he can't constantly be touching Jennifer, he's probably relieved to get out on the water to escape from Annie for a while. Did you get anything to eat?"

"A piece of chicken, the last of a little potato salad, and a brownie. Was there anything else? They were already putting everything away."

"You got the essentials."

She moved over to make room for him on the blanket. He sat down and looked to his right where he could see, at the head of the lake, the shells darting back and forth like water bugs. He watched the white hulls and brief wakes of the coaches' motor launches, circling among the crews, the drone of their engines barely audible across the water. Occasionally the unintelligible sound of a voice magnified by a megaphone drifted toward them over the sound of the engines.

"Did you sleep much last night?"

"They settled down about midnight and quit talking about three. One thing won't change when and if we go co-ed."

"What's that?"

"The language of girls in dormitories after midnight is not significantly more elevated than that of boys."

"A lot of sexist fictions are going to go by the wayside, I suppose, when we discover boys and girls are persons."

"Some differences are not fictional," she laughed.

"Differences that I did not experience last night." He put his hand on her knee.

She pushed his hand away.

"You'll have to wait until tomorrow night, I'm afraid."

"I'll forget what sex is by then. I'll forget how to do it." He pretended to pout.

"No, you won't. You can watch the young couples clinging to each other at the dance tonight and then as you lie awake in our bed tonight missing me, you can open the window and listen to the girls' naughty words to each other."

"Oh, pooh. That's no fun anymore. It used to be. Now most of the younger faculty wives use the F word, as Annie calls it, all the time in ordinary conversation. It's been trivialized by excessive repetition. I yearn for the good old days when it was used sparingly for emphasis. But, alas, another old custom bites the dust."

"You're beginning to sound like the creeping conservative Bill Henry claims you are."

"I suppose he's right. I give up fighting it. I remember the first time I heard a woman use the F word in a mixed crowd at a party in Cambridge in '61 or '62, just before I met you. She was a graduate student at Harvard, from Berkeley as I remember. I was thrilled and shocked and spent the whole evening maneuvering about the room to be in earshot of her voice. I was such a naive, silly innocent from the Midwest, even though I'd been in the service."

"You ought to write a paper on it, Jack. *The Decline and Fall of the F Word as Obscenity Symbol* or something like that."

"I'll work it up into thesis statement or abstract and file it along with my incomplete dissertation and all the other harebrained writing projects I've abandoned."

They watched the first boats leave the dock at a warm-up pace across the lake before heading to the starting line where the second and third boats had already assembled. The school owned the south side of the lake, but there were several privately owned summer cottages across the lake, their docks spaced widely along the shore.

"Did you drive over?" he asked.

"No, we hitched a ride with Maggie Henry."

"Do you want to go back with her or catch a ride with me?"

"I suppose the girls would prefer the bus. When do you make the first run?"

"I take the baseball team and dates back right after the first boats finish."

"Here they come!"

"Who?" He looked toward the starting line, expecting to see the rapid flashing of blades of the opening sprint. She pointed to the left.

"The girls."

He turned and saw Annie and Rachel emerging from behind the boathouse into an open field. Annie led the way, walking briskly along a path hidden by the shoots of rye and timothy. Rachel was running to try to keep up but was already falling behind.

"If you watch the girls for a while until I finish the shuttle runs, I'll take them the rest of the afternoon and you can take a nap. I've a date with Annie to watch the varsity baseball game."

"I don't think Rach will be very interested in a baseball game."

"Oh, we'll think of something to amuse her or else we'll bribe her with something."

"How have you and Annie been doing?"

"O.K. I guess. She hasn't shown up to practice since our second game. I take that back. She came to one game a few weeks ago and watched from the top of the hill beyond the third baseline. She left in the third inning. She didn't come near the field or the bench. I tell her about the team every so often, that acquiring Mitch Morgan has turned us around, but she doesn't seem interested. She likes to watch varsity games with me though, the real Kensington, not the stupid third form pathetics."

"Oh, Jack, forget it. You weren't meant to be Annie's athletic role model. You're her father. Someday she'll find something she admires in you to identify with. Have patience."

"I don't care if she never identifies with me. I don't want her to be a history teacher or a coach. I just don't want her to be ashamed of me, to think I'm some kind of joke."

"She doesn't, Jack. She has more common sense than that. She knows your good qualities."

"Like cheating at golf."

"Now there's an opportunity for you," she laughed. "Start playing according to the rules and you can become her moral ideal."

"And end up shooting over a hundred for the rest of my life. No thanks. I'd rather cheat."

Annie waved to them from the distance. She wore red shorts and white knee socks and a light blue T-shirt. Rachel was well behind her, walking slowly now and stopping occasionally to pick wild flowers in the field. Annie was flushed and panting when she climbed the small incline to the knoll.

"Peter's boat is in the water. Let's go to the finish line and see the end of the 3rd boat race. They're about ready to start, but we'll have to hurry to get a start on them."

"O.K., Pal." Bartley jumped up. "I'm ready to go."

"You two go ahead." Karen said. "I'd rather stay here and watch the beauty of both boats rather than have everything ruined by somebody winning."

"Don't you care if Kensington wins?" Annie put her hands on her hips.

"No, Annie. Just so both boats row well. It's one of the most beautiful things I've ever seen in sports. I hate to see it ruined by competition. From here the boats seem to be tied for the whole race. It's only at the finish line that everything is ruined."

"Don't you care if Peter wins?" She stamped one foot.

"That's O.K., Annie," Bartley interrupted, "she doesn't have to come. Your mother's an aesthete. She cares more about process than product. Now, you and me, we're bottom liners. We care about results."

Rachel arrived and dropped down to her knees on the blanket and dove forward into Karen's lap, offering a small bouquet of flowers held in one hand.

"I'm pooped."

Suddenly, they heard a small roar from up the lake and an excited voice in the distance shouting.

"The third boats are underway." Bartley looked across the water to the starting line. The oars of the two boats were beating furiously, but from the distance it seemed as though they were standing still.

"Let's go, Daddy. If we don't start now, they'll beat us. They'll beat us unless we run," Annie begged.

"It's too late now, Annie. Besides, I've just eaten. We'll stay with Mom for this race, see it the way she wants to see it. Then we'll head down to see the finishes of the second and first boats."

"But there's nothing to see here, Daddy. You can't even tell who's ahead here."

"That's your mother's point, Annie. To her its just the rowing that counts not the winning."

"And since when are you a bottom liner, Jack Bartley. You who, when we were going together, disavowed all competition as fascist. You hated football and boxing, even tennis. How do you dare claim to be a bottom liner? You have lost more games than any coach in Kensington's history. You above all should care more about process than results politically and practically."

"Well, I've changed my mind. Competition can be healthy. It can bring out good qualities in young people that might otherwise be unrealized."

"Nonsense, Jack, and you know it. Eight boys are going to row their hearts out for a mile and they're going to achieve a lovely synchronized harmony and grace and rhythm and when they get to the end of the race, one boat is going to be about two feet ahead of the other, and four boys are going to be deliriously happy and four boys are going to feel they've failed. Is that fair? No one should lose if he rows well. The mindless emphasis on competition ruins most of what we do in life. We come to idealize physical power as a solution to human problems. Everyone who is not number one is a loser. I'll watch the race from here, thank you, and if it seems one of the boats is winning, I'll just move to the left or the right until the boats look even again."

"Me, too," Rachel said, nodding agreement. "I'll stick with Mommy. I identify with Mommy."

"You don't even know what she's talking about," Annie said. "And it's 'I identify' not 'I dentify.' You are really dumb."

"I am not dumb. You always say that. Besides, you don't know what she's saying either."

"Yes, I do."

"Well, it doesn't make any difference. I don't care if I don't know what she's saying or not. As long as I don't have to walk all the way down to the end of the lake again. I've been there three times already and I'm pooped."

"I just want you to know, Karen, I take exception to what you said about my losing record. It's because of my losing record that I'm a believer in competition. Think of Bill Henry for a minute. He coached varsity baseball for over twenty years and had winning teams almost every year. Sometimes he lost only one or two games a year. Now he's quit coaching. What does he remember? His winning games? Not on your life. He's won so many games he can't tell one from the other. No, he doesn't remember games he's won. He'll be haunted for the rest of his life by the games he's lost, those few games that ruined otherwise perfect seasons. Now, take my record for the past ten years. I've lost so many games they're all one indistinguishable blur. But the few games I've won I can remember every detail—every hit, every run, every good catch, every smart play. When I retire from coaching, I'll have nothing but happy memories."

"So help me, Jack, sometimes you absolutely boggle me with your powers of bad reasoning."

"I know it boggles me too, especially lately. Each year I hear myself sounding less like Jefferson and more like Franklin. I'm sounding less like a Man of Reason and more like a Reasonable Man. It's depressing. Besides, you're not being fair. Those are my ideas about process and competition and fascism. I had those ideas first."

"You spoke those ideas first. You didn't have them first. I already believed them when we met. The only reason you think they were your ideas first is that you never gave me a chance to say anything when we were going together."

"That's not fair either. I couldn't help myself. I wanted you to know everything about me, everything I believed. All I had to court you with were my ideas and dreams and I didn't think there was enough time left in the universe to get everything out that was inside me, and I didn't think I had a chance if I didn't get everything out so that you knew me, who I was inside."

"Here come the third boats, Daddy," Annie shouted as the shells approached in invisible lanes, each cox steering toward huge round targets a half mile away. Bartley watched them go by, dead even, the four young men in each shell leaning forward, stretching, dipping, pulling, then drawing the handles of the oars into their chests. As they finished the stroke and began stretching forward again, their seats sliding backward, it seemed to Bartley that the shell stopped for a fraction of a second though he knew that was an illusion. When he looked only at the flashing oar blades, the shells moved uniformly and steadily, the oar blades entering the water without a splash, timed to enter at the speed of the shell. Karen was right. It was a thing of beauty ruined by the finish line and the declaration of a winner. As the boats passed, moving to the left toward the finish line, he could hear the rising sound of shouts of encouragement along the shore.

"They're past us now, Daddy," Annie shouted and grabbed his hand. "Let's go now so we get there in plenty of time for the next race."

"O.K., Pal, let's go." He stood up. She ran ahead of him down the path toward the boat house, and he began to follow her. After several steps, he shouted to Annie to go ahead and that he would catch up. He turned back to the top of the knoll and spoke to Karen.

"I still believe that process is more important than product and that the idealization or worship of physical power is at bottom fascist. I still believe that no matter what I've become."

He broke off when he realized he was begging, pleading his case, and turned around and hurried down the path after Annie, whom he could see in the distance already past the boat house about to enter the pine grove.

*   *   *   *

The decorative scheme of the dance held in the gym was "Old South." One of the student members of the Dance Committee from South Carolina had Spanish moss shipped from home which was hung from the imitation branches of live oaks constructed by several members of a section of fifth form art as a group project. They also painted a life-size facade of an old manse complete with columns on an enormous sheet of muslin and hung it across one wall. A rotating spot with yellow, pink, and blue gelatins played across the design. The orchestra was arranged in the foreground on a low platform creating the effect that the dance was on the lawn, but the soft and elegant moonlight and magnolias effect was diminished by the pulsing strobe lights in two of the far corners.

Early in the planning stages of the dance, Bartley had heard rumblings from a few of his Black students against the theme, implying the Afro Society might boycott the dance and might sponsor its own dance in Camden Commons, using a slave quarters decorative motif, but the rumblings disappeared a few weeks before the dance. When Bartley and Karen arrived to chaperone the early shift, they were greeted by a receiving line of Afro-Kensingtonians dressed in the pure white antebellum suits of plantation owners and their dates, each elegantly attired in a scarlet ball gown.

As usual the hit of the dance was the Chaplain, the Rev. Hal Shephard (the Whiffenpoof theologian according to George Macrakis) and his wife Barbara, who were *ex officio* members of the Dance Committee. They danced every dance, every style including the tango and the mambo, disco, lindy hop, rock, but it was their floating grace in the waltz that generated a circle of admiring students. At one point he sang a medley of Cole Porter hits. The Bartleys left just before intermission as the Shephards were leading the growing bunny hop chain.

CHAPTER 7

▼

"Did you win?" Henry asked, handing Bartley a glass of bourbon and ice. Bartley had returned on the bus from Newport at six-thirty, a half hour after the Trustee-Faculty spring cocktail party had begun. Karen had arrived earlier with Maggie and Bill Henry. Bartley said hello to her and Maggie, paid his respects to the Woodbridges, avoided trustees who might be unoccupied, and found the bar in Woody's study. He also found Bill Henry, who not wanting to get far from the martinis, had assumed temporarily the role of unofficial assistant bartender, while the professional bartender circulated among guests.

"Saturday afternoon is no time to try to make time through Providence, I can tell you. I can't wait until the final section of the interstate is completed. Can I have some more ice, a tall glass, and more bourbon, Bill?"

"Bad day, Jack?"

"No. No. A wonderful day. Had to wait for the varsity and JV games to finish since we were sharing the bus with them, so after our game I took a hike down to one of the beaches. Low tide, lovely walk. Watched the sailboats tack around a buoy. No, Bill. To the contrary, a beautiful day."

Henry poured the short drink into a taller glass, added more bourbon and ice, and handed it back, and asked again

"Did you win, Jack? Did you win?"

"Varsity took them 12-7. Decent game. Mediocre pitching though."

"I already heard that the varsity won. Did your team win?"

"What a season we had, Bill. Ever since I made that trade with Sam and picked up a catcher, a little guy, named Mitch Morgan. Tough, lots of heart, and a helluva catcher and team leader. Whole season turned around. Began to have sharp fielding drills. Worked every day, most of each practice on fielding, situations and bunting. Deferred working on hitting until we were respectable in the field. By then this gawky kid with the strong arm, Chalmers Eliot—can you believe that name?—had learned to throw the ball near the plate. We had lost four games by huge scores—suddenly we were in every game, even against Kingswood. I've never beaten Kingswood as you know. We lost that one by only three runs. Kids played their hearts out. Then, against weak opposition we won two. The important thing is, Bill, that we were playing baseball." He took a long swallow of his drink.

"I know your season record, Jack. Did you win today? At St. George's—our traditional rival? The place you just came from on the bus?"

Henry paused to mix martinis for a Trustee and his wife and mixed another one for himself as he bantered with the couple about their son, whom Henry had taught several years before.

Bartley stood to the side of the portable bar and stared at the gold-fish in a lighted aquarium against a wall behind the bar. One of the goldfish, lazily circulating among the bubbles, colorful stones, and coral trees, stopped abruptly with his nose against the glass and seemed to be staring at him. Bartley looked away and surveyed the room. It was a high-ceilinged study, its walls dominated by dark stained book-shelves. Directly across from where he was standing, a log fire burned in a massive fieldstone fireplace. Two dark green leather chairs faced the fire. Between them was a large, round oak dining table. Its legs had been shortened to form a coffee table. Bartley walked across the room and collapsed into one of the chairs and sat, quietly observing the painting above the mantle, a portrait of a Yankee Clipper underway in heavy seas. He reflected on the sense of satisfaction, of peace he always felt after the last out of the last game of the baseball season. The kids had played a helluva game. He was proud of them, of the season, of himself.

After the game he didn't want to talk to anyone. He just wanted to replay it in his imagination, over and over, again, so he took a hike to the beach and walked the hard-packed sand of the low tide for over an hour, watching the sailboats off shore, recalling each hit, each out, each catch, each run. He had sat alone near the front of the bus after declining Sam Arnold and Bob Bennett's invitation to sit further back with them. He wanted these moments alone, to savor this game, to reflect upon the season, in many ways his best ever. He had done the most with the least.

The Rhode Island countryside was as beautiful as he had ever seen it, especially the fields and woods to his left, dropping gently away to Naragansett Bay. The view from the Mount Hope Bridge was magnificent. Even the urban blight of Providence seemed quaint, suggesting the charming and antique ambience of another day, of old New England, here in the spiritual home of Separatism—America's finest moment of individualism, when Roger Williams affirmed a more profound rejection of authority than even Thoreau and Emerson could manage in their less authoritarian age almost two centuries later. It had been a perfect day.

"Did you win?" He heard Bill Henry's voice behind him. Bartley held his glass up above his head without turning around.

"I'll have another drink, Bill. The first was kind of light."

Henry took his glass, returned to the bar and poured a double shot into the glass and added ice and water. The trustee parents had left. The bartender had brought back a trayful of empty glasses and was busy mixing new orders. Henry returned across the room and placed the glass back in Bartley's hand, which he had kept in the air above his head after Henry had taken it. Henry sat in the other leather chair and watched Bartley drain half the glass.

"Trouble with you, Bill, is you always ask the wrong questions. You've got a good mind. I appreciate your tutelage. You're an expert at answering questions. But you still have to learn how to ask the right questions. When someone else asks the questions, you're a wizard at answering."

"You want the old Grantland Rice bit, eh, Jack. It's not whether you won or lost. It's how you played the game. Right? How did you play the game?"

"No, Bill, it's not winning or losing. It's not even how we played the game that matters on third form baseball. On third form baseball the only questions, the crucial question is 'Did you play the game at all or a reasonable facsimile thereof? Philosophically speaking, winning or losing are irrelevant issues and that old fiction that winning at games leads to winning in life is bunk, and you know it. Or the old bull that losing games gracefully prepares a youngster for adversity. All nonsense. When I attended good old Christian Brothers Academy, we had this monstrous football team in my senior year. Beat the hell out of everyone by forty or fifty points. We were twice as big, twice as fast. Trounced this little coeducational Catholic school, Holy Spirit High School 73 to zip. Everyone went wild. The principal, Brother John, declared a holiday to celebrate. Tell me, Bill. What did our team learn that day? What did the players of Holy Spirit learn? The star of that game, an imbecilic goon, scored five touchdowns and strutted around for the whole year like a demi-god. Last I heard he was a hopeless drunk, sentenced to six months hard labor in the county jail for wife beating and child abuse. What did he learn as the star of an undefeated football team?"

"Hey, Jack. I just asked if you won. I didn't ask for your life story or a disquisition on the morality of sports. Besides, I thought you were over the adverse effects of your Catholic education."

"When I first came to Kensington, I thought coaching was a waste of time. I coached because I had to. Gradually I've become a convert, Bill. But first I had to unlearn all my hostile attitudes. Can you believe that the nuns in grade school had us praying for the success of the Notre Dame football teams each Saturday, as though God would suspend the natural order of human events in order to bolster the morale of American Catholics, as though each victory was incontrovertible proof of the superiority of Catholic theology over secularism and Protestantism. Dreadful, Bill, dreadful. When I was twelve years old, I knew that God wouldn't assist a baseball player to hit a slider because the player had etched a cross in the dust. I knew better even then. The good hitters' prayers were answered, the poor hitters' prayers went unanswered. I knew that Babe Ruth's home run records did not constitute proof of God's special endorsement of Catholics. I had to get over the metaphorical canonization of athletes and the trivialization of prayer before I could coach in good conscience. Could you sweeten this drink Bill, and pass me the cheese and crackers? I hate to drink on an empty stomach. It goes right to my head."

He didn't tell Henry how he had himself said a prayer before every quiz or test up to graduate school when he consciously broke the habit. He had received his blue books back on a midterm examination in a course on "Reconstruction and the Rise of Industrialism." On the cover of one of the blue books his professor had circled the letters J.M.J.D. that Bartley had apparently written on the upper right hand cover. Scrawled savagely below the circled letters was the sentence, "What's this, Mr. Bartley, some kind of hex?" Bartley couldn't remember having written the letters. To his knowledge, he had not written the letters (standing for Jesus, Mary, Joseph and Dominic and affixed to the top of every piece of written work he had submitted in grade school) for over ten years. He was appalled. He had written the letters, perhaps as an unconscious attempt to relieve the anxiety of the examination and he was frightened to realize how powerful the influence of his earliest years of education had been upon him.

"Sure you haven't had too much already, Jack?"

"No, no. I'm fine. A little tired is all. Be a sport, Bill, touch it up a soupcon. You didn't put much bourbon in last time. It's almost all water. I just want to sit here and relax."

Henry stood up and took Bartley's glass. He passed him the crackers and cheese from a side table and then walked slowly to the bar. He poured himself a fresh martini and began filling Bartley's glass with ice, poured in a half shot, filled the glass with water and returned with the drink and handed it to Bartley.

"Well, go ahead," Henry said as he sat down again.

"Go ahead? Where?" Bartley asked.

"Wherever you're going until you feel you're ready to tell me whether you won or not. I can wait. We've got all evening. Sooner or later I'll get a blow by blow account of your victory or defeat. It might as well be later. Actually I've lost interest in your game, but I'm fascinated by how long it's going to take you to get around to telling me. Maybe you could just tell me the score and not say who won?"

"And that's another fiction, Bill. That athletics develops character in youngsters. Pure fiction, not one shred of proof for that myth. You'd swear if you listened to the jock philosophers that character can develop only under the savage tutelage of brutal taskmasters on a football field. I've always wondered how they handle the fact that most of the important qualities of civilized behavior have been carried on by women of strong character, moral integrity, and humanitarian ideals."

"I didn't say it did, Jack. I was just sitting here sipping my martini. I didn't say a word about sports molding character."

"But it does build the character of coaches. We learn patience and emotional restraint in the face of adversity or injustice. We learn that if we are going to hold young people up to high standards of performance—moral, academic, athletic—we must help them meet those standards. So far as most of my players are concerned, baseball's on the moon for them; just playing one game with minimal competence may happen once a year, maybe only once in two years. We come to understand their limitations. In time, we quit screaming at them, quit scapegoating them, quit punishing them for what they can't do yet on the diamond or in the classroom."

"I'd like to interrupt just for a moment, Jack. Get a word in edge-wise, if you don't mind," Henry spoke quietly, holding his hand up as though he were a traffic officer signaling a stop. "Often, over the years my students come back to visit. They like to come by the house on their way to Boston or New York or wherever. Sometimes they talk about their scars, but most of the time they brag about their trophies, granting me condescendingly a little reflected glory for victories they have won out there in the real world. I know I have been only one of many influences in their lives. Their gratitude is flattering but essentially bogus. But the fiction that I deserve some of the credit for their successes, the doctorate degrees they've earned, the books they may have written, the positions of power they have attained, is a harmless lie. I don't contradict them. They feel generous. I pretend I am honored. They go away. I usually never see them again. I know my influence was minimal.

"But, Jack, with colleagues like you it's different. I took you under my wing fifteen years ago when you first arrived, unbelievably naive, poorly educated, socially gauche—a helpless rustic from the hinterlands. I tutored you, guided you, shared my wisdom and experience. I shaped you, Jack, as best I could, in my own image. Now I sit here, listening to you talk and I feel like Dr. Frankenstein. I've created a monster. You are my monster, Jack, a monster of compulsive ideological self indulgence and I am depressed when I think how you have become a living parody, a virtual mockery of my best impulses."

Bartley waited for several moments after Henry had finished talking. He drained the last of his drink, rolling the ice cubes in his glass, set the glass on the coffee table and resumed where he had left off.

"Gradually, I began to believe in athletics for everyone—the challenge it offered the better players, the sublimation of sexual energies, the physical exercise, the psychological release it offers every youngster regardless of ability. The uncoordinated and feckless learn skills, teamwork and during the rare moment when they do something right, they sense a temporary moment of power. They feel they have controlled, however briefly or precariously, their own destinies, for one play, one swing of the bat. I have seen kids who were flunking have their sense of self worth and confidence bolstered on the wrestling mat or the soccer field just enough to struggle through the Latin or math courses to earn that D-.

"I became a convert, Bill, but it wasn't until today that I understood the ultimate lesson of third form baseball. It is the game itself that is the greatest teacher, the Great Educator of youth, not the coach. And the lesson is about life, and the game itself is an imitation of life."

"You lost," Henry interrupted.

"You never lose, Bill. Just playing the game you always win something. For third form baseball, just making it through a seven inning game can be an impossible dream. My players face circumstances raw in their existential potential. We might play flawless ball for three innings—no walks or errors, and then everything might fall apart— walks, errors, bonehead throws to wrong bases. Our only consolation is that the same disaster might happen to the other team at any time. Each inning is fraught with fear and hope.

"Athletics doesn't teach the triumph of victory or the agony of defeat. It teaches humility and hope but most of all that much of the world of chance is beyond individual control. Bill, on the third form level, baseball is a philosophical experience. For each player, a ten game season is a textbook in metaphysics, each game a chapter in the gradual unfolding of a pernicious, cosmic scheme where justice and hard work and honesty and determination perish on the swing of a bat or the errant bounce of a ball."

"You lost."

"It was a beautiful game, Bill. Tight pitching duel the first three innings, no walks, no errors for either team. We got to them first in the fourth. A lead off walk and an infield single. Men on first and second, no outs. Bunted them along, bad throw pulled the first baseman off the bag. Then Morgan hit a chopper deep in the hole and it went through. Then we bunted twice, exchanging outs for runs and we were leading 3-0.

"They picked away, scored a run in the fifth and sixth, but we held them off, leading 3-2 when they came up in the last of the seventh. Eliot had pitched a whale of a game, but he was tired. They'd been getting around on him, pulling sharp grounders in the fifth and sixth and his fast ball was coming up. He had it around the knees for the first four innings, but now it was coming in belt high and fat. He walked the first batter. We got the second on a pop-up. Then they singled sharply to left, men on first and third. There was nothing we could do but let them steal second, couldn't risk letting them tie the game on a misplay.

"The next batter hit it back to Eliot who looked the runner at third back to the bag and took the easy out at first. Two outs, Bill, and their best hitter at the plate. We walked him. Now we had a force out at any bag. We wouldn't have the pressure of tagging anyone. Put the pressure back on them. The next batter had spanked the ball hard his first two times up, pulling it sharply. We shaded the third baseman in a little and over to the line. Shortstop took two steps toward the hole. Brought the first baseman down the line a little in case they tried a bunt. Second baseman played three steps closer to the bag. Left the outfield straight away and in about three or four steps. Called time-out and told Eliot to come off the bag to the right side to cover a bunt in case they tried to fool us. Told Morgan to stay near the plate. We decided to pitch the batter inside and low. Wanted him to ground to third. Our best fielder. A sharp grounder to third and all he would have to do was step on the bag.

"Got the count to 2 and 2. Batter hit the next pitch down the line. As soon as he hit it, I knew we had the game. An easy hop to my third baseman, two steps to the bag, and the ball game's over."

"Two outs, did you say, Jack?"

"Two outs."

"Everybody running?"

"Everybody running."

"Would you like me to sweeten your drink a little?"

"I'd appreciate that very much, Bill."

When Henry returned with the glass, Bartley took a long sip and then placed it on the coffee table and resumed his narrative.

"It wasn't the kid's fault. It wasn't anybody's fault. Everyone did what he should have. The left fielder finally dug the ball out of the grass along the line in shallow left. The shortstop relayed the ball home. Morgan was standing on the plate but the second runner crossed the plate a step ahead of the throw. He would have to tag the second runner anyhow once the first run scored. He didn't know that, but it didn't make any difference."

"You lost 4-3."

"Yes. With two outs, everyone was running on a ground ball."

"You didn't tell me what happened, Jack."

"It hit something, Bill. One more bounce and the ball would be in his glove. It popped over his head. He couldn't react in time. I went out after the game and tried to find the spot. Couldn't find a thing, not a dried clod of clay, no stone, no hardened lump in the turf. Afterwards we went back to the locker and changed. Then I went down to the beach and took a long walk. Low tide. Nice hard pack of sand along the water's edge. Lots of sailboats. All in all, Bill, a beautiful day."

"What you're saying is that it was a miracle that St. George's won."

"No, Bill. You have not been listening to me, you deliberate dunderhead. I'm not saying that at all. What I'm saying is that it was a miracle that we lost."

*   *   *   *

By the next morning the game and season were over emotionally and he filed them away in his memory. This, his best season ever when he had done the most with the least, would become, like his fantasies of that perfect round of golf, the stuff of winter dreams, to be retrieved from the archives of his mind on some cold and snowy January afternoon.

As the baseball season came to an end, he regretted that Annie had not shown up for practice again. He did not broach the subject of her leaving during their bedtime chats. She did not ask him about the progress of the team. They implicitly agreed upon silence. It was as though both were ashamed—she perhaps for not sticking it out, he for persisting in an illusory, almost mindless optimism and enthusiasm for his pathetic team in the face of hopeless odds.

Had she returned, she might have understood and applauded what he went on to do to make things work: his trade with Sam Arnold, the J.V. coach, for the catcher Annie had told him about; the beginning again with a scrambled lineup; his interminable infield and outfield drills; his obsession with bunting practice using the batting machine and his emphasis on getting outs as the central point of game strategy; his bizarre triple clean-up with his only hitters in the 1,3,and 9 slots. He won two games near the end of the season and she would have understood how this had been his best season ever and why in contrast to ignorant outsiders who only understood won and loss records.

He regretted most of all that she had not witnessed that last game at St. George's. She might then have come to understand how he was different from the varsity coaches with their manhood and heroes and testosterone and hair on their chests. Had she witnessed that last game she would have appreciated how his almost pathological persistence and encouragement could instill, in defiance of all the defeats, a disposition for hopefulness if not hope itself.

With the end of the baseball season, Bartley turned his energies to his final academic and dormitory duties of the school year. He finished his American history course in the middle of the Viet Nam war when he ran out of time. He conducted amicable year end department meetings. They decided the questions on the final exam and agreed upon the texts for the upcoming year.

Even before his last class meetings, he had entered that arc of time that would lead him full circle to September. He began to make out section lists for the fall term. He reviewed his notes for his first lecture and outlined the reading assignments for the first two weeks of classes. He gathered the new books the librarian had ordered for him, to be read over the summer. As archivist and official historian of Kensington School, he began to gather the documents generated throughout the school year, all except the yearbook which had been impounded because of the picture layout of the fall dance—couples on the ground covered with blankets, ostensibly trying to keep warm as they listened to an open-air rock concert. The student editorial board threatened to resign *en masse,* but when they realized that Headmaster Woodbridge would not release the books, they relented and agreed to excise the questionable page. Bartley got a copy of each version.

At the faculty meeting before exam week, the Headmaster announced that in order to reduce some of the pressures of the exams, he was going to declare a moratorium on the dress code. The faculty wrangled for over an hour about an enforceable informal dress code. Could the students come naked? Wearing jock straps? Barefoot? How about ripped jeans or bib overalls? Collarless shirts? Was not the dress code a moral issue, a matter of respect for others? Would not an informal dress code legitimatize a defiance of authority? Would it not promote self-indulgence, exhibitionism, social competition? The Headmaster created an *ad hoc* committee of volunteers, mostly the law and order wing of the faculty, and charged them to come up with an enforceable informal dress code by the first day of exams.

The history exams were on Tuesday morning. Bartley collected the blue books and disappeared that afternoon. He posted his study door with a "Do not Disturb" sign and began reading the essays. By late Wednesday afternoon he was almost done. Most of his best students had done well. Most of his poor students had done poorly. There were a few pleasant surprises, a few disappointments, but his teaching had been validated even though like most teachers he was the sole evaluator of his own performance.

That evening he attended the final meeting of the year of the Discipline Committee unless a major case occurred to a sixth former before the graduation ceremony. It would be Bartley's final meeting forever. He had negotiated a work load exchange with Headmaster Woodbridge, accepting the chairmanship of the library committee for Woody's promise that Bartley would never have to serve on the DC again. Most of the disciplinary reports from dormitory heads were accepted without debate. There were only three cases that required DC action.

They issued a committee warning to the contrite fourth former who, during a close dorm softball game, had given the faculty umpire the finger for what the boy felt was an "egregious misjudgment," the boy's own words before the committee, on a called third strike. The committee supported the Dean's Warning issued by Phillips, along with two weeks of dormitory restrictions to be served in the fall, for three fifth formers who had been deemed the ringleaders of the food riot Sunday night. It was not really a riot—just some roll tossing and the catapulting with knives of patties of butter to the ceiling where they stuck producing yellow blotches and running stains when they softened from the heat.

Sixth formers had begun to wear shorts to the formal evening meals when the weather turned warm. No one could remember the dress code governing shorts, but Dean Phillips believed the rule was Bermuda shorts with knee length stockings as per a faculty vote of spring 1956. None of the students could remember such a rule ever being enforced at Kensington and claimed that the only restriction was against sports or athletic gear. The issue was referred to the faculty by a motion that passed without debate.

A third former lost the use of his bicycle for the remainder of the year and the first two weeks of the following fall term for driving to endanger on the path between his dormitory and the Main School Building. He claimed that he had the bike under perfect control until he skidded on some feces deposited by a faculty dog on the pathway and smashed into a tree, narrowly missing two students. A faculty witness, however, testified that the boy repeatedly drove his bike beyond safe speeds because he was almost always late to class. Dean Phillips was instructed by the committee to remind the faculty of the leash and trowel rule. The meeting adjourned at 9:10.

*　　　*　　　*　　　*

Before dinner the next evening, Bartley finally began to relax. He was sitting in the faculty corner of the Camden Commons when Steve Barber, a second year teacher in the science department and the varsity hockey and golf coach, approached him.

"Mr. Bartley. Barber here." Bartley looked up from the paper he was reading.

"May I talk to you for a few minutes?"

"Sure, Steve, but call me Jack. You make me feel ancient." Bartley stood up just as the doors opened for dinner. "I guess we'll have to wait now."

"O.K. How about right after dinner before chapel?"

"We'll meet here."

"Right.

Bartley wondered all through dinner what Steve Barber could want with him. He was one of the new Gladiators Woody had been hiring of late—mediocre classroom qualifications but excellent athletic credentials. He had played two years of Division I hockey. During his first year at Kensington he had begun an almost instant renewal of the faltering fortunes of the varsity hockey program. He had begun poorly in the classroom, teaching biology in a stiff, arbitrary, rigid way leading to a virtual student revolt. He actually did not know his subject matter as well as several students did, and he tried to hide behind a facade of authority, grading students harshly by administering tests intended to humiliate even the most diligent of students.

But once hockey season began, Barber proved to be a talented teacher, who in the context of his own expertise, was calm and flexible, full of good humor and enthusiasm. For a while, it seemed to Bartley that Barber was perfectly schizophrenic, a tyrant in the classroom, a wizard working educational wonders on the hockey rink. The varsity won its first four games before Christmas vacation, and after the return in January, managed to have a winning record in the first half of the schedule against the most important traditional opponents—Westminster, Pomfret, Moses Brown, and St. Mark's. Barber began to relax in his biology classes, asked the students to write evaluations of his performance in class, invited other teachers to attend classes and write critiques. He scaled his grades, raising the distribution patterns in line with the rest of the school, and enrolled during the second semester at Brown in the first course that would, over the next two years and summers, lead to a graduate degree.

Bartley did not know Barber well, but from what he did know he liked him and his wife, Polly, who had recently given birth to their first child. Barber didn't say much in faculty meetings, but Bartley kept a kind of private tab of his voting record, as he did of all new teachers, and was impressed by what he saw, a pattern that was liberal and fair minded. Barber had unintentionally but wisely voted with Bartley on most major issues for almost two years now.

Bartley had his reservations about the young man. He was too good looking, blond and tan even in the winter. He really was, at best, a mediocre classroom teacher, but, most of all, there were just too many new teachers just like him on the faculty. They formed a kind of clique—Barber in science, Jim Ferguson and Sam Arnold in math, Bob Gilman in English. They were all cosmetic, friendly, athletic, beautifully dressed, but non-controversial and apolitical. They had managed to go through school and college during the late sixties and early seventies as though they had an inborn immunity or insensitivity to the world beyond the narrow circumscription of places like the Dartmouth Green or the Yard, football and soccer fields, fraternity houses, baseball diamonds and hockey rinks. Most of all, though, Bartley resented their well groomed moustaches, which he had tried to grow unsuccessfully himself. They looked too much like the new wave of neo-fascist T.V. and Hollywood actors, even though they seemed to vote during faculty meetings independently of each other and of senior colleagues.

After dinner they met by the coffee cart and moved through a side door that opened on to a small raised patio. Bartley stood, uncomfortably sipping his coffee, waiting for Barber to speak. Above to his left was the chapel, its grey stones now obscured by the freshly green leaves of maples opened fully within the past week.

"Mr. Bartley. Pardon me," he laughed, "Jack, I mean, I was wondering, now that the spring sports seasons are over, if you'd like to play a round of golf. I understand you're a closet pro, hiding your talents from the rest of the faculty."

"I'm a hacker, Steve. I play alone occasionally, sometimes Bill Henry condescends to play with me, but I'm not in your class, I'm afraid. I break 50 on a good day." He paused and smiled. "Besides, I have to be candid. I kind of cheat. I play Mulligans and preferred lies, but I really appreciate your asking. I'd be happy to play but I need a few practice rounds before I could play with you."

"How well you play doesn't make any difference, Jack. Maybe I could give you some pointers. Anyhow, we're getting a game up late Friday afternoon and I was hoping you'd play. In fact, I was hoping we might play every so often this summer. Both Polly and I are taking courses at Brown, so we'll be staying on campus most of the summer."

"You know, I think you're serious. I guess if you don't mind playing with me, I sure can't complain about playing with you. I'll need Mulligans on every hole, preferred lies and two strokes on the long par 4's and the par 5. Actually, I think I'll need a stroke on the other holes, too."

"We'll just play for fun and practice to start with, Jack."

"What time?"

"3:30 Friday. The team's having a post-season informal tournament tomorrow."

"Who else are we playing with or are we just a twosome?"

They had walked back inside the Commons and placed their cups on the cart. Barber turned to Bartley. He couldn't repress the flash of a grin, which he controlled quickly and then with a slow turn, he began to walk outside again, speaking casually over his shoulder.

"Annie."

"Annie who?" Bartley asked after a long hesitation before following Barber back to the patio. "Annie who?"

"Annie Bartley. *Your* Annie. What other Annie do we both know?"

"You've got to be kidding. What does she know about golf? I took her around the course for the first time not two months ago."

"She didn't want me to tell you ahead of time, but I insisted. I told her the shock would be too much. And from the look on your face, I was right. I wish I had a camera."

"You and I and Annie are going to play golf Friday afternoon?"

"Yes, sir, Jack."

"Whose clubs will she be using?"

"Polly's. She's been using them since late April."

"Where?"

"The practice field. On the practice green. She hasn't played nine holes for score yet, only 1, 8, 9, with me after the team has cleared the course, but she's ready and she wanted you to play with her the first time."

"She's only eleven years old."

"She's a natural, Jack. She's a worker, she's more teachable than my whole golf team put together, most of whom think they already know all there's to know about golf and are just waiting for their invitations to play in the Masters."

"A natural?"

"A natural."

"How did all this happen?"

"Kind of casually and accidentally. It grew all spring. She started hanging around the lower level soccer fields where we warm up before going to the course. Then she started helping shag balls. Pretty soon a couple of the older boys were letting her hit a few iron shots. Then she was taking a regular turn and offered to shag balls for the whole team after warming up so that we could get off to the course sooner. It just kept growing. I began giving her lessons with a 5 iron, worked back and forth from there and then moved to the woods. But it was when she started coming to the course that I really became interested. Jack, Annie is more than a natural with a putter in her hands, she's spectacular, gifted. She ranks third in the varsity in lag putts. We have a little competition with lag putts from forty or fifty feet. Each player is given five lag putts. We measure the distance each ball ends up from the cup and then we add the total of the five putts. She's absolutely deadly from inside six feet too."

"You're kidding me."

"I am not kidding you. She hits irons and woods with us every day for half an hour, then she comes to the course and practices putting and chipping while we play practice rounds or a match. Her concentration and intensity are unbelievable. She has hit balls until her fingers bled."

"I wondered where she had gone." Bartley spoke aloud but to himself.

"Where she had gone?"

"Oh, nothing, Steve. I was just thinking out loud."

"Friday at 3:30. O.K.?"

"Right. Oh, by the way, could I borrow some practice balls? I better hit a few tomorrow just to get some of my timing back."

"Ask Annie. She has them for the summer. Hey, I've got to run now, Jack. See you, Friday."

"Ask Annie?" He asked out loud, but Barber had already disappeared among the students, now moving slowly toward the exit to chapel.

*　　　*　　　*　　　*

The next afternoon from the cover of a row of lilacs, he sat on the ground and watched Annie in the distance below him hitting balls across the soccer field. She hit tee shot after tee shot with a deliberate, methodical swing. She addressed the ball each time by placing the head of her club behind the ball. She held the shaft with her extended left arm only, then she lined up her body with her heels together. After a pause she placed her right hand over her left and moved her right foot to the right leaving the ball lined up directly off her left heel. She waited for several moments, then tilted her head slightly to the right so that her left eye was aligned with her left arm, down the shaft of the club. Her back swing was slow and high, and she stopped completely at the top of her swing.

Barber had taught her well. She hit the ball invariably straight out with a slight loft. Bartley guessed she was using a 3 wood. For a moment, he panicked that she might beat him in her very first complete round, but that feeling was overwhelmed by an emerging pride and then by the fear that she might not do well despite all the practice and that she would be hurt again as she was when she dreamed of playing baseball. He did not join her, knowing that she wanted their first round together to be a kind of gift to him. He felt like a spy, watching her from his cover.

Later that evening he knocked on her bedroom door and pushed the partially open door another foot or so.

"May I come in?"

"*Bien sur. Entre, Monsieur Bartley. Votre fille, Annie, ici. Enchantez...et cetera...votre connaisance.*"

"*Enchantez* to you, too. I never did learn that whole expression. You're already ahead of me."

"No I'm not. I read that from the book. Pretty rotten pronunciation, but we only have it twice a week. I guess I can't complain. It's better than no French at all."

"It's a beginning anyhow. I had Latin in high school. By the time I began French in college, it was too late for me to learn pronunciation."

She was sitting up in bed with the French text across her lap. He walked across the room and sat in the wicker rocker next to her bed and began rocking slowly. She closed the book, keeping one finger at her place.

"I saw you hitting some golf balls today on the soccer fields. I almost joined you, but I had other things to do. I was impressed."

"Oh, Steve's a super coach, and he's let me use the team's bag of practice balls almost every day when they're through with them."

"Steve?"

"Mr. Barber. Steve. He told me to call him Steve. I felt kind of funny at first, but now it seems natural."

"From what I saw, I would agree that he's a good coach."

"It's one thing on the practice tee and another thing on the course," she frowned. Then she brightened. "I'm so excited about tomorrow. Steve said not to worry if I have a poor round. It may take all summer to put everything together, but he said that I have promise. I am nervous about how I'll do anyway. For the past week whenever I think about playing Friday, I get wobbles in my stomach."

"I feel like that on the first tee every time I play even after years of playing. Especially if there are lots of people watching."

"Steve says butterflies are good to feel in sports. It's a sign you're ready. He says they disappear after the first hit."

"Yes," Bartley laughed, "with me they're replaced by feelings of disappointment, frustration, and depression which in turn are relieved occasionally by sudden bursts of elation when I accidentally hit the ball well."

"Oh, Daddy, you'd be a good golfer if you practiced. Steve says you can't just go out once every couple of weeks and play and expect to do well."

"Maybe we could practice and play some together this summer."

"Could we? That would be super. Steve and Polly are going to be here most of the summer taking courses in the morning at Brown and they asked me if I'd be their babysitter."

"Isn't their baby a little young? Wouldn't she need someone older?"

"Mom said she'd help if I had any trouble. Melanie sleeps almost all morning, and I'd only have to give her one bottle. I've already had some practice helping Polly."

"You've had a busy spring. I wondered where you were."

They sat silently. Bartley rocked slowly. Annie pretended to read.

"Are we going anywhere this summer, Daddy, like one of the battlefields in Virginia or to Monticello again. We've just been to Washington during spring vacation. I thought maybe we might stay here this summer."

"I thought you enjoyed our summer trips."

"I do, I did. It's just that I've got my first job this summer and a chance to play golf. Besides, we've been to so many battlefields and forts and historic sites since I can remember that I thought we might take the summer off or stay here in New England and do old things here for a change. Go to Sturbridge or the Freedom Trail in Boston. Day trip stuff. You know, during March vacation when Mom and I and Rachel took the Tourmobile while you were doing some research, the tour guide said that if you stood one minute in front of each exhibit of the Smithsonian, it would take over ninety years to see everything. I figure that if I had done that, spent a minute, instead of the few seconds I usually spend walking by, I'd be forty or fifty years old now. I've got enough material from all our trips to write about *fifty* history papers. I've already written three or four reports on the Civil War alone. I am the world's youngest expert on the Battle of the Crater."

"Wasn't that fun? Learning together? Walking the battlefield? Trying to reconstruct what happened? Think of all the trips we took. The whole Oregon Trail. The Mission Trail in California plus Yellowstone, Yosemite and the Grand Canyon."

"That *was* fun. I was just hoping we'd take this summer off is all."

"Well, your wish is granted. We're just going to hang around here until late July or early August. Then Mom and I thought we'd take a vacation trip to Montreal and Quebec and the Maritime Provinces. Will your job be over by then?"

"Oh, Dad, that would be super. Steve and Polly are going away in August after summer school. Kensington is a great place in the summer anyhow and I could practice my French in Canada."

"Well," he stood up and forced a laugh. "If you really like it so much, you can come to school here now if you want. We haven't talked about it much, but you know the Trustees announced that the school will become coeducational a year from now."

"Mom and I talked a little about it, and I've been thinking a lot about it recently."

"What have you been thinking?"

Her forehead wrinkled into a serious frown.

"All my life what I wanted to do most was come to Kensington. It was my impossible dream. Now that I can, I'm not so sure I want to."

"What changed your mind?"

"I don't know. I guess I'd hate to come and be a flop and embarrass you and Mom."

"You won't ever embarrass us. If we thought you'd have trouble, we'd let you go somewhere else. You don't have to come here at all. There's no pressure."

"I know. Mom told me that. I guess I'm not sure I want to be a guinea pig here. If I apply as a third former two years from now, it'll only be the second year of coeducation. I'm not sure I want to be new, like an experiment. Even though I've lived here all my life, I'd be looked on as an outsider. I don't want to come here and go to four years of high school and end up a girl version of a boy."

"You have been thinking, haven't you? What other ideas do you have?"

"Well, I suppose Misquomet Regional would be O.K. except for the long bus rides. Will the school still pay for girl fac brats to go to other schools after coeducation?"

"Not 100 per cent anymore, but there are scholarships from other schools you might qualify for."

"I've been talking to Steve and he went to Andover and it merged with Abbot, a girls' school, and it became kind of instant coeducation and it's enormous with over a thousand students from everywhere, all over the United States and the world. It would be like going off to college."

Bartley winced inwardly. One winter in one of his compulsive urges to move along to join the "greater" world, he had applied to Exeter and Andover. He wasn't even invited to Exeter for an interview and he did miserably when he met members of the history department at Andover. He talked too much, trying to sell himself. He had been intimidated by the size of the school and its reputation and in his eagerness he was too enthusiastic, too cooperative, too ingratiating in trying to impress them. He was rejected politely, in a brief note from the Department Chairman, implying they couldn't match his salary as a department chairman, but he knew they felt he didn't have it. He never told anyone but Karen that he had sought the job, but he had been hurt and his unwillingness to make himself vulnerable again was always a factor in his staying on for another year at Kensington each spring.

"There are very fine girls' schools too. In two years you might want to think about them too. Randall Hall, for example. The important thing is that you keep your mind open. You've got lots of choices now that girls just five years ago didn't have."

"That's what's fun, having a choice. Some days I think of myself at Kensington and some days I'm at Andover with a roommate from Paris or San Francisco. Do you think Andover has a girls' golf team?"

"I'm sure they have just about everything up there."

"Steve says you can go to France or Spain for one of the years. That would be neat."

"Well, keep dreaming, pal. Meanwhile, you better get back to your French." He stood up and began to leave.

"Daddy, do you think you could get me a squash ball from the Athletic Association store."

"Sure, but why?"

"Steve says I should get one and squeeze it in my left hand to build strength in my hand, wrist, and forearm."

"I'll pick one up for you tomorrow."

"Merci, Monsieur Bartley. Vous etes un bon papa."

"A Bientot, Mademoiselle Annie. Vous etes une bonne fille." He hoped she would never learn how bad his French really was. He would simply quit speaking it as she grew fluent.

"A demain."

"Oui. A demain. Trois heure y demi, O.K.?" he said, moving to the door. "On the first tee."

"Oui. On the first tee. I'm scared already. I feel wobbles in my stomach now."

"I'm scared too. *Bon soir.*"

In his study later, he felt good about their talk. He congratulated himself for not overreacting to her desire to do something else for the summer than tag along as he pursued his hobby horse. He didn't even care if she decided to go to Andover or the public high school. He did object to her use of the word "super" though. Emotionally it would always be a fascist term to him used over the years most frequently in the locker room by the more physical coaches of violent sports. He couldn't help it. He wished she had said something trite like "fantastic," or corny like "hunky dory," or inane like "great."

*　　　*　　　*　　　*

They dropped Annie off at the women's tee and walked back about seventy-five yards beyond it, up a gradual incline. Ordinarily the men would tee off first, but Annie had asked Barber if she could hit first from the women's tee alone, without them standing behind her watching, and then join them after they had teed off. Halfway up the approach to the tee they left their carts and carried only their drivers to the raised rectangle of earth, a recessed terrace of green grass hidden by a tangled and irregularly spaced copse of mixed hardwoods.

From the bench at the back of the tee, he could not see Annie, below him to the right on the women's tee. After washing his ball and resting briefly on the bench behind the blue markers, they walked back to the front of the tee to see her hit the ball. He stood next to Barber, resting his club over one shoulder and watched the ritual of her warmup.

She began by holding her driver, one hand on the neck of the club head and the other at the top of the grip, parallel to the ground. Then she began to swing it in a gentle arc from her shoulders, higher and higher until she was pivoting, shifting her weight from foot to foot and extending the length of the arc until she was reaching forward and backward. Her head remained fixed to a spot on the ground. Then she put the club across her lower back, held by her elbows stretched behind, and began to twist her body. Without her club, she stretched out her legs, leaning her body first on her left knee and then reversing to her right knee. She relaxed for several moments and then began rolling her head and shaking her hands. Then she spread her legs widely and began bobbing her head toward the ground rhythmically while bending her body from the hips. Her arms and hands dangled loosely and her limp hands brushed the ground.

"Does she need to do all that?" Bartley asked Barber, almost irritably.

"Well, it loosens her up, more psychologically than physically. It's good to have a warm-up ritual, especially in an individual sport like golf. There aren't team drills to get ready."

"I suppose you're right. I just take practice swings myself. Will she take practice swings?"

"She's beginning now."

Bartley watched her, now with the club in her hands, begin to swing the club in an every widening arc until she stopped and began full practice swings. After about twenty swings, she turned toward them and waved. Barber waved back, and she stepped forward between the red markers and leaned over to tee up her ball. She stepped back and looked up the fairway. About seventy yards off her tee a stream cut across the fairway, and to her right a row of white out of bounds stakes protected the ninth green, its flag waving beyond a field of wild grass.

For the first time Bartley sensed the wind moving the branches of the trees above him. It was a gusty wind moving from left to right across the fairway. It would surely accelerate the slice spin of his tee shot. He hated the wind except when it was at his back and even then it contributed to his misjudgments in approach shots.

Annie addressed the ball by placing the club head behind the ball adjusting her feet to the width of her shoulders. He almost turned away. He felt the wobbles in his stomach. She stepped back about a foot and took two practice swings. She addressed the ball again and Bartley, unable to bear the tension, closed his eyes.

Nothing happened. When he opened his eyes, she was striding toward them, carrying her driver over one shoulder. Two pony tails tied with red ribbons bounced off her back. She wore light blue Bermuda shorts, a white turtle neck and white knee-length stockings. As she approached them, he was startled to realize how thin she had become. Since she had abandoned baseball, her chubbiness, her baby-fat had melted away, and he in his self-absorption had not noticed until this moment.

She stopped below him, her eyes fixed on Barber. She did not even glance at him or acknowledge his presence.

"Steve. I just wanted to check. We're playing competitive rules, aren't we?"

"That's the only way, Annie, if you want to play high school or college golf or in tournaments some day."

"No Mulligans?" she asked rhetorically.

"First ball's in play," he answered.

"No preferred lies?"

"Play 'em down, as they lay."

"No gimmies?"

"Putt everything out, even hangers."

She turned around abruptly and marched back to the women's tee. She stepped directly to her ball, and without a practice swing, addressed the ball, drew her club back, pausing briefly at the top of her back swing, and laced the ball straight down the fairway in a gentle arc carrying the stream by twenty-five yards. She retrieved her tee and turned toward them, her face crinkling with happiness.

They turned back from the front of the tee.

"Blue or white markers?" Bartley asked.

"White," Barber answered.

"Want to flip for honors?"

"Show me the way, Jack."

"The circuitous route is the scenic route, I always say."

"It's where it ends up that counts, Jack."

Bartley teed his ball up, stepped a few yards behind his ball and took several practice swings. Barber stood to the side watching, the club head of his driver on the ground and the end of the shaft resting on his belt. Bartley turned to him.

"You've taught her well, Steve."

"She has a good swing. She's a hard worker."

"I didn't mean just technique, skills, practice. I mean attitudes, principles, the morality of it all.

"Thanks, Jack. Coming from you that's special."

"Why me? Why special?"

"Why, Jack, you're famous as *the* coach at Kensington who teaches attitudes, principles, the morality of it all. Character."

"Who? Me?"

"You. Why, every year at the end of new faculty orientation, the Headmaster takes those of us who are going to be varsity or J.V. coaches aside and tells us to look to Jack Bartley as a model for coaching."

"Woody does that? Every year? How do you know?"

"Well, he said the same things to me last fall that he said to Sam Arnold when he was new three years ago."

"What does he say about me? What are you supposed to look to me for?"

"He just kind of rambles along with anecdotes, but it's his way of telling us how he wants us to behave as coaches by telling us about you. He begins by saying what an awful athlete you are. He says you're not just uncoordinated, you're dis-coordinated, that you never played on an organized team of any kind when you were young, that your players are the dregs of the athletic barrel, most of whom couldn't make any other team and have to play baseball because we require participation in a team sport in the third form. He says you have never had a winning season because your schedule is so tough. Except for a few private schools, you have to play the public junior high schools and high school freshman teams whose players have been practicing together for years and not just in school but all summer when they play on little league and Babe Ruth teams. He goes on to say that you have never been known to ride an umpire or complain about judgment calls, that you have never humiliated a boy by screaming at him in practice or games, and that you teach by hard work and encouragement. Finally, he says you are the best coach at Kensington because each spring a little miracle happens on the third form diamond."

"He says all of that about me?"

"More than less. I've condensed it quite a bit."

Bartley hesitated for several moments and then took a few more practice swings before he turned back to Barber.

"He didn't tell you what the little miracle is, did he?"

"Yes." Barber stood deliberately silent as Bartley looked at him expectantly.

"Well, what is it?"

"Oh, just that fifteen kids, most of whom have never played on any team and may never play again, realize a sense of self-worth by playing correctly, if only for a few innings in a whole season, the most impossible game ever invented by man."

Bartley stepped forward and addressed the ball. He felt wobbles in his stomach and a palpitation or two. He heard the wind in the trees above him. It seemed to have increased to gale force. He looked down the fairway. The stream seemed as large as a river. The fairway was narrower. Had someone moved the out of bounds stakes to the left since he had played with Annie in April? With the concentration of a Zen mystic, he repeated to himself, "Keep your head down, Keep your head down," but his concentration broke and he stepped back from the ball and spoke deliberately to himself.

"Thus beginneth the moral education of Jack Bartley."

"What did you say, Jack?" Barber asked.

"Nothing, Steve. Nothing." Bartley looked down the fairway again. "Golf is the most impossible game ever invented by man."

"Each to his own, Jack."

"No Mulligans, eh?"

"No Mulligans."

"No preferred lies?"

"Play it down, Jack.

"No gimmies?"

"Putt everything out, even the hangers. But you can play the way you always do. It's just a friendly match, just a practice round."

"The majority rules. We can't play together with two sets of rules."

"Keep your head down."

"Right."

He stepped forward once more, addressed the ball, and drew the club back. He paused, as Annie had, at the top of his back swing. With a vision of a new heaven, a new earth fixed in his mind's eye, of the ball jumping in a line off the tee then rising into the sky and curling over at its zenith in a slightly rolling draw before dropping to the green earth in the center of the fairway, he drove the club head downward.

CHAPTER 8

▼

At a school meeting in late May, the Chairman of the Board of Trustees announced that Kensington would begin admitting girls a year hence and that the upcoming year would be one of preparation and planning. A faculty meeting was devoted to a discussion of the counseling problems that coeducational boarding was certain to produce. Mr. Woodbridge had invited a chaplain and a guidance counselor both from the Boston area colleges, to discuss their experiences with coeducation. They talked about the "profound humanity of sexuality" much to the discomfort and disdain of the conservative opponents of coeducation on the Kensington faculty. The chaplain received a particularly cold reception and the lion's share of the hostile questions because the rumor had preceded him to Kensington that on the walls of his study and on his desk he exhibited framed photographs of himself naked so that the girls he was counseling would not feel he was hiding anything. Actually, Bartley thought the man was excellent, but he wisely kept his opinion to himself. He knew the rumors were true.

The Kensington first boat didn't make it to the regatta finals for the first time in four years, but Peter took the defeat well. Except for the usual end of the year rash of disciplinary cases, mostly trivial matters—dorm masters who had finally lost their patience with loud stereos or messy rooms or classroom teachers who had exhausted their capacity to tolerate any more late homework or cut classes—the year ended smoothly.

On Memorial Day the names of each Kensington alumnus to die in the Great War, World War II, Korea, and Viet Nam were read aloud by faculty and members of the sixth form at chapel. Only two Kensington graduates had died in Viet Nam. Lt. Martin Loring, killed during the Tet offensive, had been in Bartley's dorm in his first years at Kensington. Loring was a scholarship student from a small town in Minnesota. He was tall and gawky, with a lopsided oval face and large glasses. Lonely and homesick, he had sobbed his heart out in Bartley's study often during his third and fourth form years.

He seemed happier by his senior year, but he was socially awkward, had few friends, and even in his last weeks at Kensington, after four years, confessed he was still bewildered and confused by what was expected of him by his sophisticated classmates. What should he say? How should he say it? When should he speak up? He enrolled at the University of Minnesota and joined the ROTC program, earned his degree and a commission and died eight months later in the jungle mud of Southeast Asia.

Before Bartley knew it, he had been so busy, everything was over. There were no surprises at the turnover banquet, the underformers, their rights of succession declared, were sent packing and the families of graduates began descending upon the Kensington campus. Younger brothers of graduates stayed in the dorm. Karen provided beds for two sisters of graduates in their guest bedroom, and parents commuted from motels, some as far away as Providence and Hartford.

Early in the morning of the day before graduation, Bartley took his fishing tackle to the hockey pond and began trying his lures in favorite holes along the shore. He had worked his way around half the pond when he was startled by footsteps behind him. He turned to find Peter emerging from a clump of trees to his left where a stream entered the pond.

"What are you doing here this time of day?"

Peter smiled self-consciously.

"Exploring."

"Exploring what?"

"The woods. I traced the stream all the way up the valley to where it comes from a pasture. I'm going to follow it down to the golf course in Kensington Center."

"What are you doing that for? Now, with one day until graduation?"

"After the Regatta, when four years of crew and football and wrestling were finally over, I realized all the things I hadn't done here in four years. I've spent all my time doing sports or studying. I've never seen a hockey or soccer or baseball game. I've only been down here by the pond twice. The school has five hundred acres of woods and I haven't seen anything. I've never been in dramatics, never taken an art course, never hung around the butt room. They only thing I've done is my own sports and singing in the glee club. I've been up half the night this past week in the butt room, shooting the shit with guys like Forester. I never knew what an interesting character he is. I've only seen him as a disciplinary problem. I've never sat around like that before. When I leave Kensington tomorrow, I'm going to miss all the things I haven't done as much as what I've been doing."

"That's how you feel now, Peter. But if you're lucky, you won't miss anything at all. Your college years will diminish your memories of Kensington. Then you will be busy with a career and marriage and you won't have time to look backward. Perhaps in fifteen or twenty years you may begin to feel a little nostalgia. Let's walk back to the dam. I've tried all the holes along this bank and all I've caught is snags."

"Is that what your life has been like—so busy you haven't had to look backward?" Peter asked plaintively.

Bartley laughed as they walked along the shaded path a few yards from the shore.

"You won't believe this, Peter, but I'm already looking forward to next fall. Last evening I gathered the preliminary registration figures and began setting up sections for next year and assigning teachers. I can't wait for graduation to be over with and done so I can get on with my summer."

"You mean you won't miss everything from this past year, the dorm, the guys, the fun we had. You're a lousy historian, Mr. Bartley, forgetting everything so quickly and the school archivist too. You should be ashamed of yourself."

"It's over, Peter. Another year will happen again. As an historian, one thing I know for sure, despite the faculty misgivings each spring, the fifth formers always manage to replace the graduating sixth formers. If teachers know anything, it is that nothing changes, nothing is the same, or to be more positive, everything changes, everything is the same. Let's stop here. I want to try a few casts toward the lily pads there."

He pointed and walked to the edge of the water on a small promontory of grass. He cast his line short of the floating cluster of leaves twenty or so yards off shore and began reeling in his line.

"What are you going to do this summer, sir?"

"Some fishing, some golf, lots of reading, a week or so on the Cape near Nausett Light in a cottage offered us by Bart Patterson's family. Later the Scheduling Committee. Then a Curriculum Review Committee. Helping Mrs. Bartley settle into her new job as Associate Dean in the Admissions Office."

"Mrs. Bartley? Associate Dean? I didn't know that. That's great. How come nobody knows? It wasn't announced or anything. May I say something about it when we go to dinner tomorrow night?"

"I suppose so. It's not a secret. It's just that Mr. Woodbridge doesn't want to overdo anything about coeducation. He wants to move into it quietly, matter-of-factly. By the way, when are your parents coming?"

"Tomorrow morning. They're staying at the Inn. Do you know, they made their reservations almost a year ago? And I made reservations for dinner tomorrow night three weeks ago."

"Is Jennifer coming? The Powells?"

"They're coming graduation morning. I stayed there last weekend. They picked me up Friday night as though nothing had ever happened. Mrs. Powell was friendly and talked to me a lot. You know, she's a really interesting person. She's a kind of expert on art, mainly stained glass and cathedrals. She goes to France almost every summer to study a different cathedral. I pretended I was interested, but after a while I became really bored when she showed her slides after supper. I fell asleep, you know, my eyes closed and I nodded off about ten times lying on the living room rug trying to watch all those pictures of statues and colored glass and spires."

Bartley gave up casting and returned to the trail. They walked a short way to the dam and sat on the concrete edge, their feet dangling above the water. Behind them on the downstream side of the dam, a narrow, rocky stream, barely a trickle from the overflow of the dam, fell away for about fifty yards and then disappeared among the trees.

"I hope it doesn't rain tomorrow. My mom wants to play tennis. She plays all the time, all winter in one of those metal barns and all summer at the country club where my dad plays golf. She goes to tournaments, watches matches on T.V. We used to spend our summer vacations every August up in northern Minnesota—everyone, my mom and dad and my older brother and sister—canoeing the wilderness trail, camping, fishing, portages, almost two weeks out of touch with the whole world." Peter paused but then began again. Bartley was surprised by Peter's loquaciousness. "Now just my dad and I go. We'll probably go again this August after I finish working on a construction job and before I go off to Grinnell. But my older brother and sister aren't home anymore, and my mom will go along with us as far as this tennis lodge along Lake Superior north of Duluth. She and a few friends will play tennis until we come back. She is a genuine tennis *aficionado*, Mr. Bartley. She talks about it almost like it was a science."

"Hey, I like that. *Aficionado*. Where did you pick that up?"

Peter brightened and began to laugh.

"Picked that up last fall in Mr. Henry's Sixth Form English class. We were reading *The Sun Also Rises*. God, what a class that was. We all became Hemingway aficionados. For a few weeks last fall we called everything grand. You couldn't say a thing, someone would say, 'Isn't that Grand?' At breakfast someone would say, 'Isn't the shit-on-a-shingle grand this morning?' Pretty soon everyone on the football team was using it. During practice you'd come back to the huddle after a play and someone would say 'What a grand double-team that was' or 'That trap block was grand' or 'What a grand pass, or a grand tackle, or a grand catch.' We didn't say it on Saturday during the games, but Coach got so sick of it during practice that he stopped drills once and said that if anyone said that word again, it would be two fast laps on each occasion."

"I assume that put an end to it."

"We switched to *utilize* and then it all kind of faded out by itself. Besides, we started to read *Bleak House* and that killed all our enthusiasm. It was so long and boring nothing seemed very grand any more."

"Well, Mr. Henry is a grand teacher, but teaching *Bleak House* isn't such a grand idea."

"You can say that again. But the class was so much fun, even our discussion about *Bleak House*." Peter suddenly became serious. "You wouldn't believe our last discussion of *The Sun Also Rises*. Do you know the novel?"

"Yes, we used it several years ago in a course on the Twenties. That was back in the grim, dark days of curricular stupidity when we carved up the American history course into topical mini-courses to create the illusion for the students that everything was a choice." Bartley stood up and began to cast randomly into the deepest water in front of the sluice gates. "In those days, Peter, the faculty didn't have the courage to tell the students they had to take a full course in American History before they were ready to specialize in a period or theme. We were afraid the students would think we were reactionary dolts. Forgive my editorial aside, Peter, but I'm still angry about how we were all so easily intimidated by any kid who frowned. Sorry. Tell me about your last discussion of *The Sun Also Rises* with Mr. Henry."

"Well, we had discussed the book for almost two weeks. We were winding up by reading some old advanced placement tests and discussing how we'd use *The Sun Also Rises* in answering the questions. One of the questions was about how some books over the years have been censored or criticized and we were supposed to suggest what some of the objections to *The Sun Also Rises* might be and how we would agree or disagree and use evidence to support our position. You know what those questions are like. Anyhow, Logan Ambler, who hadn't said a word for two weeks, sitting on his fat ass sandbagging, I suppose, waiting for one of us to say something stupid, suddenly dumps all over the book as immoral—a story of drunks, whores, pimps—he called Jake a pimp for fixing Brett up with Romero—who live lives of sin and irresponsibility with impunity, he said. We had to ask him what impunity meant. He said it means that nothing happens to them at the end. They weren't punished for their sins. They got off Scott free after doing nothing but boozing and screwing and fighting for two hundred and fifty-two pages. Do you know Logan Ambler, Mr. Bartley?"

"Yes, I know Logan Ambler."

"I mean, do you know him as the students know him, not like the faculty know him—straight A student and professional suck-up."

"Well, how do the students know him?"

"The students know him as the biggest jerk in the Sixth Form. For four years now he has done nothing but condescend to the rest of us, putting us down with his sneering, supercilious comments—that's another great word—I love it—supercilious. He's so hyped on the dress code he takes a shower in a coat and tie. He's such a stuffed shirt and pompous wet blanket he can kill a great bull session just by walking by in the hallway or ruin a great class with a single statement with that way he talks like William F. Buckley."

Bartley laughed.

"Yes, I know him all the ways you have described him. We're not all as blind as you might think. Besides, as a Midwesterner, I have a natural prejudice against anyone with two last names. As a matter of fact, as a Northern liberal, I have a prejudice also against anyone with two or three first names like Jim Roy or Billy Joe Frank."

"No offense to you, Mr. Bartley, but there are a lot of faculty who get taken in by assholes like Ambler. Anyhow, Mr. Henry didn't say anything for a while and let the class try to argue with Logan. I guess we didn't do very well because I could see Mr. Henry getting pissed off, sitting there listening to Logan ramble on about immorality and irresponsibility, until he began to wiggle around in his chair and shake his head, then began hitting his forehead with the palm of his hand.

"Before you know it, Mr. Henry has climbed up on his desk on all fours. You know how crowded that basement classroom is. Logan was sitting in the first row of desks, his chair's writing arm was touching the front edge of Mr. Henry's desk. Mr. Henry leaned forward and put his nose right up to Logan's tie. Logan leaned back as far as he could but he couldn't lean back far enough and Mr. Henry had his face right in Logan's.

"What the hell book have you been reading the past two weeks, Mr. Ambler?' he shouts."

"'*The Sun Also Rises*, sir,' Logan whispers."

"'What the hell classroom have you been sitting in, Mr. Ambler?'"

"'Your classroom, sir' he says. You can hardly hear Logan talk."

"All right, Mr. Ambler, what is Jake Barnes' problem? This is a quiz, Mr. Ambler, that will count 80% of your grade this semester.' Now you can see the sudden look of terror on old grade-grubber Logan's face."

"'He was emasculated in the war,' Logan answers."

"'What is his feeling toward Lady Brett Ashley?'"

"'He's in love with her, sir.'"

"'Tell us, Mr. Ambler, did Jake Barnes cause the war that emasculated him?'"

"'No, sir.'"

"'Then would you agree that Jake Barnes was punished before he had done anything wrong while serving duty and honor.'"

"'Yes, sir.'"

"'Does that seem fair to you?'"

"'No, sir.'"

"'Does it seem fair that the love he and Brett feel for each other must remain forever incomplete?'"

"'No, sir,' old suck-up Logan answered, hoping that by agreeing now he could save his grade."

"Then Mr. Henry dumped all over Logan."

"Did it ever occur to you, you blockhead, that every goddamn line of the novel is full of pain, that all Jake Barnes is trying to do is cope as best as he can with the unjust suffering inflicted upon him by a war he did not cause and that his voice is the voice of victims everywhere who deserve our compassion not our condemnation?'"

"Just then the bell rang, and Mr. Henry backed off from Logan and off the desk into his chair. None of us moved. We realized it wasn't just one of his performances. Then he said to all of us and I'll never forget what he said as long as I live. 'Don't any of you ever let your intellect or your moral principles get in the way of your sensitivity to suffering,' he said."

Bartley cast once more into the deepest part of the pond and began to reel in his lure.

"Sometimes Mr. Henry loses his self-control, especially about victims of war. He spent over three years in a German POW camp."

"I suppose that explains why he got so angry, but whatever the cause, the important thing is that a faculty member finally called Logan Ambler a blockhead—what every student in the sixth form already knew even though he got all A's in Latin and math and science. He is a blockhead and a moron in personal relations, Mr. Bartley, and Mr. Henry called him exactly what he was. His stock was never higher among the students."

"Mr. Henry is a grand person," Bartley laughed. "Hey, want to cast a few? You can say you fished here at least once in four years."

He handed the rod to Peter, who stood up on the dam alongside him. Peter walked to the middle of the dam and cast toward the shore to Bartley's left. He dropped the plug just a foot or two from the shore and then began jerking the rod and winding the reel handle. Bartley squatted on the cement and watched with admiration for several minutes as Peter worked a wide arc across the water with graceful, easy motions. His father had taught him well on the wilderness trail in northern Minnesota.

"Hey, Mr. Bartley, you want to play golf with me and my dad tomorrow morning if they get here early enough?"

"I wish I could, Peter, but I have a faculty meeting all morning. Among other things we have to vote on diplomas."

"I wouldn't want to take you away from something as important as that. How about in the afternoon?"

"Sorry. Committee meetings and then Mr. Woodbridge wants us in the dorms to greet parents."

"This pond is so beautiful. I can't believe I've been down here only a few times in four years. Maybe the reason I never came back much was because of my first time down here. It was at the height of the fall colors in my third form year. Now that I'm leaving, I can admit that my first semester was awful. I was so homesick. One afternoon I just couldn't take it anymore, and I cut third form football and came down here alone so no one would see me cry. I walked around the pond on the path and across the dam and catwalk about ten times, crying my eyes out. What made it worse was that it was so beautiful down here—the trees were in full color, red, yellow, brown, and the green pines and slanting white birch mixed in. The sky was clear, the water blue except where it was reflecting the colors of the trees, the sunlight was yellow. And everything was still, so still and quiet. By four-thirty or five o'clock the sun began going down and I could feel the air getting chilly and see everything falling into shadows and I was suddenly so lonely I became frightened. I ran up the gravel road, the whole half mile and when I came out of the woods at the top, I could see the school buildings in the distance, the lights on in the dorms, warm and cheerful, and I realized then that the school was home for me. I came across two soccer fields and the third form football field and into the dorm and up the stairs into my room and dove on my bed and lay there panting happy, so happy I could have kissed my roommate, Floyd Carlton, who I hated so passionately that I had been plotting his murder or a way he could be killed by some accident or fired from Kensington. Every night I got to sleep fantasizing his death."

Peter had walked down the dam to Bartley and handed him the rod.

"I was just too gregarious to be homesick for too long," he laughed. "That's another word I learned from Mr. Henry. Gregarious, I love it."

Bartley grinned.

"You're gregarious and garrulous."

"Garrulous?"

"Talkative."

"Not always. But I sure have talked your leg off this morning."

"Maybe that's why the fish haven't been biting."

Peter looked at his watch. "I think it's because you're using the wrong lure. I'd better be off and leave you in peace. I want to follow the stream to the golf course and maybe rent some clubs and get a practice round in before my dad comes."

Peter walked down the dam and climbed the ladder to the catwalk above the sluice gates. Bartley shouted up to him.

"When you get downstream about a quarter of a mile, the stream splits around a small island. On the island is an Adirondack lean-to the Outing Club put up a few years ago. It's a great camping site."

Peter turned around and grinned at Bartley.

"I know. Even though I've never hiked below the dam, I know exactly where it is. It's famous."

"Famous?"

"Sure, Mr. Bartley, that's where all the potheads hang out in fall and spring."

"Where do they hang out in winter?" Bartley asked, piqued that he had unwittingly revealed his naivete.

"In the empty storage room off the steam tunnel between the infirmary and the gym."

"Have a grand hike, Peter."

"Thanks, sir. Catch a grand fish."

Peter waved and strode across the catwalk and down the ladder. Bartley watched him as he plunged into the woods on the other side of the dam. He stood reflectively for several moments before he cast his lure again. Bartley didn't even know there was a storeroom off the steam tunnel between the infirmary and the gym. He didn't even know there was a steam tunnel.

*　　　*　　　*　　　*

Peter's parents arrived from Iowa on schedule and spent the day playing golf and tennis with Peter. They went to dinner at the Kensington Inn together with the Bartleys. The Colbys were a well-tanned, well-groomed, well-dressed, and handsome couple in their middle forties. Though they had exchanged letters and talked on the phone over the past few years, Bartley had never met them. They turned out to be typical Kensington parents, the kind Bartley had met often in the past, proud of their son and lavish in their praise of the Bartleys, whom Mrs. Colby declared to be, after two drinks, wonderful "role models" for Peter. Despite the embarrassing flattery, Bartley liked them. Trusting their son and the faculty, they had sent Peter away, expecting him to grow and change, and they gave the school all the credit for what had happened to him.

The next morning, try as he might, Bartley could not concentrate on his final duties. He wandered about the dorm helping students pack, checking rooms out against the inventory and condition sheet each student had signed the previous fall, but his inspection was perfunctory, pro forma at best, and his manner was distracted. Peter's room was in perfect order as he expected it would be—suitcases, trunks, and packed boxes neatly arranged at the door, the bed stripped of linen, the walls cleared of posters and draperies, rugs rolled and ready to be stored. Even his wastebasket had been emptied. He had not seen Peter all morning. Each burst of voices of a group entering the dormitory gave Bartley a brief start, a twinge of anxiety. Then he relaxed when he realized the voices did not belong to Peter and his family and that, for a while at least, the inevitable meeting with Elizabeth Powell would be deferred.

In those quiet moments, clipboard in hand, sitting on an empty desk in an abandoned room, between exercising his duties of greeting parents and checking out rooms, he rehearsed in his mind the arguments of clarification or justification he would use in meeting her challenge if she chose to turn their meeting into a confrontation. He had no idea why she might want to meet him. He had no particular desire to meet her. He felt a pressing desire to avoid a confrontation, to avoid even meeting her at all, and he didn't understand why she had told Peter she wanted to meet him. Perhaps she had expressed a merely ritualistic sense of propriety. If she were coming to the Kensington graduation, she could hardly avoid meeting him so she might as well pretend she wanted to. He hoped that was her intention.

He drew consolation from the fact that time was running out. Soon the Sixth Form would assemble on the circular steps of the sun dial for the traditional photograph with Headmaster and Mrs. Woodbridge. Soon after that would be the baccalaureate service at ten and then the procession of the Sixth Form. Soon there would be only enough time for a casual, superficial meeting with Mrs. Powell, and Bartley could forget forever one of the more unpleasant relationships of his life. He was tempted to avoid her entirely. Why not just disappear from the dorm for a half hour or so, pretend to be working in his classroom or the faculty mail room, or in an empty classroom, somewhere no one would expect to look for him? Then there would be only enough time for a hurried nod among the tumult of greetings and farewells that would follow the graduation luncheon.

But he didn't run away and he met her and they spoke. Indeed, he saw her and spoke to her even before they were introduced fifteen minutes later in front of the dorm. He had been helping one of his advisees strap a luggage carrier on the top of his car on the back side of the dorm when a dark blue Mercedes, moving slowly along the narrow crowded access road, stopped and its driver asked Bartley how to get to the overflow parking lot near the dining hall, and how after that they might find their way back to the sun dial where they were to meet the rest of their party whom they had already let off in the front of the school. Bartley gave them both sets of directions as he leaned over looking into the car past the driver to the smiling, elegant woman who was casually fixing her hair and her face in a hand mirror. It had been a cordial exchange, the man with distinguished greying curly hair and twinkling eyes and the woman not just pretty but a striking beauty, wearing a white linen suit with a high-collared, violet blouse. He realized later that he should have recognized the resemblance to Jennifer. She wore her billowing hair in studied carelessness, shaped by violet and golden combs that permitted curls to fall here and there, now and then as she pulled and gently pressed strands of hair about her head.

Peter found Bartley fifteen minutes later in the dorm where he sat in the common room, reading a three month old *Playboy* discarded hastily by a student busily cleaning out his room before his parents arrived. Outside on the walk to the chapel, under the gently swaying crowns of an avenue of elms, Bartley met the Powells and Jennifer and her younger sister. When he shook hands briefly with Mrs. Powell, she laughed and said,

"I thought you would be much younger."

He was about to say that he expected her to be much older when Mr. Powell, wearing a camera about his neck and a leather accessory case over his shoulder, broke in to say,

"Why, we've already met Mr. Bartley. He's the gentleman who gave us the excellent directions to the parking lot and back to the sun dial, for which assistance I thank you again."

"Ah," Bartley finally spoke, "the couple in the blue Mercedes." He felt his words were somehow stupid as though remembering the car revealed the triviality of his mind if not a certain class consciousness. He shaded his eyes and moved to his left to avoid a beam of light filtering through the branches of the elms, making it impossible to see Mrs. Powell. They stood silently examining each other. Then Bartley turned to Jennifer and welcomed her with an exaggerated familiarity and enthusiasm. She and Peter were holding hands and Peter wore a kind of silly grin.

"I hate to break up this congregation, but I've got to find my parents and then get to the sun dial," Peter said.

"I think we had all better begin to head for an early seat in the chapel or we'll end up standing out on the steps," Bartley suggested. Before he realized what had happened, Peter and Jennifer had run off, Mr. Powell and his younger daughter had hurried on ahead to retrieve some flashbulbs and a telephoto lens from the car, and Bartley had agreed to accompany Mrs. Powell to the chapel where they would all meet once again with the Colbys. They walked together slowly along the macadam walk and paused after a silent minute of walking to watch the laughter and commotion of the Sixth Form who were gathering chaotically on the steps of the sun dial. Then they resumed walking slowly.

"You must be quite proud of yourself, Mr. Bartley," she began.

"Proud? Me? Why?"

"Perhaps proud is the wrong word. Satisfied might be better. You must be satisfied at the end of each year by the obvious success you enjoy in influencing young people—certainly at least some sense of pride in communicating with them as teacher and counselor. You should have heard Jennifer and Peter singing your praises, and Mrs. Bartley's praises as well, last weekend."

Bartley paused for several moments, looked behind him up the walk as if he expected to discover someone he was supposed to meet. He looked at her directly and she looked at him smiling—openly? generously? playfully? sarcastically?—he could not tell.

"Don't take what young people say at graduation time too literally, Mrs. Powell. They are excited and happy and very generous and forgiving about their teachers, knowing that they do not have to face us ever again as arbitrary authorities over their minds and morals. Peter is a generous young man to start with. Yesterday morning I had a long talk with him down at the hockey pond, and among other things he said flattering things about you, that he respected your point of view and that you were a deeply interesting person, well informed about many matters he had never thought about before. I suspect, Mrs. Powell, that every adult is a teacher in some way or other all the time. Teaching isn't limited to those who get underpaid as professionals."

"Isn't that a dreadful thought," she laughed, "but it's probably true. I used to feel such a sense of relief getting the girls to bed at night when they were young. I thought then that it was physical exhaustion, but I think you're probably right. I just needed a break from being a moral model, from not screaming, punishing, or breaking into tears all day."

"Now you know why teachers need three months of vacation every summer to recover."

She laughed again—clearly, openly as though it just wasn't what he said that was entertaining. She seemed to laugh as an expression of an irrepressible happiness. They had passed beyond a moment of possible contention and she had not said what she might have.

"According to Peter I take it that he is once again a welcome visitor in your home?" He decided there was no reason to skirt the edges of the only reason they were together.

"Yes, and I think we have come to know each other better recently than we did over the two years before when he visited on weekends or during vacations. Thanks to you, of course."

"Me? I really didn't do very much." He could feel himself flushing.

"Didn't do very much!" She laughed again almost with pleasure.

"Why, Mr. Bartley. You're being too modest. You wrote me the nastiest, most insulting letter I have ever received in my life." She continued to smile, now looking at him directly. "I didn't deserve it. You had no business writing it, but I'm glad you did. You gave me an excuse to back out of an over-reaction. Other things had not been going well in my life and I guess I was trying to hold everything in place, not wanting anything to change for a while. I had entrapped myself and didn't know what to do. You gave me an opportunity to save face. Besides," now she spoke with a kind of joy, "I felt you would speak to Jennifer about certain matters more objectively, more educationally than I ever could. By the way, you did speak to them? You did carry out your part of the bargain?"

"I did. I delivered a lecture to both of them in my study and I characterized your moral point of view fairly though I did not justify it with the logic of church authorities. I'm not a theologian. I'm an historian."

"I thank you for interfering as you did and apologize for having asked for an exchange, a *quid pro quo* of sorts, in order to save face. I really didn't need my revenge and I'm sorry that I insisted you do my duty."

Bartley suddenly laughed a foolish, awkward, stuttering laugh that he was afraid was too loud and too obvious.

"I guess it's my turn to confess. I shouldn't have written that letter. I did so for reasons in some ways unrelated to Peter and Jennifer. I let some old emotional wounds get the better of my judgment. I misjudged you and tried to exorcize my demons by blaming you. I should have called you on the phone and negotiated."

"Well, everything has worked out despite our bungling and pride. 'Confess yourselves to one another' it says somewhere in the New Testament. We have done so." She turned around and looked toward the dining hall. "Here they come. I'll be saying goodbye now. We'll be leaving shortly after the luncheon."

"Yes, goodbye. He stammered for a moment. "We've just met and it's already goodbye."

"*Ave atque vale*, an expression I learned in high school Latin that I was able to translate when it showed up in a poem in college, a poem by Browning, I think. You must admit that some of our Catholic education wasn't entirely worthless." They laughed together easily.

"Hail and Farewell. Hello and Goodbye. Part of my Catholic education also." He felt a sudden wave of nostalgia as he remembered Brother Josephus, his second year Latin teacher. He was a tall, gaunt man with a shock of grey hair, deep-set eyes and the long ascetic face of a Byzantine Christ. Bartley had been Brother Josephus' prize student that year until the final examination when Bartley disregarded Brother Joe's instructions by attempting to answer every question on the test. Afterwards in a conference Brother Joe tried to explain why Bartley had scored one of the lowest grades in Latin II. "Jack," he had said sadly, "it was a comprehensive exam. Much of it was from Latin III and some from Latin IV. I told you not to guess. Had you left the responses that you didn't know blank, you'd have done fine. But you were penalized extra for wrong answers. On some sections you had a minus score. My best student with minus scores." He shook his head despairingly. Bartley had felt dreadful not so much because the grade was low but that he had studied ahead in the Latin III text and wanted to score on the next higher grade level as a kind of gift for Brother Joe for his kindness and encouragement. He would never forget the disappointment in Brother Joe's eyes.

He became aware suddenly that Mrs. Powell was speaking to him. She was offering her hand.

"Peace, Mr. Bartley. *Pax Dominus Vobiscum.*"

He took her hand in his. "Yes. Yes. Peace. I'm sorry I lost the train of thought." He laughed comfortably now. "I just remembered someone I have not thought of in a long, long time. May the peace of the Lord be with you too, Mrs. Powell."

"And also with you," she said as she turned to greet her husband and daughter now approaching the gathering area before the chapel.

*   *   *   *

Under the line of elms at the north end of the quadrangle, the grounds crew had placed a platform with a podium and several chairs. Two rows of folding chairs for the faculty flanked each side of the platform, facing the rows of chairs that had been set up on the grass across the quadrangle to the entrance of the Commons. The first several rows were reserved for the Sixth Form, which had regrouped after chapel and marched once again, this time from the entrance of the Main School Building.

Headmaster Woodbridge's introductory remarks began as a casual shopping list of bits and pieces but gradually took on a philosophic tone and focus. Bartley could sense the hand of Bill Henry emerge as Woody spoke of Kensington's origins and early history, where it was now at the moment of its most radical departure from the past, and where it seemed to be going.

He spoke of how schools reflected the values of their time and place and how Kensington had been, within the memory of most of the adults present, a pastoral escape for the sons of the very wealthy, an escape from the social changes that were happening in New England, especially in the large cities overrun by immigrants, in the last decade of the 19th century. As late as 1950 the vast majority of Kensington students were from Episcopalian families living in New York, Connecticut, and Massachusetts. There was no significant endowment. None was necessary. The cost of the few scholarship students attending was absorbed as an operating expense and paid for by the regular tuition fees.

There were no Blacks, or Jews, a few Catholics, few ethnic minorities. Faculty members were all graduates of Harvard or Yale. In 1947, Headmaster Potter undertook a radical experiment. He hired a Princeton graduate, admittedly an outstanding young man, a veteran of the European theater and one of the first Americans to enter Berlin in 1945. Before his years in the army he had been an outstanding athlete at Princeton, lettering in football and baseball. At the time there had been grumbling by old guard faculty and alumni that the floodgates had opened and that soon one could expect to find almost anyone on the faculty, graduates of Stanford or Chicago or even state universities like Ann Arbor or Chapel Hill, teachers who, not understanding Kensington's traditions, would mindlessly erode all that had been achieved in three generations. Woody commented in a humorous aside, that that first experiment from Princeton stayed only four years at Kensington, returned to finish his doctorate, and was now the Dean of Faculty of an Ivy University not far from Kensington, one that had supplied Kensington with most of its faculty in its early years.

Now, the composition of the faculty and students was national, even international—students from every state and eleven foreign countries, from every racial, ethnic, and religious heritage had attended Kensington or were attending. The faculty came from colleges and universities from every section of the country. Thirty percent of the student body was on scholarship. The unrestricted endowment was over ten million dollars and growing each year through the generosity of loyal alumni and parents.

The school was on the eve of opening its doors to young women, a decision the Trustees had made for all the right reasons: to maintain the quality of Kensington education, to eliminate the artificial and emotionally unrealistic single sex learning environment, to extend the opportunity of a quality education to every young person regardless of race, religion or gender and to recognize finally and officially four generations of Kensington women, the wives of faculty, who had gratuitously given their labor and love to their husbands, children, as well as the boys of Kensington school.

Then Woody offered a vision of a Kensington of the future—one in which the school's growing endowment would provide sufficient applicants from any corner of the country, male or female, black or white, Asian or Indian, Protestant, Catholic, Jew, and more recently Muslim, Hindu and Buhdist. It was a vision of a national, democratic, selective secondary school—private capital, run by classroom teachers who were free to shape their own curriculum without the interference of academic experts, political pressure groups, well-intentioned but often uninformed alumni and parents.

On a serious and cautious note, Woody reflected on the continuous struggle of the faculty to teach principles of integrity and service and the enduring moral and spiritual values it was its duty to perpetuate in a society of constant change of form and fashion. What had to change to be itself? What must remain the same, could not change without destroying its very being?—these were the questions central to educators, public or private, secondary or college.

In his conclusion, he warned that though he recognized the considerable educational advantages of coeducation, the *in loco parentis* responsibilities of a coeducational boarding school would not be taken lightly by the Kensington faculty. Some of the current, more liberal practices such as sign-out privileges and room visitations would by necessity have to be redefined. He also remarked, offhandedly and almost in passing, that the frequency of disciplinary cases and firing had increased in the first several years at schools that had gone coeducational. His thoughts were sobering, but Bartley understood the comments to be a sop to the conservatives though he also had to concede that the idealistic view of Kensington's future was probably intended for consumption by liberals like himself.

The valedictorian, Alan McCabe, elected by the Sixth Form, was a bright, acerbic young man with flaming red hair who had played the female lead in three musicals in the course of his Kensington career. His address was an ironic evaluation of the "Kensington System" and the Sixth Form's accomplishments according to the principles of Bentham's Hedonistic Calculus, intensity, duration, and propinquity. In his scheme of analysis the positive and negative points canceled each other out, implying that nothing had been accomplished by his class in four years. He concluded on an optimistic note, however. Had Kensington been coeducational, the positive points earned by an accessible female after dark would have had an exponential value and produced entirely different quantitative results. Bartley heard more groans than laughter in the faculty section.

During the presentation of prizes, Peter Colby won the Morgan Cup for "that senior who best combines academic excellence and athletic prowess." With what was supposed to be humor, using a beer advertisement advocating "grabbing all the gusto" as an illustration, the guest speaker exhorted the students to undertake "the real business of living" with courage and enthusiasm.

The Headmaster awarded the diplomas with the help of the President of the Student Council, Mark Adams, and his father. The audience applauded as each graduate, wearing a dark blazer and grey slacks, came forward in random order to receive his diploma. Bartley sat with his colleagues, clapping a bit louder for favorite students or advisees from Pierson.

Each year the ceremony produced in Bartley the same gloomy reflections. This rite of investiture was taking place all over America, and Bartley sadly realized that it represented the extent that the East and, in turn, European tradition pervaded American institutions and aspirations. The Hamiltonian spirit had triumphed. He knew the Jeffersonian dream was dead, had been dead for decades, perpetuated now by wistful academics from Midwestern universities and advertising executives trying to sell cigarettes. No one dreamed of being a self reliant, free yeoman farmer in the virgin land any more. No one dreamed of heading west to redeem the sordid terms of one's heritage. There was no faith anymore in the old dreams of equality, the leveling influence of the frontier.

Now we want to be level with our betters, he mourned. We aspire to the very peerage that our constitution denies us, to the forms and symbols of a title if not the title itself. We buy cars with coats of arms, imitation manor houses, schools with shields and Latin mottoes, colleges and universities that endow us with a vicarious knighthood, permit us to rub elbows with the children of the truly rich or illustrious, the barons and counts of money and power and fame.

The ceremony seemed interminable. He continued to applaud but mechanically. He longed to walk on a beach, climb a mountain, ford the headwaters of a stream deep in some forgotten woods.

During the graduation luncheon Bartley and Karen separated in order to keep the divorced parents from direct, often embarrassing confrontation while insuring that each parent received personal attention. During his first year, one of his advisees' parents had divorced and cross-married with another divorced couple. They all gathered together at one large table, parents, sisters, brothers, step-sisters, step-brothers, step-parents, grandparents—one great happy family. Liberal as he pretended to be, Bartley had never been able to deal with such casual realignments comfortably.

Back in the dormitory, Peter and Jennifer and Peter's parents said a hurried goodbye as they hauled his possessions out to the Colby's car. They were going to the Powells for the afternoon. Bartley wandered about the dorm, bidding farewell to the rest of his graduating advisees. He stopped by the double occupied by Jim Morrison and Bennett Forester, who combined had managed to accumulate more disciplinary action in four years than the rest of his graduating sixth formers combined. He drank a glass with them from their magnum of champagne as they finished packing. They lamented their four years at Kensington, thanked him for helping them through—more as skilled legal counsel than as sympathetic adviser—and at the propitious moment presented him with a half gallon of scotch and two joints, symbolizing what they had not smoked since Bartley's doomsday warning in April. Forester delivered a short speech.

"We'd be lying if we told you we liked it here at Kensington, Mr. Bartley, but the truth is we hated it with a passion. We want to thank you and Mrs. Bartley for trying to make things better." He grinned. "The joints are from us. The Chivas is from my old man."

Later, Bartley flushed the marijuana down the toilet.

The dorms had cleared by two. The station wagons, groaning under the weight of four years' accumulated possessions, glided silently down the narrow, twisting drives. The janitor made a quick run through Pierson gathering up the pornography, nude posters, and erotic magazines. Then Annie and Rachel began their annual scavenger hunt. Within an hour they had each gathered a cardboard box of treasures— discarded clothing and athletic jerseys, shampoo, soap, shaving cream, books, pens, notebooks, posters, playing cards, plants, even a bowl of goldfish. He surreptitiously removed the jocks and discarded them.

At four o'clock that afternoon Bartley fell asleep on the couch in the den as he watched a Red Sox game on TV. Karen woke him up at six for the year end faculty party. They had to dress as the title of some book or motion picture. Karen decided on *In Cold Blood*. She simply carried a pail half full of water reddened with a package of strawberry jello. When they arrived at the party, she took off her sandals, and stepped in the bucket. Later that night she was awarded third prize in the "least imaginative" category. Bartley went as *Rouge et Noire*, wearing a red Kensington t-shirt with black slacks. He won first prize in the same category.

The dining hall supplied the cement block grills and charcoal for a shish-kabob barbecue in the Woodbridge backyard. Each person brought a skewer and selected vegetables and meat from a cafeteria of bowls arranged on a picnic table by the faculty party committee under the direction of Edith Woodbridge.

As the drinking and evening progressed, small circles formed and dispersed on the porches and around the yard which had been lighted with Chinese lanterns. They talked about students and curriculum, wrangled over policies, criticized or praised the graduation speakers, looked to the potential of next year's sixth form with equal amounts of hope and despair.

At about eleven o'clock, Bartley heard a loud piercing noise, a brilliant imitation of a siren by the Business Manager and Comptroller, Jack Uppingham, which was the traditional signal calling everyone to the living room for the only formal event of the faculty party—the roasting of the Headmaster.

The room was packed. He joined Karen who was sitting on the floor to the left of the Woodbridges, already ensconced on the sofa of honor. Bill Henry stepped forward before the fireplace and raised his hand for silence. Speaking from note cards, he began with the usual opening words, "Another year, another yen."

*　　　*　　　*　　　*

The persistent ring of the phone finally woke him. He felt a dull headache as he put on his bathrobe and hurried as best he could down the hallway. He switched the light on in the study and looked at the clock. It was 3:30. At first he thought that the call might be from Karen's family in Wisconsin. Her father has not been well lately. Then he felt a tightening fear that it might be someone calling to report a car accident or some terrible disaster. When they left the faculty party, there were several colleagues in no condition to drive. By the time he picked up the receiver, he was convinced it was a prankster who would mouth some obscenity and hang up. He was already half angry when he answered.

"Jack?" A voice shouted in his ear. He recognized the voice immediately.

"You've got the right person but the wrong name." He relaxed softly into his chair.

"I'm an alumnus now. I can call you anything I damn well please. None of that *Mister* stuff anymore. No, sir, Jack. Jack Bartley. Old buddy Jack. Jack Sprat, Jack the Cat. Jack of all trades. Jack be nimble, Jack be quick. You're going to have to call me Mister Colby now. No more Peter when you come around hustling money from the alumni, Jack."

"Where are you Peter, and how drunk are you?"

"Well, Jack, I'm in Darien. At Kenny Monsons. The sixth form party. Wow! And I'm not drunk. God, that's really crazy calling you Jack. I'm only inebriated. I've consumed ten cans of beer since nine o'clock, but I've already peed nine cans since midnight, so I'm only under the influence of one can. Only one can, Jack."

"It doesn't work that way, Peter."

"I know but I'm trying to make up for lost time. I haven't had a beer since spring vacation. Kept clean all spring. Hey, clean all spring. It kind of rhymes like drunk as a skunk."

"Where are your folks?"

"They're staying in Greenwich with my mother's old Wellesley roommate. They're going to pick me up in the morning and then we're going to hit the turnpikes. Whoom! 70 MPH all the way to Iowa. ZOOM! There's only one bend in the whole road—around Chicago."

"Where are you going to sleep?"

"Sleep. Who's going to sleep. I'm just going to drink all night. But there's plenty of room here. If I pass out, I'll just lay down wherever I am. This place is enormous."

"Is Jennifer with you?"

No." Peter's voice turned serious. "I wish she were. We went to her house after graduation and had a little supper then left for here. God, I wish she were here, Mr. Bartley. I really love that girl. I'm going to marry her, Mr. Bartley. After two years I'm going to transfer to Amherst or Hampshire or U Mass, somewhere near Smith where she's hoping to go, and we're going to get married and finish out college together."

"What happened to Jack?"

"Aw, to hell with Jack. It just doesn't work. You're going to be 'sir' or Mr. Bartley the rest of my life, so I might as well resign myself to it."

"I kind of like Mr. Colby though. I'll be writing you a letter in a few years. 'Dear Mr. Colby,' I'll say. 'Would you like to contribute a few hundred thousand dollars to the Jack and Karen Bartley retirement fund. For old time's sake.'"

"I'll do it, Mr. Bartley. I'll go down and embezzle a couple million bucks from the old man's bank. He won't miss it and I'll give it to the Kensington Faculty retirement endowment with special benefits to Mr. and Mrs. J. Bartley—the world's greatest advisor and history teacher."

"How about coach? I'm a coach, too. You don't know what it's like trying to play a baseball game with third form rejects."

"Mr. Bartley. I hate to disillusion you but you are known, you are famous as the lousiest coach at Kensington. You have enthusiasm and you show up for practice all the time and you're good at keeping the box score, but the word is you are no Casey Stengel."

"I am disillusioned. I was planning to negotiate for a larger salary next year because of my 3 and 7 record this season."

"I wouldn't if I were you, Mr. Bartley. They'll cut your salary when they find out just how bad you really are."

"Am I really that bad? I mean, do the students really think I'm a lousy coach, is it accepted opinion?"

"Yes, sir. Do you want me to ask a few classmates if I can find one who isn't too drunk?"

"No thanks. Is there anything else I'm famous for now that you have this compulsion to disillusion me?"

"Oh, sure, Mr. Bartley. You're famous for having the neatest wife and best behaved fac brats on campus, and as a teacher who knows his subject and grades fairly. A lot better than half the faculty. You know, sir, old Woody confuses the students by keeping people in the faculty who couldn't get a job as dogcatcher in the real world. Take a certain English teacher who is also the yearbook advisor, for example. He dumps all over the students all the time and yet he's always late for class himself, or he misses classes, never gets papers back and in the dorm he's drunk half the time. And he isn't the only one."

"I know, Peter. But surely you are exaggerating. Half the faculty?"

"I guess I was exaggerating. There are only three or four, but the students get pissed when they realize that those people, who shall go unnamed, vote on recommendations for student discipline."

There was a pause for several moments. Then Peter spoke again.

"Sorry, sir. Had to burp. That's what's wrong with beer. It gets you coming and going. You won't believe me, sir, but I am probably the soberest member of my class at this moment."

"How many showed up?"

"Two thirds, anyhow. Some of the day students didn't come down, but there are lots of dates and some parents chaperoning. This place is a zoo. I'm calling from a study off in a corner of the house somewhere. This house is so big, Mr. Bartley, I may not find the party again for an hour or two. I didn't know Monson had this kind of money. Actually, I thought he was on scholarship until last year."

"Camden Commons is named after his grandfather—his mother's father. His middle name is Camden."

"Would you believe that for two years he bummed Cokes and candy and clothes and shaving cream from me and I thought he was some scholarship kid from Philadelphia or Chicago. I finally wised up. Right now, I'm making up for all he conned me out of. I dialed this call to you direct. I wish I could be there when they get the bill. I'm going to drink a case of beer before morning if I can and then let the water out of his pool and the air out of all the tires on their fleet of Mercedes. I wish I could eat enough to get back half the food I gave him in my first two years. I must have really been an absolute moron when I first came to Kensington."

"You were slightly naive."

"Slightly! I must have been the dumbest new third former in the history of Kensington."

"You had plenty of competition. Being naive and trusting and indiscriminate is part of the charm of being a third former."

"But I came from Iowa on top of being a weanie."

"You were lucky. You had an excuse—the same excuse I had my first two or three years at Kensington."

"That's right. You're a hick too. From Illinois. That's probably why we got along so well. Two hicks from the sticks. Hey, you don't mind me calling you at this hour, do you?"

"Not now that I'm awake and up and probably won't be able to get back to sleep again."

"Hey, Mr. Bartley. Tim Atkins is here with this absolutely gorgeous girl from Greenwich High School. I never would have believed he could get a beauty like that, he always seemed so wimpy at Kensington, always painting or sculpting. Monson invited everyone who was ever a member of our class—everybody who flunked out or was kicked out. There are some guys here I don't even remember."

"How's Tim doing?"

"Oh, he's fine. After he got kicked out, he went to his local high school and because he had taken an extra year at Kensington to start with, he went right in as a senior with plenty of credits. They only require two years of math so he'll get his diploma after a few courses in summer school."

"I'm glad. He was a good kid. Nobody wanted to kick him out, especially at the end of his last year, but going into the faculty room and stealing a copy of a math test was just too much on top of a weak academic record. He gave us no choice."

"He did it for his folks, Mr. Bartley. He didn't care personally whether he got a Kensington diploma. He didn't want to hurt them. He wasn't going to get a diploma the honest way. He knew he couldn't pass the math final."

"Peter, he didn't get fired for flunking math. He got fired for cheating."

"Yes, sir, I understand your point of view, but the students weren't very sympathetic with the firing."

"We can't decide everything according to student opinion."

"I know, but you really shouldn't fire anybody unless they absolutely flunk out or are dangerous or something."

"I didn't do it, Peter. I agree firing ought to be a last resort."

"I meant the whole faculty not just you. You're fair minded, sir, but there are plenty other faculty who don't agree with you. And as long as I'm bitching to you, who decides what students win those cups at graduation? You do more injustice with those awards than you do when you fire us."

"How can we be unjust by rewarding students for a job well done?"

"Because you don't know everything, sir. The faculty gets conned all the time. I shouldn't have received the Morgan Cup. Simmons is just as good an athlete as I am and twice the student, but he is unpopular with most of the faculty. I won because I don't give people crap all the time."

"We weren't conned, Peter. The nominations came out of the Athletic Association. The faculty simply accepted their recommendation."

"Maybe that's not a good example, but last year's Kensington Cup was enough to make the students laugh. It's supposed to be awarded to the best all around student in the sixth form by the faculty."

"What was wrong with Ferguson? His selection was one the easiest choices we had in years. He had done everything."

"Everything is right. Mr. Bartley, he was the biggest pusher on campus. He used his position and popularity to hustle drugs with the new kids until some of his classmates finally made him stop last year. He made enough money to pay for a summer trip to France."

"I am profoundly disillusioned, Peter."

"Hey, I don't want to give you a hard time. I just want you to know that the faculty isn't perfect and you can demoralize students by rewarding the wrong people as much as you can by punishing the wrong people."

"I stand corrected, Peter. I am impressed by your wisdom. I have often learned a great deal from students."

Peter laughed. "Hey, don't overrate student opinion. You remember dance weekend two years ago when about fifteen students and their dates snuck out of the dorms after check-in and had a wine party at the hockey pond?"

"Yes. You do remember that I was on the DC."

"Oh, yeah, you've always been on the DC. Anyhow, you remember Mr. Skinner found out and at assembly called for them to turn themselves in according to the honor code. Well, the Disciplinary Committee recommended suspension and probations and no firings."

"Yes, I supported the student motions in the final vote."

"All three of the student members of the DC who recommended those practically meaningless punishments had been out of the dorm and didn't turn themselves in."

"You have robbed me of all my illusions, Peter."

"You mean you didn't suspect anything when you voted? You must have thought something was strange that there were no recommendations from the students for firing. If there had been, all three would have been turned in or lynched."

"You have deepened my understanding of human nature, Peter. I may never be able to vote in a disciplinary case again."

"I'm sorry, Mr. Bartley. I didn't mean to get off on a tangent. Kensington is such a great place. It's mostly fair. I can't believe four years is over already. I'm going to miss the guys I've been with and the faculty like you. I probably won't see any of you again."

"I thought you were going to come back east in two years and marry Jennifer."

"Yeah, but I meant to see everybody together again, classmates and faculty like it's been for the past four years."

"Now, I have some wisdom for you, Peter. You can't go back in time. Even returning to a reunion can be a sign of arrested emotional development, a kind of return to the womb. Remember what Sachel Page said, 'Don't look back, something might be catching up on you.' My advice to you is don't ever come back to Kensington to try to capture the good old days. You can't. Just send a check to the faculty salary endowment fund to show your appreciation."

"I'll come back to visit you and Mrs. Bartley. Will that be O.K.?"

"You know it will, Peter."

"Once again there was a pause and the next time Peter spoke there was a profound change in the tone of his voice.

"I had to call to thank you, Mr. Bartley. I didn't have time this afternoon."

"You don't have to thank me, Peter. You did your share. You ran the dorm this year. You made my job so much easier, I should thank you."

"I don't mean just about the dorm. I mean about Mrs. Powell. You know she isn't so bad as I thought."

"She just needed time to come around, Peter."

"She didn't come around just because of time, Mr. Bartley. Jennifer told me this afternoon. She said you wrote Mrs. Powell a letter and changed her mind and that's why you gave us that dumb sex talk on dance weekend. She made you do it if she let Jennifer come to the dance."

"I used a little persuasion. She needed to be hurried a little into changing her mind."

There was a long pause on the other end of the line.

"Peter, are you still there?"

"Yes, sir."

"What's the matter?"

"I'm trying to say what I want to say, but I can't find the words."

Bartley sensed a note of sentimentality in Peter's voice and tried to avoid the certain embarrassment.

"She made me angry, Peter. I wrote her for personal reasons, not just because of you and Jennifer."

"You're the best advisor in the world, Mr. Bartley, and I'll never forget what you did for us."

"I did what I had to then, Peter."

"I have to go now, Mr. Bartley. I can't talk anymore. I...I just have to go now."

Bartley sat for several moments staring at his framed poster of Woodrow Wilson after hearing the click. Then he slowly placed the receiver back in its cradle and returned to bed.

*   *   *   *

He lay awake in bed for over an hour after Peter's call. Then he got up and dressed and made a cup of tea and sat in his study, surveying the disorganized remnants of another school year on his desk. Then with the first light beginning to grow in the east window, he stepped outside and began walking.

The lamps, attached to buildings along the way, still glowed dimly as he walked the macadam pathway that led along dorm row to the Main School Building. At the far end of Pierson approaching the upper quad, he came upon a flaming hawthorn that seemed like a torch in the slanting rays of the early morning sunlight. He took a left fork and walked across the open area toward the chapel, a replica in grey stone of an early Norman design, under the overhanging crowns of a row of elms that had managed to survive the Hurricane of '38 and the Dutch Elm disease. In front of the chapel he left the pathways and walked across the grass to the sundial and sat on its steps.

Before him was the entrance of the chapel, its rose window's color and design muted in the shadow of an enormous copper beech under whose draping boughs his children often went to play. The light was spreading across the sky now. He looked back toward Pierson, one of the several red-brick Georgian dorms that formed a crescent along one edge of a common with small hedges marking its perimeter and a large circular flower bed in its center. He could not see beyond the dorms.

Kensington was built along the ridge of a hill, but he envisioned the terraces of playing fields and tennis courts bordered by rows of cedar or poplar forming together an irregularly checkered hillside that ended in the hardwoods and the hockey pond. The lawns were rich and full and green, impeccably maintained by the grounds crew, cut and trimmed for graduation. The flower beds would continue to flourish in a grand pageant of blossoms throughout the summer.

He was awed by Kensington's beauty whatever the season: the crystalline ice storms of winter, the fiery maples in October, the flowering shrubs of spring. The school had become his home more profoundly than anywhere he had ever lived. His children knew no other home, and now with the students gone, it was a kind of Camelot, as though they had inherited for the summer a small feudal estate for their private use. The sun dial, where he was sitting, was itself perched on a platform on top of several circular steps of fitted granite slabs perhaps twenty feet in diameter. The pointer cast its shadow across hourly markings that had been etched at spatial intervals on the steps. It had always seemed to Bartley a kind of altar forming an invisible triangle with the chapel's rose window and the archway of the main entrance to the campus.

The sundial had been copied from the original at Oxford and given to the school in 1910 by the Class of '92. The main gate had also been copied from one of the Yard gates at Harvard. When he was first interviewed for a job, he had been attracted to Kensington by the age and tradition that the school had incorporated in its architecture and its institutional structure. As an historian and archivist he had gradually become the keeper and caretaker of its past. How strange, he thought, that he was both preserver and innovator, like Janus looking both ways.

But whichever way he looked at his life, it was full and rich and varied, and he couldn't believe his own luck—to have found a life's work for which he was singularly qualified. He knew he was a good teacher and a good adviser and he was valuable to the school for work on committees and his often wise and sensible counsel to younger colleagues and for the example and stability of his life for students. And the school had opened its doors to Karen, making her an equal partner in the school as in his life. He knew too that Bill Henry was right. He had mellowed and become an institutional stalwart.

But he sometimes felt a gnawing guilt that he didn't deserve this good life or worse yet that he was wasting his talent and concern and compassion on students who already had more than their share of life's advantages. Was he just another servant of the rich, a scavenger of trickle down affluence, even if those young men like Peter whom he taught and counseled were such bright and alert and honest and friendly human beings. Whenever he felt guilty for his privileged life, he consoled himself with the thought that the faculty at Ivy League universities should be required to wear hair shirts.

In his first years at Kensington how many times had he planned to leave? He had visions, or were they only illusions, of some more important purpose in his life, but nothing ever materialized. There were always convincing practical reasons to stay on. Then he no longer thought about leaving. One is what one does and he was a teacher.

Was he still the same person, he asked himself, who in his most radical undergraduate days had been a disciple of the Christian socialism and pacifism of Dorothy Day and later a sympathizer with the anti-war protests of the Berrigans? There was a time when he believed being a Republican was some kind of sin. Now he accepted the fact that there was much that he would never do with his life. Coming to Kensington was a kind of serendipity. He had read the notice of the job opening by accident. Now after fifteen years, serendipity had become destiny.

He did not have much faith in the myth that teachers shaped the future and that he might have a ripple effect on society through his influence on a handful of students who might in time have economic or political power. He did not need that illusion though in rare moments and with a certain irony he considered himself as something of a Jeffersonian subversive among Hamiltonian elitists or as a missionary of liberation theology among the children of the wealthy and powerful, trying with ideas to free his students from the bondage of materialism and class superiority that were as spiritually deadening as poverty and ignorance and disease were for the poor of the world?

Did one have to die at the barricades or be crucified on an anthill to merit redemption? Wasn't there a certain grace in ordinary acts of courtesy and friendship, in the example of one's life, in shouts of encouragement on the fields of play, in deferred judgments, in the unkind word not spoken?

Each spring, exhausted though he was, he felt a profound sense of satisfaction and accomplishment. He loved the school. His family had flourished under its patronage. Seduced by happiness he had abandoned his dreams to serve a greater purpose. In his contentment he no longer aspired to be anything but a schoolman.

HE REASONED
HE RATIONALIZED

EPILOGUE

▼

Excerpts from the Catalogue of the
Kensington School 1975-76

General Information

The faculty of Kensington School seeks to develop the balanced intellectual, moral, and physical growth of each of its students to the maximum of his ability. To realize this goal the trustees have delegated to the Headmaster and the faculty full authority in all matters of curriculum and discipline. The cornerstone of the educational experience at Kensington is responsibility. Because genuine growth cannot be realized in an artificial world, the faculty holds each student accountable for his academic performance and his personal behavior. The grading and the disciplinary systems have been devised to assess fairly the actions of students and the consequences of student behavior. The Kensington environment is real. Violation of major school rules may result in dismissal.

The admissions office at Kensington seeks, therefore, to admit students of proven intellectual commitment, demonstrated concern for others, and personal honor and integrity. The development of character is as important as the development of the mind. Individuals intending to apply to Kensington should bear in mind that such qualities as

278 \ Standing Lessons

honesty, integrity, service, and concern for others are as important as intelligence and academic achievement and that the faculty holds students accountable for their behavior in the dormitory, in the classroom, and on the fields of play.

*   *   *   *

Dormitory Life

Each student is assigned a dormitory adviser who serves as the link between the school and the parents. The adviser counsels the student in all aspects of school life: course selection, athletic activities, college placement, and matters of personal concern and anxiety. Although the adviser is obligated to report to the Dean the direct observation of the violation of a major school rule, he is much more than an enforcer of rules. Sometimes the relationship is fatherly, sometimes that of a concerned older brother. The dormitory adviser and his advisees form an extended family of mutual concern and friendship. The confidentiality rule allows the adviser to deal with a student's personal problems while it guarantees the student a trusting relationship with a helpful and often compassionate adult. Kensington School is justly proud of this guidance relationship. Adviser-student relationships have often developed into life-long friendships.